Greater Love

Judah Knight

GreenTree Publishers
www.greentreepublishers.com
Newnan, GA

No Greater Love

Thanks to 123rf for artwork:
Copyright: <a href='https://www.123rf.com/profile_ssstocker'>ssstocker</a>

Printed in the United States of America
ISBN-13: 978-1-944483-39-5

Follow Judah Knight through the following media links:
Website/blog: www.judahknight.com
Twitter: @judahknight

Greentree Publishers
www.greentreepublishers.com

Special Offer

Thank you for choosing *No Greater Love*. While you can enjoy this novel as a stand-alone book, you'll see it is connected to the previous books in the Davenport series. You can find the first five books on Amazon:

- *The Long Way Home*
- *Hope for Tomorrow*
- Finding My Way
- *Ready to Love Again*
- *Love Waits*

Special Request:

We would like to ask for a special favor. Will you go to Amazon and write a review? Your review will be such a help for someone looking for a clean and wholesome romance/adventure book. Thank you.

Offer:

As a way of saying thanks for your interest in Judah Knight's *Davenport Series*, we are offering a gift. Request a free copy of his novella, *A Girl Can Always Hope,* by visiting Judahknight.com/ free-gift.html. In *The Long Way Home* (Book 1), you learned the two main characters knew one another as teenagers, and Margaret Robertson (Meg Freeman in *The Long Way Home*) had a crush on her brother's best friend, Jon Davenport. Read the fun, short story of one awkward middle schooler's attempt to capture the impossible catch.

Now, we hope you enjoy the *No Greater Love*.

Contents

Chapter One

Fear at the Villa

Lacy felt the cold, sharp edge of the knife blade pressing against her throat as a grimy hand thrust a cloth over her nose and mouth. Eyes wide with shock, she felt paralyzed as fear raced through her mind threatening to overtake her. The knife dug into her flesh, and drops of blood rolled down her neck. The room spun as she jerked reflexively against his strong grip. *Think, stupid. Think! Don't move. He'll kill you.*

Lacy could tell he was a small man. She'd taken self-defense classes before, but now, she was frozen in terror. *What's going on?*

The man pushed her against the bathroom wall. Lacy wanted to scream, but she knew at any instant he could slit her throat. She wanted to turn her head away from the cloth, but she could still feel the knife.

Could this be one of Pedro Escobar's men? The Cartel? Her vision blurred.

"Hello, Lacy," the accented voice whispered.

He knows my name. She felt nauseous and feared she'd pass out. *Stop trembling, Lacy. You can't let him know you're afraid. Why is the room spinning? I can't stand up. What's going on?*

"I've missed you, Lacy."

Horror coursed through her body. Her mind was fading, but she knew the man. He'd taken her from Eleuthera in the Bahamas, and he'd been in her nightmares ever since. *Miguel!*

Everything went black.

@♦@♦@♦@♦

Kerrick and Jon leaned against the SUV while José spoke with the police. Kerrick couldn't help but wonder how life's twists and turns could put a person in the strangest of places. He had signed up to work on a salvage boat this summer, and now, he was in Mexico with Jon and Meg Davenport, probably the richest people he'd ever known.

Discovering treasure from the *San Roque* had changed Jon and Meg's lives. Though they had probably netted millions from the ancient treasure ship, Kerrick knew Jon's wealth initially came from real estate investments. Glancing up the road toward their vacation rental, he looked forward to spending the next couple of hours with the most beautiful girl in the world. The fact she was the Davenports' niece had nothing to do with his attraction to Lacy Henderson. He loved her and wanted to be with her.

Instead, he was stuck at a police barricade.

The light flashed atop the black pickup truck and lit the night in an eerie blue. The wind blew in from the sea, and the sky was filled with thousands of stars. Instead of enjoying the beauty of the night with Lacy, he watched policemen scouring the area like ants over their dirt mound home. The policemen made Kerrick think more of the military than a local police force. Something serious was going on in this neighborhood.

The evening had been perfect until they'd run into the roadblock near their rental. José had managed to get permission from the policemen to let the women walk up to the house. He was a great asset and a good friend to the

Davenports. He was tough, smart, and had once served in Spain's special forces. That Spanish was his primary language was a plus.

The cops had escorted the women to the house and walked through it to make sure it was safe. Kerrick could only guess what had happened to bring the police force out in such numbers, but something big had happened. He noticed several officers going in and out of the house next door.

At least, the ladies could get ready for bed. Kerrick looked toward the house and saw the light on in Lacy's bedroom. He hoped she wasn't getting ready for bed. They had a lot of talking to do. The last few days convinced him he wanted to spend the rest of his life with Lacy. He couldn't believe how his life had changed and brought him right back to the woman he truly loved.

He thought of Hannah back in Florida and felt sorry for her. The poor girl was scared and desperate. She had tried to pull him into her screwed up life by insisting he was the father of her baby. It seemed impossible, but crazy things happened when people were drunk.

That chapter is over, thank God. Now, I need to focus on what I have and not mess this up. He looked back at the house and saw the light come on in Lacy's bathroom. *She's probably taking a shower. Maybe by the time the cops let us drive the car back to the house, she'll be ready to talk.*

"It's great to have you back, Kerrick," Jon said as he patted Kerrick's shoulder. "That whole story about Hannah is bizarre."

"Yeah, crazy," he sighed. "My parents will help her find a home. My mom knows several places that take in new mothers when there's no father in the picture."

"So, will Hannah keep the baby?"

"She hasn't decided yet. I suppose if she can figure out who the father is and get a little financial support, she may keep him."

Jon leaned against the car and crossed his legs. "If she can't take care of the baby, I hope she'll let a good family adopt the child. A lot of fine people could give him a great home."

"True. You have no idea how relieved I was when I figured out I wasn't the father."

"I'm sure. I guess she came clean about her scheme to ruin your life."

Kerrick laughed. "I hate to say she would have ruined my life, but I have other plans than being Hannah's husband." He looked back toward the house.

Jon flashed a knowing smile. "Lacy's special."

Kerrick looked back at his friend and mentor and nodded. "Yeah. She's special."

"What are you thinking?" Jon asked.

"I'm thinking I nearly lost her, and I don't want that to happen again. If you think about it, I almost lost her on Coral Cay this summer, too. Hannah was just a different kind of predator than Miguel and his flunkies. Different, but still dangerous."

Kerrick looked up and saw José walking toward them. He looked formidable and dangerous. Something about José sent a message that said *don't mess with this guy*. Lacy once told

Kerrick how José saved Meg's life when she was attacked by three men. He managed to take out all three of them even though at least one had a gun. José had even been shot in the process. Kerrick was glad to have José on his side.

"So, what's all the fuss about?" Kerrick asked. "Did they tell you?"

Slipping his hands into his pockets, José said. "They didn't want to at first, but I finally got enough out of the bigger guy to know there's a dead body in the house next to our rental. Family members came to check on their grandfather and found him dead."

"People die all the time," Kerrick said. "What's the big deal?"

"The big deal is most of them aren't wrapped up in plastic."

Kerrick shivered. "He was murdered?"

"Maybe," José replied. "The captain told me we could drive the car back to the house in just a little bit. I don't like the ladies being in there alone. He said I can go to the house, but someone needs to stay with the car. I think he had sympathy for me when I told him Ann was expecting. I suggest you both hang out here until they let you pass."

Jon nodded, and Kerrick wished he'd insisted on staying with the women. He hadn't felt good about them going to the house alone in the first place, police escort or not.

José walked up the hill toward the rental, and Jon leaned toward Kerrick. "The cake idea was pretty creative, Kerrick."

"*Pastel de tres leches*? I have a few good ideas now and then." Kerrick smiled as he thought back to the restaurant scene just an hour earlier. He regretted no one had videoed Lacy's face when she saw the cake and realized he was back from Florida. Her look had been priceless. The thought crossed his mind that he and Lacy could have *pastel de tres leches* for a wedding cake. *Whoa, Kerrick. Let's not get ahead of ourselves.*

The phone call Jon received while they were having cake and coffee at La Parroquia came to Kerrick's mind, and he thought about the boy he'd saved while diving on a shipwreck that summer. Randal turned out to be a tough kid, and the boy had a good heart. Now, his older brother was in trouble.

He smiled as he thought about Jon Davenport. He always helped people, whether he knew them or not. They had never met Freddy, but he was Randal's brother, and that was all that mattered to Jon.

"So, what do we do now, Jon? About Freddy."

"I don't know. I need to think about the situation, but we don't have a lot of time left. We need to get home. You guys start class in a few days."

"I bet we could get the University to put class off a week for us," Kerrick said with a laugh. "Surely, you have some pull."

Jon grinned. "Not likely."

"Too bad we have to go back to school. I'm not sure I'm ready for another semester."

"You only have two semesters left. Right?"

"I think so," Kerrick agreed, "but you never know. I have to meet with my advisor this week to make sure I'm on track to graduate in May."

"That will be great. Graduation, I mean. We should return to Miami on Tuesday as we planned. José and I might come back to Veracruz toward the end of the week or maybe next week. Maybe, we can put feelers out tomorrow so we can at least know where to start looking for the kid when we return."

Kid? He's probably close to my age. "Mexico is a big place. Freddy could be anywhere."

"True. It's like looking for a piece of rice on the ocean floor."

Kerrick stared at the flashing blue lights for a moment. The whole Mexico trip was supposed to be about looking for the lost city and King Harold Bluetooth's treasure, not searching for a guy hooked on drugs. Thanks to Hannah, nothing had worked out like they had planned. Oh well. Since money was no issue for Jon and Meg, maybe they could come back over winter break. Kerrick felt a little funny spending their money, even if they did have millions. Maybe billions.

"What about the city?" Kerrick asked.

"We don't know if there is a city. I know the clues we found on Coral Cay said there was, but we don't know if that information is dependable. I'd still like to come back and look for it sometime."

"Ancient city or not, this has been a memorable trip."

Jon glanced over at Kerrick. "I'd say you found something more valuable than King Bluetooth's ancient city."

Kerrick smiled and looked back toward Lacy's bedroom. "Yeah. I have to agree with you. Old Bluetooth's treasure pales in comparison."

"If there's a city filled with treasure, it's been tucked away for a long time. I bet it will sit there and wait on us to find it."

"I hope so."

It still blew Kerrick's mind they possessed a clue as to the whereabouts of an ancient, Mesoamerican city filled with gold and jewels. It wasn't much of a clue but a clue, nevertheless. What were the odds it existed and was still undiscovered?

"Have you heard anything from your friend in Spain? About the scroll we found in the cave?"

Kerrick marveled that Jon seemed to have just the right connections. Jon knew a woman from grad school who was an expert in ancient languages.

"I need to call her. Maybe she can decipher that scroll. It was messed up, but she's good at what she does. If anyone can find a faded message on a piece of animal skin, Cindy can."

Kerrick heard a police officer rattling something off in Spanish. When he and Jon stared at the man, the officer pointed to the vacation house and waved to them. They were cleared to take the car back to the house. Finally. Kerrick was dying to spend time with Lacy. They'd been separated too long.

Chapter Two

Taken

Miguel caught Lacy as she slipped unconscious to the floor. He knew if someone was downstairs, and her body slammed to the floor, he might have unwanted company. He had watched from the upstairs windows earlier as Lacy and the redhead walked up toward the house. Meg was farther behind them, carrying her kid and walking beside an older woman. He couldn't believe his luck. It was like someone giving him their winning lottery ticket because they didn't need the money.

Fortunately, he also spotted the police officer walking just ahead of the women. Because Miguel had already spent a significant amount of time in the house, he knew he could hide in a ventilation shaft. He easily squeezed through an opening in the bathroom, and the cop never had a clue. Climbing back into the bathroom before Lacy entered the room was a piece of cake.

Until the Davenports returned to the villa, the whole afternoon and evening had been a near disaster. What were the chances of the police discovering the old man's body? When he left the neighbor's house earlier, the dead guy was wrapped up tight, so there was no way anyone could have smelled him. The thought crossed Miguel's mind that someone saw him entering the house, but in all likelihood, the old man's family probably came by and discovered him. Too bad. If he could have gotten rid of the body, that house would have been a perfect hideout.

The whole episode at the La Flor club almost ruined his plan. He should have gone into the place, made contact with the guy who had the drugs, and left. He needed something to knock Lacy out for a while. Luck had smiled on him when he managed to find someone with chloroform and a syringe filled with propofol as well. The loser was a nurse, but he probably made more money on the street selling the hospital's drugs than he made at his job.

He picked up Lacy's limp body and laid her on the bed. He removed his shoes, eased to the door, and locked it. Turning to stare at the beautiful girl, he couldn't believe he had her. Excitement rushed through him with thoughts of the fun he was about to have. As much as he wanted the party to start, he had to get out to somewhere safe.

Miguel reached into his backpack and pulled out the syringe he had gotten from the idiot at the club. *What was his name? Pablo? He nearly got me killed.* Being an emergency room nurse had its perks. He said the drugs would be clean. He told Miguel to jab her upper arm and empty the syringe. He knew the chloroform would be wearing off soon. Good thing he had something stronger. He should have enough propofol to keep her out for at least a little while. Pablo told him this drug was used for surgeries all the time and guaranteed it to be effective.

Miguel saw Lacy's head move. He needed to inject the drug. He reached for the needle, removed the cap, and stuck it into her arm. She flinched a bit but never awakened.

"Sleep well my beautiful Lacy," he whispered. "You're mine now. We'll find a nice villa where we can really get to know one another."

His eyes slid down her body and back to her flawless face. Her cheeks glowed. He slowly reached his hand out to touch her soft cheek. She was warm and inviting. He stared at her pink, full lips and imagined kissing her.

He bent over her sleeping form and cupped her face. Just as his lips were about to touch hers, he heard steps outside the bedroom door. Hurrying into the bathroom, he turned on the shower. *Hopefully, they'll hear the shower and leave me alone.* He stepped back to the door and listened. A smile spread across his face as he heard whoever it was walking back down the stairs.

How am I going to get us out of here without being seen? He sat down on the bed and touched his swollen cheek. If Pablo hadn't pushed so many drinks on him, Miguel knew his experience at the club would have ended quietly. He shouldn't have told the nurse about Escobar, but Pablo should have kept his mouth shut. What happened to Escobar's son was a private matter.

Miguel shook his head. He had been stupid to tell anyone about killing Escobar's kid. Of course, Miguel had been smashed by that point in the evening. He didn't even remember how many beers he'd had before starting on the strong stuff. Good thing the club was dark, and no one got a good look at him. The last thing he needed was Escobar's men finding him.

He took Lacy's hand in his. "We've got to get out of here," he whispered. "Me and you, Baby." A breeze blew through the open sliding glass doors that led to the balcony, and Miguel looked out to the sea. He walked out and peered down the street to his right. He could see the Davenports car a block away at the barricade. If he didn't have to worry about being seen, he could easily climb down from the balcony. He looked to his left and wondered about Kerrick's room at the end of the hall. They could get out his window and be hidden by the house. He remembered some bushes being in the backyard. *I bet I could get through those bushes to the yard behind this one. The cops are busy at the other house.*

Easing back to the bed, Miguel picked up Lacy and laid her over his shoulder. She was light but firm. Her leg muscles were well defined, adding to the intoxication of her shape. She smelled good, like...like something really nice. Not only would he get the medallion and all the treasure, but the next few days would be the most memorable of his life.

He grabbed his shoes, stepped from the bedroom, and moved like a wraith down the hallway. Kerrick's bedroom door was ajar, and he pushed it open further with his toe. Once inside, he closed the door behind him. He laid Lacy down on a rug near the window and grabbed the sheets from the bed. He tied at least twenty feet of sheets together and figured that would be enough.

He created a sling in the end of the sheets, slipped it under Lacy's arms, and lowered her from the window. With her full weight pulling against him, Miguel struggled but maintained control. He eased her to the ground before slipping into his shoes. He climbed out the window, dangled from the ledge, and dropped into the soft grass beside Lacy.

Within minutes, Miguel had carried Lacy into the bushes and was making his way through the darkened backyard of another house to a nearby street. Now, he just had to steal a car.

@♦@♦@♦@♦

Eduardo Perez pulled Pablo into the alley behind La Flor and delivered a massive blow to Pablo's nose. Three of his men stood in a loose circle to make sure no one interrupted the action. Perez pulled him back to his feet and punched him in the gut. Pablo vomited and fell again, moaning and holding his abdomen.

"I want to know who this guy is who killed Escobar's boy," Perez said through gritted teeth. "I saw the video of him in the club. I don't know him."

Pablo crawled backward toward the building, blood spurting from his broken nose. He heard the door to the club close and knew no one was coming to his aid. He was as good as dead. His breathing was labored, and he was certain he had broken ribs. He should have left the club after the fight earlier between Miguel and Escobar's men. How Miguel had gotten away was a mystery.

"I told you," Pablo whimpered. "I don't know who he is. He just said his name is Miguel, and he's not from here. We did some business. That's all. I do business all the time with people I don't know."

Perez slapped Pablo's face and screamed profanities. "Where's he from?" He pulled a pistol from his waistband and pressed into Pablo's neck.

The nurse whimpered and took a deep breath through his mouth. His teeth were busted. "He sounded Cuban, maybe." Blood and saliva dribbled from his mouth. "He just said killing Javier Escobar had been a mistake."

"It was a mistake, all right," Perez growled. "My boss will make this Miguel pay dearly."

"I think he meant he killed the wrong person," Pablo said weakly.

"Miguel whoever he is will regret the day he was born. Why were you meeting with him?"

"He bought propofol from me. He said he had a job to do up near the Walmart in Villa Nueva, or something like that. It involved a girl. I needed her weight to give the right dose, but he didn't know it. He just said she was around nineteen or twenty years old and perfect."

"Propofol? The date drug?"

Pablo nodded in agreement. "I know. Sounds pathetic to me. He was a creep."

"Did you say Nueva?" Perez scratched the stubble on his chin and turned toward the muscle-bound man next to him. "Hey, Marco. Didn't we just hear somethin' about Nueva on the radio? Somethin' about a dead body?"

"Yeah. We did. Some old man bought it and got wrapped up in plastic."

Perez turned back to Pablo. "If this doesn't add up, we'll be back. You better hope we find this guy."

Eduardo jumped into an Audi and tore out of the parking lot with the other three men following close behind him in a black SUV.

Pablo collapsed against the building. How had he allowed himself to get involved in something with the Los Unidos Cartel? He needed to leave town. Maybe the country. He could take a short leave from the hospital.

If he could drive himself home to pack, he'd head north to the States. He had dual citizenship, so he could hide out in Texas until everything cooled down. He vomited again before getting to his feet and staggering toward his car.

Chapter Three

Missing

Kerrick knocked harder on the door, but Lacy still didn't answer. He tried the knob. Locked. When he leaned his ear against the door, he heard water running. The light had come on in the bathroom earlier, so maybe she was taking a shower. He returned to the first floor where he found Jon sitting in a chair in the living room talking to José.

"Where's Lacy?" Jon asked.

"I guess she's in the shower. I think I heard water."

"Ann said she checked on her earlier, and the door was locked," José said. "Of course, that's been at least thirty minutes ago."

"Are you talking about me?" Ann teased as she joined them.

"We were talking about Lacy."

"I knocked on her door a while ago," Ann said, "but she didn't answer. I heard the water running. She should be out of the shower by now, though."

Kerrick went into José and Ann's bathroom and could hear water flowing through the pipes from upstairs. He had gotten to know Lacy well over the last few months and knew she didn't take long showers.

"Something's weird," Kerrick said as he returned to the living room.

José jumped up and headed to his bedroom, where he grabbed something from his luggage. "I can get into the room. Ann, come with me, and you can go in and check on her."

Kerrick watched as José turned something that looked like a strong, skinny nail. The doorknob twisted freely, and Ann hurried into the room. Kerrick and Jon heard her gasp and ran toward the steamy bathroom.

"She's not here," Ann shrieked. "The shower is running full blast, but no one's here."

"Where is she?" Kerrick asked. He hurried over to the sliding glass doors and looked out toward the street. He ran out of the room, down to his bedroom, and saw his window open. Fear wrapped an icy hand around his heart and made him go to the window and look out. "Oh, my God."

"What is it?" José said from behind him.

Kerrick stepped aside so José could look.

Ann grabbed Kerrick's arm. "What, Kerrick?"

"Someone got out of the window by using sheets tied together."

José turned and bolted from the room, followed by Kerrick and Ann. They ran out the door into the backyard.

Jon rushed out to them. "What's going on?"

"Lacy's gone," José said. He bent to examine the sheets and held the sling up for everyone to see. "Someone was lowered from that window, Jon."

Kerrick felt sick. This couldn't be happening. How could someone have taken Lacy when police were all over the place? It had to be Miguel.

Jon looked up and ran toward the bushes lining the yard. José and Kerrick followed.

José pointed. "There's some broken branches. They went through there, all right."

Kerrick pushed through the bushes into the backyard of another house. The lights were on, but he didn't see a car in the driveway. The three men ran through the backyard to the empty street. When they turned to go back through the yard, a man stepped through the door of the house onto the porch.

"*Buenos noches*," José said.

Kerrick could tell that something was wrong.

"*Mi carro!*" the man yelled. "*Mi carro!*"

José listened as the man chattered in Spanish and gestured wildly with his hands. José said something else to him, and the older man hurried back into his house.

José turned to Kerrick and Jon. "Someone took his car. He said his father has a habit of leaving the keys in the ignition. I told him to call the police."

❀❀❀❀❀❀❀

Lacy felt like she had fallen into a deep, dark tunnel, and she either didn't want to come out or couldn't. Her body suddenly shifted, and her head banged against something hard. She groaned and felt around her. *Where am I?*

She fought to open her eyes. She was somewhere dark, but she was moving. *I'm in the back of a car!*

Lacy struggled to remember what had happened. She felt the blood drain from her face. *Miguel. Oh, my God. Miguel.*

The car swerved and something slammed into them on the side. *Oh no!* Metal scraped against metal as Miguel slammed on the brakes.

Lacy felt another huge impact on the side of the car and then seemed momentarily weightless before the car crashed hard. Her head hit something solid, and everything went black.

She awakened to screaming. *Is that Miguel?* She could hear the voice of another man, maybe two. It sounded like someone was begging for mercy and screaming in pain. Lacy felt sick to her stomach. *Someone must be hurting Miguel.* Whoever was out there would not only hurt Miguel but would also hurt her. Unless…they didn't know she was there. She couldn't let herself get sick. She held her breath and thought for the first time in her life she should pray.

The only prayer that came to mind was "Now, I lay me down to sleep." *God, please help me. Please.*

She thought of her mother and wondered why the one person who cared the least for her popped into her head. It was possible her father cared less than her mother, but why couldn't she think of her wonderful Aunt Meg or Uncle Jon? Tears rolled down her cheeks. Whether her mother hated her or not, Lacy still wanted her.

She heard someone's fist hit the trunk. *I'm dead. If he opens this trunk, I'm dead.* The unmistakable sound of keys jingling sent ice through her veins. A hand slammed down on the trunk again, and Lacy heard rapid-fire Spanish. She didn't understand it all, but thanks to the boy who sat next to her in ninth grade, she knew enough to know the man was cursing.

Then, she heard the sweet sound of sirens. *Thank God.* Whoever was outside ran away.

Within a few minutes, Lacy heard men talking as they walked around the car. Someone knocked on the trunk. "Señorita Lacy?"

She hoped it was the police. For all she knew, it could be another Cartel member. *They wouldn't have used a siren, though.*

"I'm here!" Lacy did her best to shout, but it sounded more like a whisper.

The trunk popped open, and Lacy stared into the beam of a flashlight. She covered her eyes. Spanish words flew around her, and she couldn't concentrate enough to know what was being said. She sat up at the same time Kerrick ran into the middle of the officers.

"Lacy! Oh, thank God! Are you okay?"

"I think so," Lacy said. "My head hurts."

Kerrick smothered her in a hug.

"Señor, Señor!" a police officer warned him.

Kerrick wouldn't let go. Lacy heard another siren and realized she was about to be hauled off to a Mexican hospital. A hospital was the last place she wanted to go. She saw someone else forcing her way through the cops. Meg! Lacy began to cry.

"Lacy," Meg said as she pulled Kerrick away and put her arms around her niece. "Oh, Lacy."

Tears poured from Lacy's eyes as she noticed Jon and José standing beside the wrecked car. The whole scene was overwhelming.

"I don't want to go to the hospital," Lacy pleaded, her speech a little slurred.

"You just need to be checked out," Meg insisted. "Are you okay? Were you drugged?"

Lacy tried to think of what Meg had just asked. *Was I drugged?* "My head hurts a little, and my shoulder...the cloth. He gave me something, and I must have passed out."

"You've got to go the hospital, Meg said again. "They won't keep you overnight. We'll make sure you're okay and then go home."

Lacy's body stiffened. "I can't go back to that house."

Jon stepped forward. "You won't need to go back to the house. We'll get a hotel room. Okay?"

"That's fine," Lacy said. She thought of her friend she met when they first arrived in Veracruz. "Maybe Meson Del Mar. I'd like to see Ruth again."

After a few minutes, the EMTs helped Lacy out of the trunk and onto the gurney. When she turned to look back toward where she heard Miguel's screams, Jon stepped forward.

"It's probably best not to look over there, Lacy," Jon said. No need for you to have that memory lodged in your mind."

Lacy shuddered as she imagined what had happened to her captor. At least, he was dead. Of that, she was sure. He wouldn't be chasing after her and her medallion anymore.

"Who did it?" Lacy whispered to Jon as she lay down on the gurney. "Who killed Miguel?"

"The police think it was members of a cartel. Someone reported to the police Miguel may have been the one who killed the cartel leader's son. Do you remember that being on the news a couple of days ago?"

Lacy thought for a second. The last few days were a blur. The main thing on her mind was that Kerrick had left her because of that girl and her baby. She vaguely remembered José saying something about a murder when he and Ann first arrived. "Maybe."

"The way Miguel was killed shows a motive of revenge."

Lacy closed her eyes. *No one deserves to be tortured. He was a bad man, but…*

"I'm riding with you in the ambulance," Kerrick insisted. "If they let me."

After a little negotiating, Kerrick jumped in and rode off with Lacy as the ambulance sped toward the hospital.

@◆@◆@◆@◆

Jon, Meg, Ann, and José stepped into a crowded waiting area. It took them an hour to go back to the house, secure the place, grab some clothes, and head to the hospital in Veracruz. By the time they arrived, Lacy was in an exam room.

The waiting room smelled of sickness. Jon imagined all sorts of germs floating around the place and wondered if they should wait outside. Ever since practically living at Emory Hospital in Atlanta during his first wife's illness, he had hated hospitals. Being in one brought back a lot of sad memories.

"I'm guessing Kerrick is with her, so we may as well stay here," Meg suggested.

Jon guided Meg to a chair. "Too bad we don't have our scuba tanks."

"Scuba tanks?" She asked.

"Yeah. No telling what germs we're inhaling. It is a hospital emergency room after all."

Meg smiled. "I'm sure the doctor will want to fill us in when they're done. If we don't stay here, he won't know where to find us."

"Other than the lingering effects of whatever drug Miguel gave her, she's probably just bruised up a bit," José offered. "It had to be something pretty strong."

Meg put her hand on Jon's leg. "What are we going to do, Jon?"

"I suggest we get Lacy home, as in Miami. She's been through a lot over the last few months. She needs to rest and to somehow get mentally ready to start class."

"What about Freddy? Do we need to alert the authorities?"

"If he came down here of his own free will, the authorities can't do anything about him. I suppose if he came into Mexico illegally, they might be interested."

"I doubt the authorities will be too worried about an American kid slipping into the country," José said. "They have their hands full with other matters."

"Maybe José and I can come back in a week or so and do some poking around," Jon suggested. "We can at least get some ideas on where to start our search. If he got messed up with one of the cartels, he's probably farther north than Veracruz. Those groups usually hang out around Mexico City or the northern border."

"Miguel is dead," Meg said, "so they must be around here."

José leaned forward. "They were here because Escobar's son was killed in Boco del Rio. I don't think they normally work this area."

Jon looked up to see a short but pleasant looking man in a lab coat walking toward them. Jon watched him stop to speak to a family in the waiting area. After patting the older woman's shoulder, he turned toward the Davenports.

"Hello, I'm Dr. Rodriguez," he said as he extended his hand. His grip was strong. His English was accented, but Jon figured he would have no problem understanding him.

"Lacy is a strong young lady. She's been through a traumatic experience, but physically, she's going to be okay. It seems her captor gave her propofol, which is a drug we use for surgeries to put patients to sleep. She has a slight concussion, but she should be fine. I suggest you wake her every two hours through the night, just as a precaution. If you can't awaken her, call an ambulance. It also seems she got bumped around a good bit in the trunk of the car, so she'll be sore with some bruises. All in all, she's a fortunate girl. I think she'll be fine."

"That's great news," Meg said.

"I understand the cartel was involved," Dr. Rodriguez said. "Her story could have been very different. I suggest you wait a couple of days before flying and then follow instructions I'll leave for you." He extended his hand. "It's a pleasure to meet you and to be able to share good news. Please call me if you have any additional questions."

"Thank you, Dr. Rodriguez," Jon said as he reached for the doctor's hand. "We were supposed to fly home Tuesday, but we can wait until Wednesday, if needed. Thank you for your help."

"I guess our Mexican vacation just came to an end," Meg said as the doctor walked away. "I doubt this trip will go down as our most enjoyable one, but maybe our most memorable."

"Memorable, indeed," Jon agreed.

"I think every day with you, Jon Davenport, gets more memorable. Let's try for a few weeks of boring."

Jon leaned over and kissed his wife. "Let's go get our patient."

Chapter Four

Home Again

Lacy sighed as they drove down the driveway to the beautiful home in Miami Beach. The bright moon lit the entire front yard. A slight ocean breeze blew the fronds of the palm trees. Lacy felt like she was home when in fact, she'd only lived in the house for about a week before leaving for Mexico. Her body hurt in places she'd never noticed, and she longed for a good night's sleep. Sunday night had been rough. Poor Meg had to wake her every two hours, and the little sleep she had was filled with nightmares of Miguel's screams. Monday night was better. Dr. Rodriguez agreed for them to fly home Tuesday.

At least, she could wake up knowing Miguel could hurt her only in her dreams. It was crazy how she could see him lying on the ground, tortured. She hadn't seen his body beside the car, thanks to the police officers and Jon. It was probably best she hadn't.

They crawled out of the limo and grabbed luggage. Kerrick insisted on carrying Lacy's suitcase into the house, and she didn't refuse. Just over a week ago, she'd made a big deal about carrying her own luggage. Now, she decided she kind of liked being pampered. It was sweet.

Once inside the house, Lacy stopped and watched Meg come out of the master bedroom where she had put Carla to sleep. She thought back to the first time she had walked into the cavernous entry way of the Miami Beach house. The tall ceiling and tile floor made it feel so cold, but now it felt warm and inviting. She was home.

"Uncle Jon and Aunt Meg, thanks for everything. Thank you for being there for me in Mexico. I don't know what I would do without you. I wouldn't even have a place to live if..." She felt her eyes brimming with tears. "Thank you for loving me when I'm not always so easy to love."

Meg pulled Lacy into her arms. "You are so easy to love, Lacy, and you always have a home with us. What you need right now is a hot shower and a lot of sleep. I'll have a big breakfast ready in the morning whenever you get up."

José came in, his arms filled with luggage. "Where would you like for me and Ann to sleep tonight?"

"Judy has her suite downstairs. I'd suggest you sleep upstairs in the room at the end of the hallway."

Judy was a special part of their family. Though not related, Lacy loved her like she was her real grandma. When Jon and Meg got married, Judy came along as a package deal, and everyone knew she was a special package.

Ann stepped through the front door. "I didn't hear everything you said, but I heard end of the hallway upstairs. I'm so tired I could sleep on the kitchen stool."

"Lead the way, Sweetheart," José said. "I've got about seven minutes left in me before I collapse."

The two climbed the stairs and disappeared down the hall.

Lacy hugged Jon and followed Kerrick and her luggage up the stairs. Her bedroom was just as she'd left it. Kerrick set the suitcase down onto the bed and turned to Lacy. He took her hands, and she looked up into his blue eyes. They stood still as if in a trance. Lacy examined every inch of his face. Strong, pronounced chin, in need of a shave. She was drawn to his lips like a magnet to steel.

Lacy stood on her toes and slipped her arms around his neck. She pressed her lips against his, sending an explosion of passion through her entire body. She melted into him as he pulled her into a tight embrace. Strong, protective, tender Kerrick. So many words described this wonderful man. Her man.

Their kiss deepened, and all her senses were afire. She wanted nothing more than to spend the rest of her life in his embrace. Lacy pulled her mouth an inch away from his. "We're breaking the rules."

Lacy's mind flashed back to the discussion she and Kerrick had less than two weeks ago, though it seemed like years. Knowing Meg and Jon had strong opinions about sex before marriage and especially since Lacy was staying in their home, she felt they should honor her aunt and uncle's wishes. Besides, her mother had abandoned any rules, and Lacy didn't want to be anything like her mother. If she had to pick, she wanted to be like Meg, and she wanted her future marriage to reflect Jon's and Meg's marriage. Kerrick agreed to establishing some boundaries, though on more than one occasion, they leaned hard against them. So far, they had managed to maintain their commitment.

"The rules didn't say anything about hugging you or kissing you."

"No, but they do say something about you being in my room."

"We made the rules, so we can break them."

He moved his lips to hers again. Hungry. Desperate. She felt all six feet four inches of his hard body clinging to her as if he might lose her. Never again. She would never be separated from him.

"I brought fresh towels," Meg said from the open doorway.

Lacy pulled away from Kerrick. Her cheeks were hot with embarrassment. She wanted to crawl under the bed. What did she expect? They could have closed the door. Now, that would have been great for Meg to find them behind a closed door making out like they had no tomorrow.

"Thanks, Meg." Lacy looked at the floor as if counting the carpet fibers. "I was just about to take a shower."

"That's what I thought," Meg said as she eyed Kerrick. "Kerrick, you're welcome to stay tonight in the guest room downstairs, unless you'd rather go back to your dorm."

Kerrick cleared his throat. "Uh, yeah. I mean, yeah, the guest room will be great. I'd like to stay if you don't mind. I can go back to the dorm tomorrow night. I've got a meeting on campus with my advisor tomorrow, and Lacy has orientation on Thursday."

"I think I'll shower, too," Kerrick said. "I mean, not…you know…downstairs."

"Good night, Kerrick," Meg said with a grin. She walked over and hugged him. "I'm so glad you're in our lives."

"Me, too," Lacy said. "Good night."

@◆@◆@◆@◆

José slid closer to Ann and inhaled the scent of her clean hair. He had managed to stay awake until she'd gotten out of the shower and into bed. He wrapped his arms around her allowing his hand to slip down to her belly.

He didn't think loving her more was possible, but over the months of their marriage and her pregnancy, his love for Ann had grown. Over the years, he never thought marriage was a possibility because of his line of work. Members of Spain's Special Forces or bodyguards for government leaders didn't get married, but now he had a wife and would soon be a father. It all started when Jon Davenport became his best friend, and he became Jon's partner in the salvage business.

"How's he doing today?" José whispered into her ear.

"You sure are going to be surprised if he turns out to be a she."

"He's a boy. I'm sure of it."

Ann laughed and turned to face her husband. She traced the outline of his face and stared into his dark eyes. José felt the warmth and familiar thrill he experienced every time he looked at his wife, and now that she was carrying his child, she was irresistible. It seemed she grew more beautiful each day.

He leaned toward her and kissed her. He slipped his right hand through her auburn hair and pulled her against him.

"Seems like I remember hearing you say downstairs you only had seven minutes before you collapsed," Ann said with a grin. "I took at least ten minutes in the shower."

"The shower was a God send. It gave me ten minutes to get refreshed."

Ann laughed as José kissed her neck. "You know, José, I think we're going to be having a wedding before we have a college graduation."

José leaned back and grinned. "Are you trying to change the subject?"

"Oh? I didn't realize we had a subject." Ann winked and kissed him again. "I just can't quit thinking about Kerrick and Lacy."

José thought about the young couple. "No doubt they're in love, but I think Kerrick will graduate first, and the wedding will follow a week later."

"Do you want to place a bet on that?"

"I'm not a gambling man," José said as a smile spread across his face. "I've also learned it's best not to place a bet against my wife."

"Oh? You've learned that?"

"Yes. I find you are right eighty percent of the time."

"Only eighty?"

José laughed. Ann was so much fun, and it was a privilege being married to her. The day she had accepted his proposal was the best day of his life.

"I'm so glad we didn't have to struggle through some of the things Lacy and Kerrick have had to face," Ann said. "They are so young, and poor Lacy has been through so much."

"She's lucky to have Kerrick," José said. "Of course, Kerrick is also fortunate to have Lacy. When I first met her, I didn't think I'd be able to stand being on the same boat with her, but she has made a dramatic turn around. I've never seen anything like it."

"Kerrick has done a lot for her, but I think Jon and Meg are mainly responsible for the Lacy we see today."

José placed a kiss on her forehead and cupped her face. "You've played a part in her change as well, Sweetheart. You've been such a good friend to Lacy."

"She's a sweet girl, José. Well, she's sweet now. Before this summer, she would have made a sailor blush."

José's mind went back to the first time he could remember meeting Lacy. Though Jon insisted he'd introduced José to Lacy at his and Meg's wedding, José only remembered meeting her the time she first stepped aboard Jon's yacht, the *New Beginnings*. He didn't think she would make it on the salvage team a week because of her foul mouth. Meg had a very strict rule about bad language, so Lacy's transformation was miraculous.

"I suppose being kidnapped and having your life threatened more than once is enough to bring about some changes," Ann thought aloud.

José's mind returned to the time he and Jon rescued the girl from Coral Cay. She had been a mess. When Kerrick had fallen from the cliff, she would have gone after him if her leg hadn't been broken.

"Tragedy makes you grow up fast," José agreed. He thought back to the tragedy in his own life. Growing up without parents had made him a man. "From what Meg told you, it seems Lacy is well acquainted with tragedy. She's fortunate to have you and Meg."

"And you and Jon," Ann said as she leaned over and kissed his cheek.

José pulled Ann into his arms and thought he was the luckiest man on earth. Ann was a gem, his priceless treasure. She was going to be such a wonderful mother. She was kind and tender, but she could also be as tough as nails.

Their little boy would not get away with anything. At the same time, he would be strong, secure, and independent. Exactly what they wanted for their son. *What if it is a girl?* In that case, José hoped she would be just like Ann.

Ann placed her hand on his cheek. "Now, about that subject."

He pulled away for a moment and turned out the light.

Chapter Five

Kitchen Talk

As the morning sun peeked through the windows, Lacy came downstairs wearing white shorts and a baby blue tank top. Other than every muscle in her body hurting, she felt refreshed. A dark bruise on her shoulder stood out against the blue of her shirt. She saw Kerrick and Jon sitting on the back deck with mugs of coffee. Meg was in the kitchen at the sink.

Lacy noticed flour and eggs on the counter, but Meg hadn't cooked anything, yet. She saw a steaming mug of coffee beside the sink where Meg stood washing out a pot. The fresh coffee smelled good.

"Good morning, Meg."

Surprised, Meg turned. "Well, good morning. I figured you would have slept till at least ten o'clock. It's not even nine."

"I thought so too, but I woke up at seven thirty and couldn't go back to sleep. I slept some on the plane yesterday, so I guess I wasn't as tired as I thought. Where's Carla?"

"Judy took her down the street to the park. They ate earlier. How do you feel?"

"Like I got in a fight with a bull, and the bull won."

Meg laughed. "Dr. Rodriguez said you'd hurt for a few days. What are your plans today?"

"I guess I don't have any."

"Why don't we go shopping and leave the guys alone for a while? Doesn't Kerrick have something at school?"

Lacy looked toward Kerrick on the back deck. "He has to be on campus later today for some meeting or something."

"Oh, that's right. He said last night he has to meet with his advisor."

Lacy looked back at Kerrick and could tell he and Jon were in a deep conversation. "You said we need to leave the guys alone? So, the interpretation is Jon wants to talk to Kerrick?"

"Very perceptive," Meg said with a grin. "You could probably use some clothes for school too. Right?"

"What does he want to talk to Kerrick about?" Lacy asked, ignoring Meg's question.

"His intentions."

Lacy felt her heart skip a beat. "What do you mean? Or do I want to know?"

"You are a special girl, Lacy, and Jon wants to make sure Kerrick knows that and is willing to be the kind of man you deserve."

"It's not like we're about to get married, Meg."

Meg put a K-Cup in the Keurig and placed a mug underneath for fresh coffee. The silence was thick, and Lacy thought Meg would never reply. She obviously had something on her mind too. She finally turned with a fresh cup of coffee, handed it to Lacy, and walked toward the kitchen table.

Oh, boy. Here comes a sermon from Pastor Meg. Lacy took the seat across from her aunt. Though she'd never admit it to

Meg, these conversations with Meg were life-giving. They reminded her she was loved, and Meg's advice was always good.

"Do you love Kerrick?" Meg asked.

"Yes. You know I love him."

"And he loves you, Lacy. I have no doubt about that. Your love for one another doesn't necessarily mean you'll get married, but it could. It also means you face some significant relational challenges between now and then."

"Then? As if we're going to get married?"

"It's quite possible."

"And the challenges? Why don't you come right out and say you're worried we're having sex?"

"I'm not worried you're having sex, Lacy. Listen, I'm not that much older than you are. What, fourteen or fifteen years? I'll be the first to tell you sex is a wonderful thing. I also believe it should be enjoyed within the committed relationship of marriage."

"I know you feel that way, Meg, and I'm okay with you having your beliefs."

"It's not just about my faith, and there is a good reason God said sex is right and good when experienced between two people who love each other and are committed to one another for life. Sex should be a regular expression of that commitment. If it's as common as holding hands or even sharing a kiss, then it loses that expression of a life-long commitment. I can tell you that expressing my life-long commitment to my husband through the most intimate of experiences takes the meaning of sex to a different place. For me, it's not only physical and emotional. It's also spiritual."

Lacy took a sip of her coffee not knowing how to respond. *Sex is spiritual? Meg could have said one hundred things, but
I never would have imagined hearing that one.* "I know sex is sacred
to you, or whatever. I'm still working through all that, but I
can tell you that Kerrick and I have an understanding about
the issue."

"I remember. You told us you and Kerrick created
rules."

Lacy was sure her face was glowing. "Yes. We have an
agreement. Partly out of respect for you, but he and I are
also trying to come to terms with the whole sex thing. You
know, how it fits into our lives or whatever. I'm sorry, Meg.
Talking about this is a little awkward for me."

"I understand. This is not really what's on my mind or
Jon's, for that matter. We love you, Lacy, and we want to
make sure Kerrick is willing to take care of you like he
should. Jon wants to help him be the best man and husband
possible. He also wants him to know how serious it is for
him if he wants to marry our niece. Jon says you are special,
like a precious jewel, and he wants to make sure Kerrick un-
derstands just how special."

"Jon said that?"

"Yep. And he means it."

Lacy stared down into her cup. No one had ever said
anything like that about her, and she didn't know what to
say. Her eyes started to water. *Why doesn't my father think I'm
a jewel?* She bit her lip and reached for a napkin from the
holder on the table. *Come on, Lacy. Cut it out!*

"Where's Ann?" she asked after blowing her nose into
the napkin.

"She and José went up to Ft. Lauderdale to see Ann's aunt. She's in her 80's and not doing so well. Since it's just the two of us, I thought we should do something fun. You want to go shopping?"

Lacy opened her mouth, and Meg held up her hand. "Don't bring up the money issue. Ok? I'm grateful you don't like spending our money. It speaks well of your character. I want to buy you some clothes. Period. There's nothing wrong with an aunt taking her niece shopping."

"Sure," Lacy said. *How did she know what I was about to say?*

"Let's cook some breakfast, and then we can go check out The Shops at Midtown. Judy said she'd watch Carla for me so Jon and Kerrick could have plenty of time to talk."

"Doesn't Judy want to go shopping with us?" Lacy asked.

"Her definition of shopping is a little different than ours. Besides, she has a friend in Miami she wants to visit this afternoon, and she'll probably head out to see her after putting Carla down for a nap. Kerrick will be on campus, so Jon can take over Carla duty."

By the time Lacy and Meg returned from shopping, Jon and Kerrick had grilled steaks and pulled baked potatoes from the oven. Kerrick had also created an amazing salad that looked colorful enough for Bon Appetit magazine.

Lacy walked behind Kerrick in the kitchen and slid her hand over his broad back. "You're handsome, strong, and you can cook. I'm amazed at your hidden talents."

Kerrick turned around and kissed her. "Jon did the cooking. I just made the salad."

"And you kissed me only because Jon and Meg aren't in the room."

"No. I kissed you because you're beautiful, intoxicating, I love you, and we happen to be alone."

"I'm guessing that means your talk with Jon didn't dissuade you from pursuing me."

He pulled her into his arms and kissed her again. When he finally pulled away, he held her face and stared into her eyes. "No. It reminded me how fortunate you are to have someone like Jon and Meg in your life. They love you so much. It almost makes me want to follow our rules even more."

"Almost?" Lacy laughed. "I figured Jon would have that kind of effect on you. He can be persuasive."

Jon came in from the deck with a plate piled with four huge steaks and another plate with a single hotdog rolling around on it. The aroma from the steaks was incredible, but Lacy wondered how in the world she could ever hope to eat one. One was big enough to feed her for two or three meals.

Jon looked toward Lacy. "Would you mind finding my beautiful bride and telling her dinner is served?"

Lacy hurried out of the room and found Meg in the master bedroom brushing Carla's hair. Lacy, Meg, and Carla joined the men and sat down to a wonderful meal. Jon told the group his version of how Meg asked him to marry her.

"That's not how I remember it, Uncle Jon."

"It's the gospel truth. Any other version must have come from a revisionist."

"You know where you go for lying," Lacy said with a grin.

"Yeah," Jon said. "Washington, D.C. That's my joke."

"Whatever you did to convince Meg to marry you, I'm glad you did," Lacy said. "You guys have taught me so much. When are you heading back to Pirate's Cove?"

Lacy loved Jon and Meg's house on Great Exuma in the Bahamas. It was like the most exquisite pictures on Pinterest, but it was also filled with love and laughter. She felt safe there. Safe from parents who didn't love her, bad guys who wanted to hurt her, and a world that didn't seem to care about her. Somehow, this house in Miami felt like an extension of the wonderful compound they called Pirate's Cove.

"We figured we'd at least wait until you finished orientation at the university," Meg said. "I guess that means we'll go home Friday morning."

"Yeah," Jon agreed. "I wish we could stay longer, but we need to get back home. If José and I are going to return to Mexico soon, I have some business that needs tending. Besides, I think Judy is past ready to get home."

Meg got up and began to clear the table of dishes. Lacy joined her at the sink and started rinsing the dishes and loading the dishwasher.

Kerrick walked into the kitchen and put his hands on Lacy's hips. "You want to go for a walk down the beach?"

"Sure. That sounds great. I feel like I just ate a whole cow."

Kerrick laughed. "I'll need to head back to my dorm before long."

"Y'all go ahead," Meg suggested. "I'll finish up in here."

Chapter Six

A Man's Man

The evening was still quite warm, but a pleasant, steady breeze blew through Lacy's hair. They passed several middle-aged couples, and Lacy wondered what it would be like to be married to someone for so many years. She hoped to learn from experience. She thought of her parents and felt sad for them. How could two people love each other at first and then hate one another so severely just a few years later?

She didn't know if marriage to Kerrick was in her future, but if it were, it would be forever. No matter what challenges they may encounter, she couldn't imagine anything that would make her not want to always be Kerrick Daniels' wife.

Dinner lasted longer than any meal Lacy ever remembered. She'd stared at Kerrick throughout the ordeal hoping for a hint of his conversation with Jon, but all she got was an occasional wink and leg squeeze. Thinking about the conversation she was about to have made her feel like a million butterflies had landed in her stomach.

They stepped onto the white sand, and Lacy pulled the sandals from her feet. Sand filled in the gaps between her toes, and she had a brief memory of burying her father's legs in the sand when she was a little girl. He suggested they build a sandcastle, and she could be the sand princess. How could that man have gone from being a doting father to a class A jerk?

"Why don't we leave our shoes over by that post," Kerrick suggested as he pointed to their left. "No one will bother them."

He took their shoes and dropped them beside the post. They joined hands and walked south down the beach toward the state park. Lacy grinned as she thought about their night together, being locked inside the lighthouse at the state park. She would never forget it—it was quite romantic. Kerrick's friend who let them slip into the park after hours didn't think to tell them not to close the door of the lighthouse. No one else would consider falling asleep on a concrete floor romantic, but she would always remember being held in Kerrick's strong arms as she drifted off to sleep.

"What are you thinking?" Kerrick asked.

Lacy looked down the beach in the direction of the lighthouse. "Other than the obvious? I was just thinking about our first night together."

"Our first night?"

"Yeah. Have you already forgotten?"

"Oh, that night. I'd rather not remember that experience as our first night together. I figured you were thinking about my conversation with Jon."

"*That…*" Lacy paused and made quotation marks in the air, "…is the obvious."

"Got it. The obvious. The story of the lighthouse will be an amazing story to tell our children."

Lacy stopped and stared up at Kerrick. "What did you say?"

He grinned at her. "How many do you want to have?"

"Children?"

"Yeah."

"Who says I want to have children?" *Not to mention the fact that you're actually talking about marrying me.*

"You do. Every time you're with Carla, it's obvious."

Lacy looked down at the sand and wiggled her toes. "I've never been able to think of myself as a mother. I'm afraid."

"Afraid of what?"

"Afraid I'll be a terrible mother."

"No, you won't. Just learn from Meg. She's an awesome mother."

They turned and continued walking down the beach. The sun had already dropped out of sight, though they still had daylight left. They walked in silence down the beach for at least ten minutes. Lacy considered the fact she was walking with the guy she loved, and they didn't even have to talk. However, she was still dying to know about his conversation with Jon. Why didn't he go ahead and tell her?

"So, what did you and Jon talk about?" Lacy said, breaking the silence.

"Well," Kerrick said, drawing out the word. "A lot of things."

"Like what?"

"Well," he drew out again. "Like women. We talked about women."

Lacy stopped and looked at him. "You talked about women? You've got to be kidding."

"Nope. We specifically talked two particular women, but maybe some of it was women in general."

"And what did you have to say about women?" Lacy asked with a smile in her voice.

"Jon quoted some Bible verse about women being weaker."

"You've got to be kidding!" Lacy said again. "For starters, there's no verse in the Bible that says that."

"Actually, there is, but it doesn't mean what you think. Jon told me it doesn't mean weak as compared to strong, but rather delicate and priceless, like fine china. I already know you're priceless. I've just never thought of you as being like fine china."

Lacy started walking again, pulling Kerrick along with her. She had heard a woman once talking about how chauvinistic the Bible was, but that verse didn't sound chauvinistic. It sounded sweet.

"We talked a lot about what it means to be a man. For a man to love his wife sacrificially and selflessly. He said my first priority other than God should be you."

"Me?"

"Yes, when we get married. I suppose that even applies to now, before we get married."

Lacy stopped again. "Where did all this marriage talk come from?"

Kerrick stared into Lacy's eyes. "It's a topic I want us to talk about one day."

"Oh," Lacy said, and they both started walking again. "About three months ago, or so, I wasn't ever getting married."

"I know. I'm hoping you will eventually change your mind."

"It's possible."

They walked together until the beach was dark. She felt warm all over and proud to be Kerrick's girlfriend. The more he spoke of his time with Jon, the more Lacy loved her uncle, if loving him any more was possible. She liked the fact Jon wanted to help Kerrick be the kind of man she wanted for a husband, if she wanted a husband. *Of course, I want a husband, and I want him to be Kerrick.*

Her love for Kerrick had grown, and this episode with Hannah the Husband Stealer let her know she didn't want to lose Kerrick to anyone. She had never known any other guy like him. Most guys were jerks, hung up on themselves, but Kerrick was considerate and humble. He never pushed her for anything—even the one thing every guy wanted. His priority seemed to be her and her needs. No way in the world was she letting him go.

Back at the house, Kerrick hurried inside to gather his things while Lacy strolled into the living room where José and Ann were talking with Jon and Meg. Kerrick joined them and said his goodbyes, and Lacy followed him out to his car.

"I enjoyed our walk," Lacy said. "It means a lot for you to share things so openly."

"You're easy to talk to, Lacy. The more I talk to you, the more I want to talk to you. We've spent so much time together over the last few months, I don't want to be separated from you."

"You don't have to be."

"I'm not moving in."

"I didn't mean that, but you can come over any time."

"Jon says we need to be careful. He warned me about building our relationship on emotions and physical…you know."

"Kissing? Are you saying you don't want to kiss me?"

"Heavens no, Lacy. One problem I have is I want to kiss you all the time."

"That's a problem?"

Kerrick laughed. "Not for me. Jon just encouraged me to make sure our relationship was growing deeper emotionally and even spiritually."

Lacy looked down at her feet. *There's that word again—spiritual. Conversation is spiritual. Sex is spiritual. It sounds like everything is spiritual.* "How do you do that?"

"I'm not one hundred percent sure, but I'm determined to figure it out. I don't want our relationship to be built solely on sex."

"Being we haven't had sex, I don't think you need to worry about that right now."

"You know what I mean, Lacy. I want to know you. I want to know how you think and how you feel. I want to be the man you've always dreamed of. If you haven't dreamed of having a husband, then I want our relationship to birth that dream in your heart."

Lacy felt a lump form in her throat and Kerrick's face became blurry. *I cannot start crying. Come on, Lacy. Get a grip.*

He placed his hand on her cheek and slowly bent until their lips met. Her heart pounded in her chest as she slid her hands through his hair.

Kerrick finally pulled back and looked into her eyes. "One thing Jon said really stuck with me. He told me I need to be the kind of man who will help you become the best possible version of yourself. I want to do that, Lacy Henderson." He kissed her again. She felt numb, stunned. She didn't know how to respond. She'd never had anyone say something like that to her before.

"I love you," Kerrick whispered, and he turned to go.

Lacy stood on the front porch as Kerrick turned his truck around and pulled out of the driveway. He was the sweetest guy she'd ever known. If he had asked her to marry him tonight, she would have said yes without hesitation.

She walked back into the house and slipped upstairs to her room. Lacy didn't even want to speak to the four most important adults in her life who sat in the living room. She didn't want any part of this evening to slip from her memory. She wanted to seal this night up and treasure it for the rest of her life.

@◆@◆@◆@◆

"What did you and Kerrick talk about all afternoon?" Meg asked as she crawled into bed and snuggled against Jon's back.

"Oh, we mainly talked about what it means to be a real man."

"Sounds interesting. If anyone could have that talk, you could."

Jon rolled over and took Meg into his arms. She could feel his heart beat as if it were hers. She supposed in a way, it was.

"Kerrick is a fine person," Jon finally said. "If anyone can understand Lacy and help her figure out her life, he can. He has character."

"He really does. Did you talk about marriage?"

"A little. I mainly talked about what kind of man he wanted to become, and I planted a few thoughts. Some of them are already true about him."

"Like what?"

"Like being selfless. Kerrick is not a selfish guy. I see him focusing his attention on Lacy. I can honestly say I don't see him thinking only of his needs."

"I agree. You're that way, Jon. You always have my needs first in your mind. I'm very blessed and fortunate."

"I'm the one who's blessed, Meg. Being your husband is the greatest thrill I can imagine."

Meg lay still, secure in her husband's arms. His body was firm, but his heart was soft. "Is that all you talked about?"

Jon chuckled. "We talked about a lot of things, like being a servant leader and how a man walks point for his family."

Meg thought back to a talk she heard Jon give at a conference in Georgia. He compared a husband to a soldier who walks point for his squad. She still remembered Jon saying a real man accepts responsibility for the whole squad, willingly sacrifices for the good of his team, maintains laser focus on the objectives of the mission, and leads his team strategically while understanding the success of the mission rested upon his shoulders. She had been so proud of him that night.

"Are you and José really planning to go back to Veracruz?" Meg said softly.

"I don't know about Veracruz, but we need to return to Mexico. But before going, we need to visit Randal and his mother in Virginia. I'd like to get as much information about what Freddy said he was going to do. His girlfriend knows more than she's saying."

"Probably," Meg agreed. "Aren't you bothered by the Cartel? I mean, doesn't what happened to Miguel worry you?"

"I don't plan to knock heads with the Cartel. I just want to meet with Freddy and try to talk him into going home. That's all. I can't force him to leave."

"Please don't take risks, Jon. Carla and I need you."

Meg snuggled closer into Jon's arms. Her life had changed because of this wonderful man. After Steve died, she didn't think she could ever be happy again, much less remarry. Saying her vows to Jon had been one of the happiest days of her life. She was so fortunate. So blessed. She wanted to grow old with Jon. He didn't need to end his life trying to save a boy from the Mexican Cartel.

She trusted her husband. Jon never did anything without forethought. Well, that wasn't exactly true. Her mind went back to the bus station incident in Veracruz. He acted out of love. He even took dumb risks sometimes out of love.

"Jon?"

"Hmm?"

"Please don't take any risks. Do you promise?"

"I promise. If I do, it will only be because I have no choice."

"What does that mean? I want to grow old with you. Really old."

"We will, Sweetheart."

Jon reached over and turned out the bedside lamp. Meg felt his hands on her back causing a shiver to run through her. She slipped her hands under his shirt and melted into his body. They entered into the familiar place a husband and wife knew, and they knew it well. It was a place of abiding joy and relational intimacy. It was a place called love.

Chapter Seven

Trouble at Home

Turning the final page of the *Curious George* book, Meg pulled Carla into a hug and kissed the top of her head. She loved reading to her little girl and was thrilled Carla loved books so much. However, she hoped Carla wouldn't develop the wander lust of the little monkey. They had enough adventure in their lives.

Meg was glad this most recent adventure was about to end. She was exhausted and ready to get back to their home on Great Exuma. She loved living in the Bahamas, and at that moment, there was no place she'd rather be. When she and Jon first talked about relocating to the island, she wondered if she'd miss living in the Atlanta area. She didn't. Never sitting in another traffic jam on Interstate 285 was reason enough.

"Sweetie, Mama has to get dinner ready," Meg said. "Lacy will be home from school shortly, and Daddy will be back soon, too. Can you play with your blocks in the kitchen?"

"Unc A?" Carla managed.

Meg smiled down at Carla. Her little girl loved José and Ann like they were family. José gave her special attention and made up the most wonderful stories for her. Meg told him he should write a book.

"If I put my stories in a book," José had once said, "they wouldn't belong to Carla."

Meg came to understand José didn't want to write a book. He was well read and brilliant. He never talked about his military service in the Spanish special forces, but Jon said he had experience in some very dangerous missions. Many people who served in the military didn't talk about what happened on the battlefield. She supposed they didn't want to relive the bad memories.

"Uncle A and Aunt Ann will be here for dinner, too."

"Gama?"

"Yes, Sweetie. Grandma Judy is here. Hopefully, my spaghetti will pass her approval."

Meg enjoyed cooking sometimes and giving Judy time on her own. Meg tried to make her feel she wasn't a maid or a cook, but Judy insisted on cooking, cleaning, and taking care of Carla as much as possible. Carla loved her as though she were her real grandmother.

Meg looked at her watch and checked the clock on the stove. Lacy would soon be home. She dreaded telling her about the phone call from Liz. Seeing her sister's name on the caller I.D. that afternoon surprised her. Liz never called unless she wanted something. Jon was well off before they married and found the *San Roque* treasure, and Meg wondered how long it would be before Liz started asking for money. It wasn't long.

Jon was gracious to Liz from the start. When her car broke down, he bought her a new one, but when she called needing money for rent, Jon insisted she read Dave Ramsey's *Total Money Makeover* before he'd help. He helped her get on a budget last year and told her he would only help in the future if he saw she was following her budget. Jon could have told the sun to quit setting for the good that did. Liz was bitter toward Rick, her ex-husband, mad at Meg and Jon because they wouldn't help with her credit card payments, and angry at the world.

When Meg called her sister from Mexico to tell her what had happened to Lacy, Liz was more concerned about getting dressed for a date than the well-being of her daughter. Before answering the phone earlier, Meg thought maybe Liz was feeling bad about being so selfish. Maybe she was calling to check on Lacy. That was not the case.

This phone call had been different. Liz seemed broken up by the news she shared. Meg didn't know if Lacy could handle anymore upheaval, but Meg had no choice. She considered getting her niece out of orientation but decided waiting a few hours wouldn't hurt. It was Lacy's first day at her new school, and she didn't need anything derailing her.

Meg called Jon earlier, but he didn't answer his phone. He told her before he left he may not be available for a while because he would be in a meeting with a couple of CEOs who wanted to be a part of their program to help inner-city boys. So, she kept her conversation with Liz to herself. She dreaded dinner.

Everyone at dinner was bubbling over with excitement about the day, everyone but Meg. She knew her bombshell would certainly change the atmosphere. If Jon knew the news, it would somehow be easier to talk with Lacy about it. Maybe she should tell him before talking with Lacy. She was aware of the sound of conversation around her but had a hard time focusing on what was said.

"You sure are quiet, Hon," Jon said. "Carla must have worn you out today."

Meg jumped as she realized her husband was talking to her. "Sorry. My mind drifted. So, Lacy, are you going to like your classes?"

Lacy looked amused. "I think you're somewhere else, Aunt Meg. I just said I didn't get any classes I wanted and this semester was going to be a disaster."

"Oh, sorry Lacy. What are you going to do?"

"My advisor said I could take some of them online and possibly make changes during drop/add."

"What did you learn about graduation, Kerrick?" Jon asked.

"Looks like everything should be in order to finish up in May. I can't believe it's finally here."

"What are you going to do after graduation?" Judy asked.

"I know of a salvage company that pays top dollar," Jon said with a wink. "Of course, that's not exactly marine biology."

"Jon," Meg interrupted. "Don't put Kerrick on the spot like that. He may want to get another job."

"It's okay, Meg. It's not awkward. I'll figure it out before May."

After dinner, Jon helped Meg clean up while the rest of the group played a game. Lacy, however, read a book to Carla.

Meg leaned over to Jon. "I need to talk to you, just not with everyone around."

Jon's face grew serious. "After we get Carla to bed, we'll have a few minutes alone."

Once Carla was asleep, Meg told Jon about the call from Liz. He listened in silence, but she could see the weight of the issue on his face. They heard laughter around the table, and Meg knew she had to get Lacy alone.

"Kerrick needs to be a part of this conversation," Jon said. "Judy has already gone to her room, and I think I can get José to end the game early and leave us alone. I'll send him a text."

"What will you tell him?"

Jon pulled out his phone and began typing. "I'll just say we need to talk with Lacy about some difficult information, and it would be best if he and Ann left us alone. He'll understand."

As Jon and Meg returned to the dining area, José said. "Hey, I'm ready for bed. Let's let this round be the last."

"You're sleepy?" Ann asked. "Since when do you go to bed before ten o'clock?"

Lacy smiled conspiratorially. "He said he was ready for bed, but he didn't say he was sleepy."

Meg cleared her throat. "Well, uh, who's winning?"

"Lacy!" Kerrick said. "She always wins at Phase Ten. I don't know how she does it."

"Too bad we have to quit," Lacy said. "I'm on a roll."

"Don't count your chickens," Ann warned. "You're only on the fifth phase."

After a few more minutes of play, Lacy smiled as she went out again. "Like I said, I'm on a roll."

"I'm done," José said. "We'll pick up here another time."

José and Ann said goodnight and climbed the stairs to their room. Meg made a cup of coffee. She was putting off

the conversation and knew she had better start talking before Lacy and Kerrick decided to walk down the beach or
something.

"Lacy, do you or Kerrick want any coffee?"

"I'll take some, Meg," Kerrick said.

Meg handed him the first cup and began making another. Jon sat down at the table, and Meg walked over with
his coffee, as well as her own.

"I feel like something's up," Lacy said. "You guys are too
quiet."

"Lacy," Meg began. "I got a phone call from your
mother."

"I don't think I want to hear it," Lacy interrupted. "Let
me guess. She promised to come down for my next birthday
because she feels so badly about missing it last month, or…
wait, does she need money to repair a broken fingernail?"

"I know you and your mother have issues, and she's not
always at her best, but your bitterness is not going to hurt
anyone but yourself."

Lacy looked down at her coffee cup. "Sorry. That was
rude. Do you want to give me the grace and space sermon?"

"Grace and space?" Kerrick asked.

"We need to give everyone grace to mess up and space
to grow up," Lacy replied by rote. "I've heard that sermon
several times from Meg over the last year or so, and it's actually worth hearing. Seems like Mom should have grown up
by now, though."

Meg smiled. A few months ago, Lacy would not have
admitted the grace and space talk was worth hearing. She
had made wonderful progress.

"Her call was nothing about herself," Meg said. "It was about your father."

"Now there's a vast topic," Lacy said. "He definitely needs grace and a lot of it. I haven't even heard from him in what, two years? No, I think it's been over three years."

Lacy's relationship with her father was worse than her relationship with her mother. He slipped out of her life after divorcing her mother and had not bothered to stay in touch. He married the woman he was seeing while still married to Liz, but they had divorced. He was now on wife number three.

"He's sick, Lacy." Meg said. Silence filled the dining area.

"What's wrong with him?" Lacy finally asked.

"It seems he's been sick for a while and hasn't told anyone. He has cancer. Colon cancer."

Lacy looked as if someone slapped her. "He's dying?"

"I'm not sure, but he's really sick," Meg said. "He's at Emory hospital, and he asked if you would come see him."

"Let me get this straight," Lacy blurted out. "He runs around on my mother and leaves us to marry his bimbo. He ignores me for over three years, and I'm supposed drop everything and run to his hospital bed because he's feeling guilty about being a crappy father?"

"Something like that," Jon said. "You know, Lacy, your father has had serious issues."

"Got that right," Lacy said.

"The fact is we all have issues," Jon continued. "I'm not excusing your father's faults, but you need to think about your feelings. We feel anger when we've been mistreated. Forgiving someone is one of the greatest, most selfless things we can do, but the truth is, we are the greatest beneficiaries of having a forgiving spirit."

"Meg's told me that before," Lacy said as a tear ran down her cheek.

"I know you have a lot of hatred toward your father," Meg said, "but it is hurting only yourself."

"After what he has done to me and Mom, he doesn't deserve to be forgiven."

"Do any of us deserve forgiveness?" Jon asked. "Frankly, we all deserve hell, but we're offered grace instead."

"I don't know if Rick is going to die, but I know from experience you don't want to leave anything unsaid. The only way you can truly heal is to lay it all on the table and forgive your father, whether he wants it or not."

Lacy got up from the table. "I'll think about it."

Kerrick stood up beside her. "Why don't we go for a walk?"

"I think I just want to go to bed," Lacy said.

"I suggest a walk," Kerrick insisted. "Fresh air always gives me a better perspective." Silence filled the room. "Please?"

"Okay," Lacy mumbled. "I'll get my sandals."

When Lacy left the room, Kerrick looked at Meg and Jon. "I'm sorry you had to break that news to her."

"I'm sorry, too," Meg said, "but I'm glad Lacy has you."

"I don't really know what to say," Kerrick acknowledged.

"Just love her," Jon suggested. "Just love her."

Chapter Eight

Night Stroll

Kerrick looked up at the starlit sky as Lacy stared at her feet. They walked down the short street to the beach without saying a word. He took her shoes, placed them beside the familiar post, and reached for her hand. As they splashed through the receding tide, he heard her sniff. He was prepared for tears.

"You want a tissue?" Kerrick asked as he held one out to her.

"Thanks. When did you become a Kleenex dispenser?"

Kerrick looked at his watch. "Exactly fourteen minutes ago. You want to talk about your dad?"

"Not really. I'm not ready to deal with my parents right now. I've had so much hate in my heart toward them the last couple of years that there's no room for grace, space, forgiveness, or even love. My father's been such a jerk, and my mother…Don't get me started."

Although Kerrick had known Lacy only a few months, he knew quite a bit about her parents. His parents were so full of love and support he couldn't imagine what it was like to have a mother and a father who didn't care about their child. He winced at the memory of Lacy leaving for Florida without telling her mother, and her mother not realizing she was missing until two days later. Her father was no better. Maybe worse.

"The thing is, Lace, the only way to work through your anger and bitterness is to somehow find a way to forgive your father. The sooner you do that, the better."

"You sound like Meg."

"Maybe that's because what we are both saying is the right thing. Holding onto bitterness never resolves anger, and nurtured anger only hurts you in the end."

"I don't want to forgive him. He's getting what he deserves."

Kerrick knew Lacy didn't mean what she said, but he didn't know what to say or how to help her. "Maybe he doesn't deserve your forgiveness, but you deserve being free from the pain caused by his failures."

Lacy stopped and looked up into Kerrick's eyes. "Do I? I'm part of the reason my father left in the first place."

"You can't say that, Lacy."

"Yes, I can because it's true."

"Your father is a messed up, broken man. He left because of his own selfishness, lust, and maybe impatience with himself and your mother. I don't know the details, but I can tell you fathers don't leave because of their daughters. I don't know your father, but the fact he hasn't called you in three years tells me he's been consumed with himself."

Lacy turned and started walking down the beach again. Kerrick hurried beside her and took her hand.

"I have a feeling lying in a hospital bed with a terminal illness has caused your father to do a lot of thinking about his life and his decisions."

"So, I'm supposed to go help rid him of his guilty conscious so he can die in peace?"

"Not necessarily, but you should go and at least take a small step toward making things right with him. If he really is dying, you won't have a second chance."

The next twenty minutes passed in silence as they trudged down the beach hand-in-hand. Kerrick felt helpless and totally inept. How could he help her carry this load and work through her problems? They turned around to head back to the house before he spoke again.

"Will you at least try?"

"How do I do that?"

"It has nothing to do with feelings. It just starts with actions. Will you take a step toward reconciliation by going to see him? I'm not saying you have to forgive him or that everything will suddenly be all daisies and roses. Sometimes, forgiveness takes time."

"I don't know, Kerrick. I'll have to think about it."

"I'll go with you. You won't have to do it by yourself."

"I'll think about it."

@◆@◆@◆@◆

Meg watched Lacy descend the stairs the next morning. The dark circles under her eyes and her uncombed hair told Meg all she needed to know about Lacy's night and current state of mind. After Kerrick and Lacy left for their walk the previous night, Jon had talked to José and Ann. They all knew Lacy needed to go see her father, but it would have to be her decision.

Meg and Jon waited up a while on Lacy and Kerrick to return but finally went to bed. They heard the door open around midnight, but Jon suggested they let her slip upstairs alone.

"Good morning," Meg said. "You want a cup of coffee?"

"Sure."

"Did you have a rough night?"

Lacy sat down at the table as if in a trance. She combed her fingers through her long, blond hair and stared out the kitchen window. Meg placed Lacy's coffee cup in front of her and sat down beside her.

"I'm going to go see my father," Lacy said after taking a sip of her coffee.

Meg waited to see if she wanted to say anything else, but she was quiet. "Would you like for me and Jon to go with you?"

"No. Thanks. Kerrick said he'd go with me."

"I'm glad to hear you're going."

"I don't want to talk about it right now," Lacy said. "I'm somehow going to go see my father because…well, because it's the right thing to do. It's certainly not because he deserves it or because I'm going to forgive him. He deserves to be in…"

"We all deserve to be there, Lacy," Meg interrupted. "I'm glad you're at least going to see him. That sounds like a good plan."

Lacy stared at the floor for a full minute. "Meg, I've hated him for so long that I think hate has become my comfort zone. How dysfunctional is that?"

"It's understandable. I think you're doing the right thing."

"I suppose if you feel like praying for me, that would be okay."

Meg smiled as she pulled her coffee cup to her lips. Lacy never suggested prayer in her life. She had attended church a few times as a teenager, but religion and spirituality had never been much of a priority. Meg knew the abuse and emotional pain she had experienced for so long had jaded her against relationships, including a relationship with God.

"Of course, I'll pray for you. I have been for a long time."

"Funny. I said I didn't want to talk about it, and here I am talking about it. I think I'm going to take a shower."

"When do you want to leave for Georgia? I'll get Jon to buy plane tickets to Atlanta for you and Kerrick."

"I'm sorry I'm such a financial burden to you and Uncle Jon."

"You're not a burden, Lacy. We'll work it out of you this summer. Trust me."

"It's going to take the next thirty summers to pay you back for what you've spent over the last couple of months."

Meg put her hand on Lacy's. "Jon and I think you're worth the investment. When do you want to go?"

"I think I should leave early in the morning and come back tomorrow night. I'd rather not spend the night at home and get caught up in my mother's drama."

"Sounds good. Jon and I have decided to wait until Sunday afternoon to go back to Pirate's Cove. Maybe we could all go to church Sunday morning here in Miami."

Lacy grinned at her aunt. "You're pretty smooth with that church stuff. I ask you to pray for me, and next thing I know, you have me in church."

Meg laughed. "You don't have to go. Jon and I enjoy attending Journey Church when we're in Miami. I just thought you and Kerrick might like to go."

"The last time I went to church, I swear you got the preacher to preach about forgiving my mother. How close are you to this preacher?"

"You know that's not true," Meg said with a laugh. "I do find coincidences happen a lot more when I'm praying about something or someone. I guess you know I don't really believe in coincidences."

"And you were praying for me?"

"Of course."

"I'll think about church." Lacy got up from the table and slid her chair back into place. She picked up her coffee mug. "And Meg."

"Yes?"

"Thanks for loving me and being patient with me. I know I'm quite a project."

"You're not a project, Lacy, and I do love you."

Lacy's smile lit her face. "I think I'll take a shower before Kerrick sees this wreck. He may decide he doesn't want me after all."

"I don't think that's likely. It seems he loves you whether you're a wreck or not."

Meg left the kitchen, coffee in hand, and went to find Jon. She heard the television in the living room. He was so focused on the weather report he didn't seem to notice her entering the room. When she sat down beside him, he flinched in surprise.

"You sure are jumpy. I must really look scary this morning."

"You look radiant, as always. I was just watching the weather report. It seems we have some trouble coming."

"What kind of trouble?"

"Hurricane. They're calling it David, and they're predicting it will be a category three sometime today. It's still a few days out, but it's heading for the Bahamas. They're even saying it could hit south Florida if it doesn't turn north."

Meg was alarmed. When they left for Mexico, they did nothing to prepare for a major hurricane. "If it's a three now, it could gain strength."

"The meteorologist said he expected it to become a four before making landfall. It could even become a five. I think we'd better get home and prepare."

"Okay. I'll pack."

Meg heard the front door open and passed Kerrick coming through the foyer as she raced toward her room.

"Good morning," Kerrick said. "What's the hurry?"

"Morning, Kerrick. A large hurricane is heading toward the Bahamas. Jon says we need to go home to get the house ready."

"I can go with you," he offered. "You'll probably need all the help you can get."

"I'm sure Jon would appreciate it."

Kerrick looked up the staircase toward Lacy's room. *I wonder if she's up yet. She got to bed late. Maybe I should give her a little longer.* He hoped she slept better than he. She was so broken last night his heart hurt for her. He knew it was past two thirty in the morning before he fell asleep. He went into the kitchen to make a cup of coffee and saw Jon in the living room on the couch with his laptop open.

"Hey," Kerrick said. "So, what's the latest?"

"Good morning, Kerrick. They're saying it's headed toward the Bahamas, and it will be a cat three. I have maybe three days to get everything ready at Pirate's Cove."

"Sounds to me like you can use help. Want me to come along? Lacy might want to come, too."

Kerrick realized he offered to go with Lacy to see her father, but they had never said when they should go. The obvious time would be this weekend, but they couldn't be in two places at once. As important as Lacy's trip was, getting the compound in the Bahamas ready for a major storm was more important. He and Lacy could fly to Atlanta from Nassau as soon as they finished storm preparations. *I wonder what will happen with classes on Monday. If there's a chance a hurricane could hit south Florida, I bet classes will be canceled.*

"That would be great," Jon said. "I was looking at more information on this storm, and it could really get rough." He turned his laptop toward Kerrick. "This article says it could even become a category five. The path could come toward south Florida. That would be devastating. You weren't alive when Andrew hit in '92. It was bad, but Miami narrowly escaped. Over 700,000 homes were damaged or destroyed. If

it had hit a little further north, Miami would have been ruined."

Kerrick leaned over and scanned the article. He saw mul-
tiple path predictions with the most likely going through the
southern Bahamas, skirting the bottom of the Keys and
heading into the Gulf. He thought about the people of New
Orleans. Although he wasn't around for Hurricane Andrew,
he remembered Katrina. He'd never forget the horrific pictures of New Orleans and the other coastal cities in the
aftermath of that storm.

"Hopefully, this prediction is correct," Kerrick said. "At
least, Miami could be spared. If it follows Andrew's track,
though, Great Exuma could have some damage."

"True. Hurricanes are so unpredictable, especially when
they're still this far out. A lot can change in three days."

"What will you do? I mean, to prepare for the storm?"

Jon sipped his coffee. "I'm sure Diego has started preparations, but he'll need help. We have plywood in storage, so
we can cover all of the windows."

"That task itself is monumental," Kerrick pointed out.

"True. I'm about to call him to make sure he's started
working on it. We'll want to get as many things as possible
into sealed plastic crates. We built the storage building with
hurricanes in mind, so we'll park the truck inside of it."

"What about the boats?"

"Thankfully, *The Discoverer* is in Miami for now. I'll have
Captain Buffington watch the weather and prepare to move
it north or south, depending on the direction of the storm.
I'll plan to take the *New Beginnings* somewhere out of harm's
way."

"Where will you go?"

"I could take Meg and Carla to Titusville or Jacksonville. I need to visit Randal's mother. If the storm stays south, I could dock in Titusville and fly to DC for a couple of days. I'd like to drive out to Belmont and talk to Randal and his family. I may want to visit with Freddy's girlfriend, too."

"Are you and José really going back to Mexico?"

"Maybe. We can take a few days to try to locate Freddy. I think Meg and Carla would rather stay home. I doubt Ann wants to go. She's been struggling with morning sickness and seems glad to be back in the States."

"I wish I could go," Kerrick said. "I guess I don't need to start my last year of college by skipping class. I think I'll go upstairs and talk with Lacy about going with you guys to Pirate's Cove. I'm sure she can help get ready for the storm, too."

"The more the merrier," Jon said as he reached for his phone to call Diego. "I heard her tell Meg she was going to shower, but surely, she's done by now."

Chapter Nine

Change of Plans

The door to Lacy's room was closed when Kerrick made it upstairs. She was not one to take a long time to get dressed. He tapped on the door.

"Who is it?" Lacy said behind the closed door.

"It's me. I need to talk to you. You decent?"

The door opened and Lacy stood before Kerrick in a bathrobe with wet hair. Her suitcase sat open on her bed.

"I can come back," Kerrick suggested, "when you get dressed."

"So, this isn't decent?" Lacy said with a grin.

Kerrick took Lacy's hands. "You are more than decent. I can barely see your neck. Whose robe is that?"

"I don't know. I guess it's Jon's. It was hanging in the bathroom when I first came to Miami. You like it?"

Lacy turned as if modeling an evening gown.

"Uh, well, I think you could put on a gunny sack and be the most beautiful woman in the world."

Lacy stopped spinning and stared up at Kerrick. Her cheeks began to glow. "A gunny sack?"

"You know. Farmers put potatoes in them. I think."

"I thought those were burlap sacks."

Kerrick took Lacy's hands and stared into her glacier blue eyes. Soft, expectant. Her full lips invited him closer. He leaned in and kissed her. It was natural. It was right. It was good.

He pulled away and saw Lacy's eyes closed as if savoring the moment. She was a beautiful angel. *His* angel.

Her eyes popped open. "That's the first sweet thing you've said today."

"That farmers put potatoes in gunny sacks?" Kerrick teased.

Lacy pushed against his chest. "No, silly. You know what I mean."

"You're keeping score?" Kerrick asked as he pulled her into his arms.

"Not exactly," she said staring up into his eyes. "Meg once told me love doesn't keep score."

Lacy smelled like lilac, and Kerrick felt like metal being drawn to a magnet, a fish being reeled in by an angler. He knew he should come back after she had dressed, but he couldn't take his eyes from her. She was magnificent, beautiful, alluring, and exotic. Her cheeks were pink, and her lips slightly apart. Her tongue slid across her top lip.

The silence was deafening. Kerrick could hear his own heart pounding against his chest. He pulled her close, and their lips met again in passion and heat. He felt her hands slip into his hair, and he slid his hands down her back. He wanted to hold her.

He pulled his head back but felt drawn to her. He belonged here. She belonged here in his arms. "Okay," Kerrick said and took a deep breath. "We're definitely breaking a rule, and I'm about to fall off the edge."

"If you fall, I'll catch you."

He smiled down at her. He traced the side of her face with his finger and cupped her chin. "I think you've already caught me, and I don't want you to let go." Kerrick cleared his throat. "I am under your spell, Lacy Henderson."

"So, I'm a witch now?" Lacy smiled and placed her hand on his chest.

"Couldn't Aphrodite cast a spell?"

Lacy laughed. "For starters, she wasn't real."

"You are definitely real." Kerrick took a deep breath and stepped back. "I hate to change the subject, but we need to talk about something. Why don't you get dressed and meet me in the kitchen?"

Kerrick would have sworn Lacy's lower lip stuck out like she was pouting. He couldn't stand it. He kissed her again, savoring her smell and enjoying her taste. He finally pulled away and whispered, "The kitchen," before leaving the room.

Ten minutes later, Lacy stepped into the kitchen wearing white shorts and a pink tank top. Her wet hair hung straight down her back. She was radiant. Kerrick's heart skipped a beat, and he sloshed hot coffee onto his hand.

"Ouch," Kerrick yelped. "That's hot."

He hurried to the sink and put his hand under a stream of cold water. He knew their relationship had moved to a new place, and he was going to have a hard time controlling their certain destiny. He looked forward to that destiny, but they were going to have to gain control of their emotions and tame their passion.

Lacy leaned against Kerrick to inspect his hand. "You okay?"

"Fine. I think you have me a little rattled…in a good way."

Lacy touched Kerrick's face and lightly kissed his lips. "You rattle me, too."

"Uh, well, I need to tell you about what's going on. Jon told me a hurricane is heading toward the Bahamas. We have maybe three days before it could hit the Exumas, and we did nothing before leaving Pirate's Cove to prepare the compound."

"How big is the hurricane?"

"It will become a category three today. It will probably intensify before making landfall. Jon is about to head back to Great Exuma now, and he could use our help."

"Let's go, then. I'll just need to put on different clothes."

"What about your father?"

"I need to talk with you about that. I decided to visit my father, but visiting my father can wait. The storm won't. It's as simple as that. I'll throw some clothes in a bag. Hopefully, I have enough clean clothes. Maybe I can wash a load while we're working on the house."

"I'm sure Meg would be fine with that," Kerrick agreed. "If we work fast, we may be able to finish in time to fly to Atlanta to see your father on Sunday."

"I doubt it," Lacy said. "I can't imagine getting that place ready for a storm by Sunday morning, and we're supposed to start class on Monday. We can go see my father next weekend."

"I wonder about school. What will they do with a hurricane bearing down on us? I have to pack a few things myself, but I'll need to run back to the dorm to do it. I'll tell Jon we can be ready in an hour."

The flight to the Great Exuma airport didn't take long. Fortunately, Jon had been able to secure a private plane that could handle four adults and a child. Judy insisted on going, but the pilot didn't want to risk taking one more adult. Ann woke up sick that morning, so Jon insisted José stay with her in Miami.

The hectic George Town Airport buzzed with activity. People arrived to work on vacation homes in preparation for the storm. Many were trying to evacuate. Diego waved to them as they crossed the terminal and hurried to the F-250. In less than twenty minutes, Diego pulled into the driveway of the compound they knew as Pirate's Cove.

"Oh, it feels so good to be home," Meg said. "I can't believe we're going to have to turn right around and leave again. I'm getting tired of all this traveling."

"Sorry, Sweetheart," Jon said. "I know you want to stay here, but right now, it's not safe."

"I know. I'm just desperate to find normalcy again. The weather is so beautiful. You'd never know we're about to be hit by a category four hurricane."

"They're still saying it's going south of us," Jon reminded her, "and I think it's still a three."

"I just pulled up a weather update," Kerrick said. "It has moved slightly north, and they're expecting it to become a four by tonight. I also saw the governor has called for an evacuation of south Florida."

"I saw that earlier," Jon admitted, "but I didn't realize it had gotten stronger. It's reminding me of Andrew's path back in '92. The Exuma islands missed the worst of Andrew, but it was still bad. I'm hoping we can get the windows of the main house covered by midnight. We can work on the guest house in the morning."

"I started yesterday, Jon," Diego said. "My son helped me a little, but it's difficult work on only one ladder. He will help us today, too, and I picked up another ladder in George Town."

Kerrick thought about all the men on the island who would normally be available to help, but they were probably working on their own homes. As Diego stopped the truck in front of the house, Kerrick marveled at this incredible place. Jon had remodeled the home and turned it into a show place. The swimming pool looked like a small pond in a beautiful garden, and even the guest house looked like a work of art. It would be a shame if any of it were destroyed.

He stepped toward the edge of the bluff and looked down toward the water. The *New Beginnings* bobbed up and down, and the little Robalo was tied up farther down the dock. Kerrick hadn't thought about the smaller ski boat. *What will Jon do with it?* Kerrick looked up and saw Jon backing the truck down the drive to the storage building. He hurried to help him.

Hours later, the group stopped for a late dinner of barbecue sandwiches Diego's wife prepared and served them on the screened-in porch. A gust of wind blew an empty garbage can toward the swimming pool. Jon managed to run it down before it took a plunge off the bluff. Dinner was good but brief, and they went back to work.

By mid-afternoon the next day, all the windows were covered with plywood, and Meg had managed to get most of their personal belongings stored into plastic tubs. Because the threat of a hurricane was a seasonal reality for anyone who lived in the Bahamas, Jon and Meg were prepared.

Kerrick drove the Robalo to the marina in George Town in growing seas with heavy sprays of water blowing across his face. He had to wait in line at the marina, but before too much time had passed, he floated up onto the submerged boat trailer, and Jon pulled him out of the water. When they returned to the house, just after two a.m., it seemed the house was ready. Jon backed the ski boat into the outbuilding he said should hold up pretty well under a hurricane. He had told Kerrick earlier that day they built the storage building with hurricanes in mind.

"We wouldn't have made it without you two," Meg said to Lacy and Kerrick, exhaustion written all over her face. "I'm sorry I messed up your trip to see your father. I suppose you can still go tomorrow, but you may have a hard time getting a plane out."

"We are where we need to be," Lacy insisted. "It's not like my dad is dying right now. He just wants to see me. That's all. I can go up next weekend or even the next. He hasn't been in a hurry to see me over the years, so why should I hurry off to see him?"

Kerrick squeezed Lacy's hand, and their eyes met.

"I'm sorry. I shouldn't have said that. Waiting a week won't matter. I'll get my first week of school behind me and then head back to Atlanta. No big deal."

"We won't be having school this week," Kerrick said, "at least, not on Monday or Tuesday. I saw that class was canceled, and students are leaving the city."

"What will they do?" Lacy asked. "I mean, about class?"

"I guess we'll make it up somehow," Kerrick suggested. "Hopefully, the storm will pass south of the Keys, and everything will be back to normal by Wednesday."

"I suggest we get some sleep," Jon said. "I figure we'll have a few more details to take care of early in the morning, and then we can head to Titusville. Diego, why don't you and your family go with us? We have room on the yacht."

"Thank you, Jon. Maybe Isabell and Gregorio will go. I'll stay here and make sure the compound is secure."

"That's not necessary," Meg said. "Your safety is more important than this compound."

"I'll be fine. I'll go to bed now and see you in the morning. Good night."

❀◆❀◆❀◆❀

Meg collapsed into bed determined to wait on Jon before going to sleep. She watched his masculine form in the bathroom as he stood at the sink brushing his teeth. Because he was shirtless, she could make out the distinct muscles on his back and thought it odd how many muscles it took to brush teeth. Thanks to regular exercise, he was strong and healthy. He still thought of himself as an athlete, and he certainly had the body of one. Thirty-six-years-old wasn't ancient, and he could make young men look silly on a soccer field.

Her phone buzzed with another missed call from Mexico. This was the second one of the day. She had ignored the other one, too. She didn't know anyone in Mexico, so it was probably a prank call. If it were important, they would leave a message.

"Jon?" Meg called from the bed. "Are you sure it's safe for us to wait until morning to leave?"

Jon spit toothpaste into the sink and rinsed his mouth. "We'll be fine. For starters, it seems likely the storm will stay south of us, and it's not supposed to come through our area until Monday afternoon. Besides, I'm exhausted. I don't think I can make it to Titusville without a few hours of sleep."

"You're right about that." Meg looked at the clock and saw it was almost three o'clock. "I suppose we're only sleeping for a few hours anyway."

"Yep," Jon said as he slipped into bed and took Meg into his arms. He kissed her gently. "I'm getting up at six. I'd like us to be pulling off by nine. Will that work?"

"The sooner the better, as far as I'm concerned." Meg scowled as her phone buzzed again to remind her that she had a missed call. "That's the second call I've had today from Mexico. Who would have my number there? I didn't give it to anyone."

Jon reached to the bedside table to retrieve his phone. "I've got some missed calls, too. It's too late to worry about it now. I'll call whoever it is in the morning."

Meg nuzzled into Jon's neck. He was warm and inviting. His arms were strong, and his quick shower left him smelling like Old Spice. She traced the outline of his chest and reached up to kiss his neck and behind his ear.

"I thought you were exhausted," Jon said and grinned down at his wife.

"I am. That's just a goodnight kiss."

Jon turned off the lamp beside the bed and pulled his wife back into his arms. "I love you, Sweetheart. You've worked hard today. We make a great team."

"I'm so glad I'm on your team, Jon Davenport. Get some sleep. You're going to need it."

Chapter Ten

Ready for Anything

Lacy took the final plastic tub from Kerrick and carried it into the salon of the forty-four-foot Carver yacht. She noticed the bullet hole in the floor and felt a shiver run down her spine. Jon kept saying he'd repair it. That hole was a constant reminder of what could have been a deadly encounter with the drug lord, Alvaro Lopez. Jon always shrugged off comments about the event and said it was a turning point in his relationship with Meg. Lacy had never met the evil man, but Meg's stories both thrilled her and scared her to death. Thankfully, the creep was locked away for a very long time.

Looking at the bullet hole, she knew the gun firing into the floor of the boat was not the turning point in Jon and Meg's relationship. The plane crash was. How could so many crazy things happen to one couple? Their lives blew her mind. Of course, since hanging out with them in the Bahamas, her life had gotten a little crazy too. She smiled. *I suppose I must like crazy.*

It seemed as if Jon and Meg's marriage had been plagued with danger, and now, her life was no different. Still, she wouldn't trade it for anything else in the world. She'd rather face the whole Mexican Cartel with Jon and Meg than be back under the roof with her pitiful mother. Although her life seemed to be in constant danger, she never felt safer.

The boat rocked, throwing Lacy against the table. *We've got to get out of here.* She hurried back out on the deck and saw Jon and Meg coming down the steps toward the dock.

"Everything loaded?" Jon asked.

"Loaded and ready to go," Kerrick acknowledged. "We've got room for more plastic tubs if you want to bring them."

"We're good," Meg insisted. "The four I'm bringing have the only irreplaceable items we own. I think we need to leave. Jon and I made it through one hurricane, and I don't want to have to go through another one. This storm is turning into a monster. We saw it's now definitely a four and gaining steam. We've got to go now while we still can."

Lacy gasped. "What about Isabell and Gregorio? Don't they need to go with us?"

"They decided to go with the rest of their family on the ferry. Diego still insists on staying."

She didn't understand the man. Why would he choose to stay when his life could be in danger? Lacy looked back to the top of the bluff and wondered if Jon and Meg's home was the most beautiful on the island. Probably not, but it had to be in the top ten. She was sure as soon as people left the island, looters would have a heyday. That meant Diego could be in danger from the storm and the riffraff on the island. He was either stupid or loyal. She knew it was the latter.

A sudden thought rocketed through Lacy's mind making her gasp for breath. She jumped back onto the dock and turned toward the boat. "I'll be right back. I'm forgetting something really important."

A few minutes later, she returned, grasping the object that had nearly gotten her killed this summer. She did not know the value of her medallion, but it was her most treasured possession. Meg had given it to her as a graduation present, but it symbolized much more than a simple gift.

"Diego gave me my medallion last night, and I nearly forgot it. After all we've been through because of this thing, there's no way I'm leaving it behind, especially now that we know Miguel is…" Lacy looked down at Carla and realized her little cousin didn't need to hear what she was about to say. "Now that we know Miguel is no longer with us," she concluded.

She hurried toward the taut rope at the stern of the boat. Once Jon was secure on the bridge, Lacy pulled the rope free from the cleat and threw it into the boat. Kerrick motioned for her get aboard before he released his rope, and within a few minutes, Jon guided the boat through the choppy sea toward Titusville. It would be a long twelve-hour ride, but at least, they'd be safe.

Lacy and Kerrick climbed the ladder to the bridge and sat down on the vinyl couch behind the main steering wheel. She watched her aunt force Carla's arms into a miniature lifejacket and then stare back toward her island home. She must be wondering if the beautiful compound would survive the storm. Lacy figured this was the price of living in paradise. Carla sat on Meg's hip jabbering away as if they were taking a Sunday spin around the island. *Oh, the bliss of being a baby.*

Meg looked back at the ladder leading to the lower deck. "Lacy, would you mind closing the gate at the top of the ladder? I'd rather Carla not take a tumble."

Lacy chided herself for not thinking to do that on her own. She secured the gate and returned to the couch beside Kerrick. She wondered if her aunt and uncle enclosed the bridge as a safety precaution for Carla or if the boat came that way.

Meg looked out toward the open sea and turned toward Jon. "What about Judy and the house at Miami Beach?"

"I called her a little bit ago to tell her we were about to leave. She's quite industrious. She managed to hire some college students to cover the windows, and one of the boys offered to drive her to Orlando."

"Wow. How did she manage to rope students into helping her?"

"She's got her ways," Jon said with a grin. "I also called Don to have him fly the jet down to Titusville. I figure since Kerrick and Lacy won't have to worry about school on Monday, he can drop them off in Atlanta and take us to D.C."

"Did you call that number back from Mexico?" Meg asked. "I don't feel comfortable calling."

"Oh, no. I forgot about that call. Please help me remember to do it when we get to Titusville. Well, I suppose it will be too late tonight. Help me remember tomorrow."

Exhausted, Lacy leaned against Kerrick. She felt his arm slip around her, and she laid her head on his shoulder. Storm or not, the best place to be was in Kerrick's arms. She smiled as his lips pressed against the top of her head. How could she be so fortunate to have him beside her. After noticing her aunt and uncle were both focused on the sea in front of them, she turned her face toward Kerrick, and his lips were on hers. Their kiss was tender but short. Carla giggled.

I wonder what Meg meant when she said something about a call from Mexico. Lacy considered the possibility someone was calling them with information on Freddy. That seemed unlikely. She didn't remember Jon talking with anyone in Veracruz about Randal's brother. Could the call have been about Miguel? No, he was dead, so they shouldn't have to worry about him for the rest of their lives. *Thank God!*

She closed her eyes and breathed in Kerrick's familiar scent. Even with the salty wind, she could still recognize the distinct smell that would always belong to the man she loved. A smile spread across her face as that thought sunk deep into her heart. *The man I love.*

❦❦❦❦❦❦❦

Meg stirred as she felt the boat slowing. They must be in Titusville. Finally. She looked at her little girl sleeping. Carla had never been bothered by choppy seas before, but this time, they'd faced significant swells. The poor child had cried for two hours after leaving Freeport. Meg began to wonder if something else was wrong with her until she went to sleep. The only problem now was her nap started so late she may not sleep tonight.

Freeport had been a pleasant surprise. Jon had been concerned about getting fuel, but there was plenty at Port Lucaya Marina. Jon had allowed a fifteen-minute break to walk around, which had been a lifesaver. Carla's crying had started, however, when they returned to the yacht. Meg didn't blame her. She felt like crying, too.

She slipped out of bed, noticing that it was nearly eleven o'clock. The seas had slowed them down a good bit. She eased out onto the main deck and saw Lacy and Kerrick leaning against the side rails looking up the Indian River. Meg had never been to the Titusville Marina, but Jon mentioned it was in the lagoon just behind the Kennedy Space Center. She briefly wondered what they would do if the storm turned and headed north. They'd be in trouble. Right now, all she wanted was a firm bed that didn't move.

The tops of masts loomed in the distance, and she knew they had arrived at the marina. It was probably filled to capacity, but Jon mentioned he knew the manager quite well. She assumed that meant there'd be an available slip. She looked up and saw Jon on the bridge talking into his cell phone. He was laughing and carrying on like they'd been sailing across smooth waters for only a few minutes.

She smiled at her wonderful husband. He had the ability of turning everything in a positive direction. He told her all the time they had no control over their circumstances, but they did have control over their actions and attitudes. That attitude worked for him, and she discovered it worked for her, too. She figured his laughter meant they'd be able to dock.

Ten minutes later, Jon steered the Carver into an empty slip, and Kerrick threw a rope to a boy standing on the dock. Once the boat kissed the rubber against the side of the dock, Kerrick leaped onto the wooden dock and grabbed the rope from the boy, who had been trying to wrap it around the cleat. He pulled the rope tight and secured the boat before hurrying toward the rear of the yacht to catch the rope Lacy threw him.

As Jon stepped onto the dock, a large, red-faced man walked toward them with a big grin on his face. "Well, well. If it isn't the golden boy."

"Hey Jeffery," Jon said, slapping the big man's back. "How's life treating you?"

"Right now, I'm about to lose my mind, and then I get a distress call from my dear friend who needed an empty slip."

"I'm surprised you had an empty slip," Jon admitted.

"I happened to know a man who had planned to leave for Jacksonville in an hour. I called and asked if he wouldn't mind leaving a little early. When he heard it was you, he gladly accommodated us."

"Do I know him?"

"Nah. But everyone knows you, so enjoy it while it lasts." Jeffrey slapped Jon on the back again, causing him to stumble forward.

They talked for a few minutes about business and weather, and Meg hurried back toward the cabin to gather their luggage. Kerrick must have read her mind because he was there to help her carry their stuff off the boat.

"What about Carla?" he whispered.

"As soon as I know where we're going, I'll get her up. I just hate to wake her right now."

Kerrick stepped toward the door leading to the salon. "I think we're going straight to a private airport about twenty minutes from here."

"You've got to be kidding," Meg groaned as she tucked a strand of hair behind her ear.

"Jon told me he talked to Don before calling the marina, and Don said he would not be able to leave the plane at the airport overnight. He said the place was a madhouse with everyone trying to escape the storm. We have to leave right away."

"Oh, well," Meg sighed. "I guess that makes sense. I hoped Carla would be able to get a decent night's sleep. Is the boat safe here?"

"Odds are it is," Kerrick said. "Although the storm could turn north, forecasters think it's going to catch south Florida or maybe miss it and slip into the Gulf. It's going over Turks and Caicos right now and it's been upgraded to a five. One forecast has it jogging north as it goes past Cuba. If it turns too much, it could be a disaster for Miami."

Meg felt like she wanted to cry. This storm could do some serious damage to Pirate's Cove. The last weather report she saw showed the storm was quite large. It wouldn't take much for the outer bands to go right over her island, bringing significant storm surge and major wind damage. At least, their compound was high up on the bluff. She thought of all the people who were going to be affected. Some of the poor people on the islands would have nowhere to go. She prayed for no loss of life.

Jon came toward Meg. "Honey, I'm going to get Carla. We need to get to the airport and fly out of here tonight."

"Kerrick told me. Please try your best not to wake her."

The flight was a little over two hours, and about an hour after that, the limo driver pulled into the Hilton Garden Inn just outside of McDonough, Georgia. Meg knew that in the morning, she'd be glad they chose to drive close to the hospital before getting a hotel. She also knew deciding to go to the hospital with Lacy would be the best idea. Their trip to Washington could wait a few hours.

She looked at Lacy as she climbed out of the car. The girl looked horrible. The right side of her face was red, and her hair was a fright. Kerrick had his arm around her, oblivious. He was a keeper. Now, they needed to get some sleep. *Tomorrow's going to be a tough day.*

Chapter Eleven

Painful Reunion

Lacy stared into the mirror at her bloodshot eyes. She couldn't believe she was about to go upstairs to see her dying father. Was he really dying, or was her mom just being dramatic? Of course, colon cancer was serious. Did Meg say stage four? Maybe not. Lacy couldn't remember. Jon said he would be starting treatment, so there was still hope. Right?

Through the mirror, she scanned the stalls behind her and saw no feet visible beneath the stall doors. Lacy blew out a breath of air, lifting still damp strands into the air. The women's restroom was cool and smelled clean. Clorox, maybe. Lacy wished she could somehow make her past smell the same way. Sanitized.

She splashed water on her face while staring down into the sink. She hadn't bothered to put on makeup and now decided a little something might help. She gasped when a hand slid across her back.

"You going to stay here all day?" Meg's voice echoed in the bathroom. "I figured I'd better come in here and check on you."

"I'm fine," Lacy lied. "I just thought I might put on a little makeup. Anything's better than this," she said, pointing at her face.

"You look fine, Lacy."

"You're either lying or you need to see an optometrist."

Meg laughed. "You just need more sleep, not eye liner. Then again, I've seen makeup do wonders on me."

A few minutes later, they walked out of the bathroom to find Kerrick and Jon standing in the vast lobby of the hospital. Some interior designer team thought if they made the place look like the Garden of Eden, everyone would feel happy. Unfortunately, her family found the tree in the center of that garden years ago and chose to eat the fruit. *There's one Sunday School lesson I remember from somewhere. Meg would be proud.*

Kerrick gave her the once over and grinned before taking her hand and walking toward the elevators. He leaned toward her and kissed the top of her head. "He's on the third floor. While you were in the bathroom, I had time to review the intimate details of every patient in the hospital, and I found your father's room."

"You're a real comedian," Lacy said, punching him in the ribs.

"Whoa, now. Quite a hook you've got there." His arm slipped around her shoulders. "You ready for this?"

Lacy stopped five feet from the elevator. "No. I don't know what to say. Just because he's got cancer doesn't make him less of a jerk. He ran out on us and said I was to blame for getting raped by my cousin. How was it my fault?"

Kerrick pulled her into his arms as her eyes filled with tears. So much for the makeup.

"It wasn't your fault. You know that. Just remember, how you feel about the past and the present is your choice."

Lacy reached into her purse for a tissue. "I know. I've already read that chapter in the Meg Davenport book, *How to Love Your Father no Matter What.* I will no longer let him shape how I think or feel."

Lacy heard Meg's footsteps and felt her aunt's arm around her. "I heard that, Lacy, and that's really good. Something else you might want to think about…"

"I'm not sure I want to know," Lacy said, "but go ahead."

"When you choose to let him make you hate him, he's still controlling you. Don't choose to hate him. Choose to forgive him whether he deserves it or not. Remember bitterness only hurts you."

"I know, I know. It's the old gasoline in the Styrofoam cup. Bitterness destroys the container, and I'm the container."

Meg moved Lacy's hair out of her eyes and kissed her cheek. "I marvel at the woman you've become, Lacy. I'm so proud of you."

Lacy felt fresh tears on her cheeks. Why couldn't her mother or father be proud of her? "Now, I'm going to have to go back into the bathroom."

Kerrick pulled her toward the elevator. "No, you're not. You look beautiful."

After getting off the elevator on the third floor, Lacy paused in front of room 311 and bowed her head. It crossed her mind that it looked like she was praying, and the thought had some appeal. She reached for the doorknob. It felt cold against her palm. Maybe as cold as her heart. Rick Henderson didn't deserve to be loved or forgiven. She remembered one of Meg's sermons. *No one deserved to be forgiven, but God offered forgiveness to anyone who'd take it.*

Is that true? She thought back to some of the dumb things she'd done, like the time she'd lied about Aaron Hersey just to get him in trouble. He hadn't touched her, but all it took was an accusation, and the boy was expelled from school. She didn't mean to get him in that much trouble. She had been a real jerk in her past, too. *I guess the apple doesn't fall far from the tree.*

She pushed the door open and heard a few curse words come from the bed as her father looked toward her. This room didn't smell as clean as the restroom.

"Well, hello, Darlin. I was hoping you were that little nurse. What's her name? Megan. Yeah, Megan."

Lacy felt sorry for the poor nurses having to work with such a pervert. He was still being a jerk, but the man lying in the bed didn't resemble the large man who'd stormed out of their house two years ago. Now, he was shriveled up and bald.

"Hello, Dad." Lacy looked down at the floor. "I heard you were sick."

The room was still. She heard beeping, CNN, and heavy breathing. The door clicked closed as Kerrick walked in behind her. She looked up at her father's face and thought she saw a tear running down his cheek. Probably not.

"I didn't figure I'd ever see you again."

"Well, here I am."

"Thank God you're not that other nurse that's been messing with me. She's like Godzilla with a needle. I swear, if she sticks me one more time, I…"

"You know she's only doing what she has to do," Lacy interrupted. "And of course, they're trying to help you."

"Whatever. I heard you was in college. Kind of surprised me."

Lacy felt her stomach tighten and couldn't believe her father was still putting her down. "You didn't think I could do it, did you?" Lacy felt Kerrick's hand grasp hers.

"Honestly, Darlin. No, I didn't." Rick motioned to Kerrick. "And it looks like you got what you went to school for."

"I went to school to get a degree in exercise science, and that's what I'm getting."

"Hello, Mr. Henderson. I'm Kerrick Daniels. You'll be proud to know your daughter has a 4.0. She'll probably get a scholarship at the University of Miami. She just transferred down there."

Lacy looked up at Kerrick. She wasn't getting a scholarship, and how did he know her GPA?

"The surprises keep comin'. I figured you'd grow up to be just like your mama."

Lacy felt the heat rising up her neck. She couldn't stand her mother, but now, she couldn't stand her father insulting her.

"Actually," Kerrick continued, "her mother encouraged her to pursue her dream of being a physical therapist, and if Lacy continues down that path, she's going to be an awesome therapist. I've seen her do anything she puts her mind to."

"That a fact? What did you say your name is?"

"I'm Kerrick Daniels. I've been working with Lacy this summer on the Davenports' ship."

"Yeah. Liz told me a little about it. Somethin' about being kidnapped and a broken leg. My girl's always been a tough one. Cain't always believe her, but she's tough all right!"

Lacy thought she could feel steam blowing out her ears. What did he mean he couldn't always believe her? She knew in his mind, his nephew had always been telling the truth and had never touched her. It didn't matter that a couple of years later, the same thing happened to another girl, and her stupid cousin had gone to prison. Her hands balled into fists as she stepped closer to the bed.

"Well, hello, Sweetheart," Rick said, looking over Lacy's shoulder. "I've been wonderin what happened to you. I'd hoped my little comment earlier hadn't scared you off."

Lacy turned around and saw a cute, petite nurse standing behind her. Lacy didn't ask the poor nurse about the earlier comment. The look on the nurse's face said everything. She headed toward the door as the nurse mumbled something about needing a machine that was in the corner.

Once in the hall, she felt Kerrick's arms slip around her. She gulped in a breath of fresh, antiseptic air as salty tears stung her eyes.

"You okay, Lacy?" Meg asked as she hurried toward her.

"I hate him! Coming here was a mistake."

Meg reached out to hug her niece, but Lacy stomped toward the elevators. She couldn't stand to be in the hospital another minute. As far as she was concerned, she never wanted to see Rick Henderson again.

As the limo pulled out of the hospital parking lot, Jon looked over at Lacy. "I'm guessing that didn't go well. You okay?"

Lacy sat up straight and adjusted her seatbelt. "I don't know what I was thinking, Jon. I guess I thought when a person knows he's dying, he'd be a little sorry for the jerk he's been for the last ten years."

"I'm sorry, Lacy," Meg said, touching Lacy's arm. "You did your best."

"*Did* is right. I won't be doing anything else related to him."

They rode in silence around the hospital searching for the proper way to exit. Lacy leaned her head back and closed her eyes.

"Since we're done here, do you two want to go with us to D.C. to see Randal's mother? I'd value your insight, and it would be a great way to get all this off your mind."

"Sure," Lacy said. "I don't suppose we have anything better to do."

"Seeing Randal again would be nice," Kerrick added. "What's the latest on the storm?"

Jon's face grew still and serious. "It's slowed down just north of Cuba, but it's turning north. One of the models suggested that might happen, but I don't believe anyone thought it would."

"That could be disastrous," Kerrick said. "Does that mean it's heading toward Miami? What about the house in Miami Beach?"

Jon nodded his head. "Yes. They're now saying it could hit anywhere from Key Largo to Boca Raton. Regardless of where it hits, the winds are going to pummel the land for a long time. It's become a monster, and it's slowing. The weather service is predicting serious damage."

"What about Great Exuma?" Meg asked.

"I don't know," Jon admitted. "Even though it passed south of our island, I'm sure we still caught some strong winds. That thing is so massive, the outside edge easily hit Pirate's Cove. I tried to call Diego, but there's no service."

"I hope he's okay," Meg said.

"This isn't the first hurricane he's ridden out. I'm sure he'll be fine."

"I'm sure we won't be able to get back to the island for days," Kerrick said.

Jon took the ramp onto the interstate. "Let's rescue Don from child duty and head toward Washington. I'd like to talk with Randal's mother and his brother's girlfriend if we can find her. We're not going to be able to go to Miami or Pirate's Cove anytime soon, so we've got all the time in the world. Worrying about what can happen also won't change anything. Let's hope for the best."

"Maybe we should go back to Mexico," Kerrick suggested.

"Mexico!" Meg gasped. "I need to return that call."

"Let's go to our room first," Jon suggested. "We can call that number from the room. I think Don would appreciate it if we'd hurry. I don't think babysitting is his specialty."

When they walked into the room, Don held Carla in his lap, and they both were covered in syrup. Carla's face lit up when she saw Jon and Meg.

"Mama!" Carla cheered.

Meg laughed. "What happened, Don? It looks like you two took a bath in syrup."

"That about describes it," Don admitted. "She needs a bath, but I wasn't about to attempt that."

"You're a dear for watching her," Meg said with a grin. "I'll take her from here."

Jon reached for his phone. "I'll return that call from Mexico." He walked into the bedroom of the two-room suite.

Lacy could hear Jon talking to someone but couldn't make out what he was saying. She saw him walking toward her, telling someone to hold on for a moment.

"Lacy, I hate to ask you to do this, but the police in Mexico need you to identify Miguel. I told the investigator you weren't ready to see pictures like this, but he wants you to look at this man's face and tell them if it's Miguel. It seems you're the only one who's seen him."

"You mean, they want me to look at his…his messed up…?"

"They just need you to look at this picture of his face and identify him. He was cut there, too, but they said you should still be able to identify him. Most of the rest of him is covered up."

Lacy stilled herself. "Ok." She swallowed down the bile she felt rising up in her throat. The only dead body she'd ever seen was her grandfather's, and he was in a casket. Of course, there were the men José had killed on Coral Cay, but she hadn't really looked at their bodies. "Show me the picture."

Jon spoke back into the phone. When she heard the buzz of a received text, Jon looked at the picture and grimaced. "Are you sure you're okay with looking at this?"

"If it means I can free myself from Miguel once and for all, then I'm okay with it."

Jon turned the picture toward Lacy, and the color drained from her face. She felt faint.

"What is it, Lacy?" Jon asked. "You're white as a sheet."

Lacy steadied herself, sat down, and mumbled.

"I couldn't hear you," Jon said. "Sorry, Lacy. I don't understand what you're saying."

Lacy looked up into Jon's eyes and stared. "It's not him."

Chapter Twelve

Resurrection

"What do you mean it wasn't him?" Meg said as she sat down hard on the closed toilet lid. Carla splashed water out of the bathtub and soaked Jon's foot.

Jon knelt in front of Meg and took her hands. "I spoke with the detective in Veracruz," he said just above a whisper, "and he sent me a…" He stood up and pulled her toward the open bathroom door. "He sent me a picture of the dead man's face. Lacy is confident the man is not Miguel. It must have been someone with the Cartel."

Meg felt sick and leaned against the door jamb. "I can't believe it. This means our nightmare isn't over."

"Maybe, maybe not. One thing for certain is the Cartel is after Miguel, so I doubt he'll survive."

Meg rubbed her eyes and leaned her head back against the hard wood. She thought they could live in peace and move on with their lives, but now, they couldn't. She'd already been kidnapped, accosted by a drug lord, and chased through the Bahamas by terrorists. She'd also faced the possibility of her niece being murdered by these thugs. Now, not only were Lacy and Jon in danger, but Carla was too. *How much more?*

"We won't be safe until Miguel is captured," Meg whispered. "We're not safe anywhere."

Jon pulled Meg into his arms, and she felt the familiar warmth and security. She was safe with Jon. She believed that. He had always protected her. He and José risked their lives to save Lacy, and they succeeded. She had to believe her husband could protect them.

"I don't think Miguel will be following us to Washington. He won't have any idea where to find us. By now, he's got to know we left Mexico and returned to Miami."

Meg looked up into Jon's eyes. Determined. Strong. How could he be so calm and confident? She needed some of what he had. "Okay. Whatever you think, Jon. I guess this could be the one bright spot of this horrible hurricane. Miguel won't know where to find us."

"He wouldn't know to go to Washington," Jon said. "That's for sure. Even if he did know when we left Mexico, there's no way he could have followed us from Pirate's Cove to here."

"What are we going to do, Jon? We can't live like normal people knowing this wacko is trying to kill us."

"We'll have to let the authorities do their job. They'll catch him. I'll call someone with the FBI or Homeland Security. I'll just call my father-in-law. He'll be able to do something about it."

Meg loved President Randall Johnson and thought about the first time she'd met him. He was only a former governor with presidential hopes. She'd never forget interrupting their honeymoon to celebrate his presidential victory. He and his wife, Gina, had welcomed her into their family as if she could somehow take their daughter's place. It was like they were relieved Jon had remarried after their daughter's death. The president still considered Jon their son-in-law. Meg wasn't sure what that made her. Of course, he had walked her down the aisle when she married Jon.

Jon scanned through the numbers in his phone, pressed send, and winked at Meg. "It's not every day you call the president's private number."

As Jon walked away, Meg could tell it wasn't the president who answered. So much for his private number. *I suppose when you become president, nothing is private any longer.* She turned back toward the tub and saw half of the water was on the floor.

"Okay little mermaid. Let's get you out of the tub and clean up this mess."

As she walked into the bedroom toweling off her little girl, Jon walked toward her with a grin on his face.

"Apparently, you can't just call the most powerful man in the free world," Jon said. "His assistant, or whoever was answering his phone, said she would have him call me back at twelve thirty. I imagine we'll be driving back toward the Griffin airport about that time."

"Jon, shouldn't we check in with Liz while we're in Griffin? She is Lacy's mother, after all."

"And your sister," Jon added. "Why don't you call her and, at least, let her know we're nearby. Maybe we can have lunch with her in Griffin."

Meg handed the squirming little girl to her father. "You can have the honors."

"My pleasure," Jon gushed as he nuzzled Carla's neck. Carla squealed with delight.

Meg pressed her sister's name in her phone and was instantly connected. After several rings, the phone went to voicemail.

"Hey Liz. It's Meg. We happen to be near Griffin for a little bit, and I thought we could go to lunch. It's a long story, but Lacy came up to see Rick. Call me."

"She's either on a date or hasn't gotten out of bed yet," Jon said.

"Jon, be nice."

"I was being nice. Let's get packed up and head to Griffin. If she doesn't call back, at least, we tried. I doubt Lacy would be too thrilled about seeing her father *and* her mother on the same day, anyway."

"You said you were being nice."

"Now, I'm being honest. Let's get packed."

While Meg made sure all their clothes were packed, she thought about Liz. Why were they so different? What happened to make Liz so selfish and clueless? Poor Lacy.

It amazed Meg that Lacy had made such progress. Meg hadn't heard a curse word in a couple of months, which was quite a change. When they had been together at Christmas, the girl needed a major mouth cleaning. It didn't help that Rick's language was horrible, so Lacy sort of inherited his potty mouth. The fact she had somehow overcome a horrible habit was nothing short of a miracle.

When she pulled the luggage back into the living area, Lacy appeared ready to go. She mentioned Kerrick had called from his room to tell them he would wait on them in the lobby.

The drive to Griffin was quiet until Jon mentioned Meg had called Liz. As predicted, Lacy was not happy, but she consoled herself by saying she was confident her mother wouldn't be calling. So far, she was right. At exactly twelve thirty, Jon's cell phone rang.

"Hello. This is Jon Davenport."

Meg grinned. *As if he didn't know the president of the United States was calling him.*

"Mr. President!" Jon said and listened. "Okay. Randall. I feel funny calling the president of the United States by his first name." He listened and laughed. "I know you'll always be Randall. Thanks for calling. Did your assistant tell you what happened?"

Jon lowered the phone and mouthed to Meg, "He already knew."

"Yes, sir," he said into the phone. "We're heading to our plane now. We should be in D.C. this afternoon…uh, well, sure. We'd be honored…Okay. We'll see you this evening. Goodbye."

"What?" Meg said running her hands through her hair. "Let me guess. We're going to the White House."

"Good guess."

"Jon! I don't have anything to wear to the White House."

"Meg, we can't go to Washington and not stop by to see Randall and Gina. We can go in the back door. No one will see us."

Meg laughed. "That place doesn't have a back door. No one can sneak into the White House."

"He's busy until kind of late tonight. He said we could have a late dinner with Gina, and he would see us before we go to bed."

"The poor man. I bet he never sleeps."

"Oh, you'd be surprised. His physicians work hard to make sure he stays in top shape, and a good night's sleep is an important part of that regimen."

"Do you realize how confusing it is that the two Randalls we know both live in Washington?"

"Yeah, but one of them has only one 'l'."

"Got it," Meg grinned. "That clarifies things."

"We'll go up to South Kensington and see Randal, with one l, and his family and then head back to D.C. Maybe we'll get lucky and find Freddy's girlfriend before leaving tomorrow."

"Where will we go tomorrow?" Meg asked.

"I'm not sure. Somewhere safe."

@◆@◆@◆@◆

Miguel slammed down the phone in disbelief. He had to get somewhere safe, and nothing was working. The walls of this hotel room were closing in on him. If one more airline agent told him his flight was canceled, he'd go ballistic.

The only thing that had gone right for him was killing the Los Unidos jerk who ran him off the road. The idiot thought he could cause Miguel Martinez to wreck and then slit his throat. Not in this lifetime. That knife work wasn't murder. It was vengeance and vengeance with a pleasure.

Other than the roadside incident, he'd had the worst luck on this trip. Killing the son of the leader of Los Unidos was an unfortunate miscalculation, and everything went downhill from there. Of course, it was his luck some guilt-ridden daughter decided to come check on her sick father, whom he happened to wrap in plastic. *So, what's wrong with wrapping a stiff in plastic? Beats smelling it.*

And now, a hurricane! Who would have guessed a freakin' hurricane would pick now to hit the Bahamas and head toward Miami? He flung the lamp at the wall and watched it shatter.

Okay, okay. Get a grip or you're going to be in worse shape. He lay down on the bed and closed his eyes. The Aero Mexico rep told him the Miami airport was closed, but he could fly to Houston. He decided the cancelations may be good news after all. The airport was probably crawling with Escobar's men. He'd love to get back to the States, but that might not be the safest move. He had to think.

He needed a place to hole up for a few days, and then, he could leave the country. He had to get out of Veracruz City. Mexico was a big country. He could find a nice, safe town to visit until the weekend. How hard could that be?

One problem was authorities would soon have all exits blocked. Traveling under his real name could be dangerous. He needed a decoy. Dumping out his luggage, he tore the edge of the liner and pulled out a passport. He stared at the name: Miguel Ramírez Martinez. He hadn't used this passport in years.

He hurried out of his room and caught a city bus to La Flor, the club where he'd purchased the propofol he'd used on Lacy. Before meeting the nurse who sold him the drug, Miguel remembered talking with a guy who said he could get

Miguel anything he wanted. *What are the odds Javier will be at the club this time of day? Are they even open?*

Forty-five minutes after stepping through the back door of La Flor, Miguel stared down at a fake visa that looked as authentic as he'd ever seen. Of course, it cost him nearly $1,200 in American bills, but it was worth it. The only problem Miguel had now was he would soon be low on cash. He grinned. Getting money shouldn't be a problem.

He started to take a cab to the airport but decided it would be safer to take the city bus. He didn't think it was a good idea to be near the airport, but then again, it wasn't safe to be anywhere.

He walked into the main ticketing area of the airport and scanned the crowd. He saw a couple huddled in one corner saying their goodbyes. He could tell they didn't have much money.

Miguel guessed the woman was leaving on a trip, and the rest of the family couldn't go. He wondered how they'd gotten the money for her ticket. She must be going to the United States because when she headed toward the line, he heard her say, "Houston."

Miguel looked back at the heartbroken husband, noting he was maybe a few years younger than himself. He stared at the man's face and then down at his passport. He looked up again. *This could work.*

He approached the Mexican and made an offer. Fortunately, Miguel still had some cash. He gave him enough for a ticket to Houston as well as an additional thousand dollars.

"The only condition is that you must be Miguel Martinez." Miguel needed a good excuse for giving the man his passport and money for a ticket. He hadn't thought enough in advance about his reasoning or that this guy would question his motives.

"My wife thinks I'm going to the states," Miguel lied with ease, "but I need to stay here for a little…business. You understand? You are Miguel Martinez, originally from Columbia. Don't ask any questions, and you can go to the States. Deal?"

The man reached out and took the money, passport, and visa without a question. Miguel stood in a corner and watched him receive his ticket from the agent and disappear up the escalators. The poor man was too stupid to realize how he was breaking the law, but no great loss. Miguel headed out to catch a bus back to his hotel.

Back in his room, he grabbed his phone and scrolled to Google Maps. He had to find a landing spot where he could disappear for a week or two. He scanned the whole state of Veracruz. He needed a city off the Pan-American Highway. He could go north to Xalapa, but that was too risky. He was sure the Cartel would have the capital city of the state of Veracruz covered up. He'd be dead thirty minutes after arriving. That meant his option was either west or southwest.

He scrolled around the map and noticed the state line to Oaxaca was not far away, and the first city in Oaxaca was Tuxtepec. It looked to be a good size place. He looked toward the east and saw a large lake on the map. *Catemaco. I've heard of that place. Seems like a big tourist area. I could get lost around a bunch of tourists.*

Because it was possible he had shown up on some hidden security camera before he killed Escobar's son, he

figured he better not try the main bus station. He got out of
bed and grabbed his few belongings. He figured he could
pay someone to get him to Catemaco. How hard could that
be?

Two hours and 500 pesos later, Miguel found transportation as far as Alvarado. *Why does everyone have to be paid for a
little information?*

Catemaco was about two hours south of Alvarado, so he
ought to be able to take a bus the rest of the way. He should
be checked into a hotel before nightfall. He got into the
truck with the old farmer and thought of killing the guy and
taking his truck. *I probably shouldn't do anything to draw attention.
I suppose it's grandpa's lucky day.*

Chapter Thirteen

The People's House

Meg stepped out of the rental car and surveyed the Schmidt's new house and nice neighborhood around it. Simple yet elegant. The yards were nicely kept. No cars on blocks and kids played in the yard next door. Randal and his family had to be thrilled with their new home. What a change from the dangerous apartment complex they used to call home.

Jon was amazing. He had somehow managed to move this family to a beautiful new home without making them feel they were getting a handout. Of course, Betty made her first monthly payment, as promised. Meg couldn't wait to meet her. She turned to retrieve Carla from the car seat.

"Randal!" Lacy cried out when she saw her friend at the front door. She hurried across the tiny yard toward him.

Grinning from ear to ear, Randal stepped off the porch. He embraced her. "I can't believe you're here."

Meg noticed Randal look around, and she wondered if he was checking to see if anyone was watching. He seemed taller. Surely, he wouldn't be embarrassed to be seen hugging Lacy. He probably wanted his friends to see him hugging a beautiful girl.

Lacy was instrumental in helping to shape Randal's life this summer, but Meg knew Lacy's life was impacted by their relationship as well. She wondered if his life would be permanently affected by his summer on *The Discoverer*. She hoped so. A movement in the front doorway caught her attention, and she turned to see Randal's mother appear.

Betty's bright, blue eyes opened wide, and she pulled her hands up to her pale face. "Dr. Davenport. I can't believe you're here."

"Hello Betty. I don't think you've met my wife. This is Meg, and this is our little girl, Carla."

"Hello Mrs. Davenport." Betty's hands rubbed down her dress as if she were trying to iron out wrinkles before shaking Meg's hand. "An honor. 'Tis a real honor. And what a beautiful child!"

Carla ducked her head behind Meg's neck.

A smile spread across Jon's face as he turned and looked at Randal. "He is doing so well."

"Thanks to you, Dr. Davenport…"

"Betty," Jon interrupted, "please call us Jon and Meg. We're your friends."

"Ok, Jon and Meg." Her cheeks turned crimson.

"We only played a small part," Jon said. "Randal is a fine young man. Betty, this is Lacy Henderson, our niece, and Kerrick Daniels. He's one of our interns."

Stepping onto the porch, Betty wrapped her thin arms around Kerrick and wept. "You saved my boy. I cain't never thank ya enough."

Kerrick hugged her and patted her back. "He would have done the same for me, Mrs. Schmidt. You have a wonderful son. We all love him, and we know you are so proud of him."

"I am. I really am." Betty stood back and wiped her eyes. "Oh, what's wrong wi' me? Please come in. I need ta show ya around. We so proud of our home."

"It's beautiful," Lacy said. "I'm glad you were able to move out of the city."

"We didn't know how to act our first night. No shootin', and we didn't have to stay away from windows. And Lord, look at our yard! We got grass. Had to cut my grass las' week, and I loved it. I ain't never cut grass before in my life. What a blessin'."

Meg squeezed Jon's hand and wiped a tear from her eye. Helping this sweet family was one of the best experiences of her life. Losing Freddy would be devastating. Randal lost one older brother because of drugs. He didn't need to lose another one.

Betty led them into the living room and invited everyone to sit. The house was clean and orderly. Two little girls ran into the room and stared at the group.

"That's Layla," Randal said, pointing to a skinny girl with tight, curly black hair, "and she's Andrea." He motioned to an olive-skinned girl, maybe a year older than Layla. "My sisters."

Meg noticed the girls came from different fathers. One father must have been African American, and the other, Hispanic or Indian. They were both cute as a button and not used to having guests.

For once, Carla sat quietly on Meg's lap and played with her hair. She slipped her thumb into her mouth.

Betty offered everyone something to drink, but they declined. "Please, sit down," she urged them a second time.

"Thank you for your hospitality, Betty," Jon said. "We want to talk about Freddy. I'm glad you called my office to tell me he was missing."

"Yo secretary was so kind," Betty said. "Sarah, right?"

"Yes," Jon said. "She is a wonderful person and a great assistant."

"Randal made me call. I hated to bother ya. You been so good to us. If anyone can find my boy, you can."

They talked with Betty and Randal for nearly an hour and didn't learn much they didn't already know. Freddy disappeared with his girlfriend and hadn't come home. She returned a couple of weeks ago and said she doesn't know where Freddy is, but she left him in Mexico.

"Why did he go to Mexico?" Meg asked.

"He knows Spanish," Randal said. "That may be why. He was friends with some of the Puerto Ricans—a gang in the projects. He'd also been hanging with a couple of guys in D.C. They part of another gang from Mexico."

Jon leaned forward. "Do you remember the name of the gang, Randal?"

"Los…something. I can't remember."

"Los Unidos?"

"That's it! How did you know?"

"Uh, well, it's a group I've heard of in Mexico," Jon said.

Meg looked over at Betty and saw hope written all over her face. This poor mother had no idea her son may be involved with one of the fiercest cartel groups in the world. Dealing drugs was calm compared to many other things they did. Fear and dread filled Meg's heart. Jon would be heading back to Mexico to find the Cartel. How could she stop him? Should she even try?

"Why do you think he left?" Kerrick asked.

"He said he was goin' to make it big," Randal said. "Didn't know he meant he was leavin', but he tol' me to watch 'n see. He was goin' to be drivin' a Hummer."

"What about Freddy's girlfriend?" Jon asked. "You think she'd talk with us? Do you even know how to find her?"

Randal and Betty looked down at the floor. They knew how to find the girl and seemed ashamed of it.

"I know how ya can find her," Betty admitted. She turned to Meg. "It's best for ya and little Carla not to go."

"So, it's not safe?" Meg asked.

"It's…Well…it just ain't right for a respectable lady. The only girls in that area are…well, they for sale. You understand?"

Meg had been protected throughout her life, and what she knew about the sex industry could fit on a postage stamp. She understood enough to know Freddy's girlfriend was a drug addict and a prostitute.

"She'll be at Logan Circle most nights. Drive down the street. If you don't see her, just wait. She'll be back."

"We don't know what she looks like," Jon said. "I'm not sure that will work."

"I can find her," Randal offered.

Betty bristled at the idea. Meg knew the last thing she wanted was for her boy to go back into D.C.

"I've lost two boys. I don't need ta lose another."

Randal looked at his mother, pleading. "You won't lose me, Ma. I'll stay right with Mr. Jon and Kerrick."

Jon smiled. "Of course, if you go with us, you'll have to spend the night with us. You'll have an experience you'll be able to talk about for the rest of your life."

"What kind of experience?" Betty wanted to know.

Meg smiled. "He'll get to meet the president and stay in his house."

"You mean *the* president?" Randal asked.

"The White House?" Betty wondered. "The real White House on Pennsylvania Avenue?"

"President Johnson is Jon's father-in-law," Lacy said. "Or ex-Father-in-law," she clarified. "Jon's first wife died a few years ago, and her father was Randall Johnson."

Randal grinned. "So, you named me after the president, Ma? Now, I gotta meet him."

"I didn't know yo wife died, Mr. Jon," Betty said.

"Yes, my wife died, and later, the good Lord blessed me with Meg." He reached out and took Meg's hand. "For Randal to be allowed into the White House, we'll need to take along some identification, and I'll need to call ahead. Because he's under eighteen, a certified copy of his birth certificate should work."

"I know where it is," Betty said. "My son ain't no Republican though."

"Ma, I ain't nothin, but if I can spend the night in the White House, I'll become a Republican."

"You'll see Randall and Gina will welcome you no matter what," Jon said. "I promise. We can have dinner in the White House, meet the president, and make a quick visit to Logan Circle. Are you okay with that Betty? We can have him home first thing in the morning."

Betty thought for a moment. "If he'll stay with ya the whole time, Jon," Betty finally said. "He's my last son. Please be careful."

"You still have Freddy, Ma. We just don't know where he is right now."

"I'm prayin' for that Randal. I'm a prayin'."

❁◈❁◈❁◈❁

Once the Secret Service thoroughly searched the car, Jon drove up toward the East Wing Entrance of the White House. Everyone sat in reverential silence, and Lacy felt she needed to pinch herself to make sure she wasn't dreaming this whole experience.

When the car stopped in front of the entrance, Lacy got out and began digging through her purse. She had never been to Washington, D.C. before, and now, her first stop was to spend the night in the White House. She had to get a picture.

She gripped Kerrick's arm as he stepped out of the car. "Hey. Let's get a picture with the White House behind us. I'd say this is a once in a lifetime shot." She turned to Randal. "You want to take our picture?"

"Sure."

She held her phone out for Randal, but a large hand came over her shoulder and snatched the phone.

"I'm sorry, M'am," a short, clipped voice sounded behind her. "No pictures allowed. You'll have to leave your phone with us here at security. We'll safeguard it for you."

No pictures? You've got to be kidding me. "Uh, well, I'm sorry. I didn't know."

"It's okay, M'am. Most people do exactly what you did. I would do the same thing. We had to stop pictures a few years ago for safety precautions. I'm sure you understand. We'll have someone inside snap a few pictures for you."

Additional Secret Service personnel searched them, and a young woman approached from the polished brick hallway leading to the Executive Residence. She appeared to be in her mid-thirties and smiled as if she were welcoming old friends.

"Dr. and Mrs. Davenport. A pleasure to see you again. And this must be Carla"

"Hello Laura," Meg said as she hugged the woman from the side so as not to smash Carla. "Since when have we been Dr. and Mrs. anything? And yes, this is Carla."

Laura squeezed Carla's arm, and the little girl reached for Laura's necklace.

"No, M'am," Meg said, grabbing Carla's little hand. "Laura, I want you to meet our niece, Lacy Henderson, and one of our staff members, Kerrick Daniels." Laura shook their hands before Meg turned and motioned to Randal. "This bright young man is Randal Schmidt. He lives just out of the city in South Kensington."

"Pleased to meet you. I'm Laura Gordon. I'm Gina Johnson's personal assistant. I've known Jon since our college days. Of course, he's a lot older than I am."

"Right," Jon laughed. "Older by two years."

"The First Lady is expecting you for dinner, but you have time to stop by your room. Jon, you and Meg will be in the Lincoln Bedroom. Lacy, you will be our honored guest in the Queen's Bedroom. And you guys," motioning to

Kerrick and Randal, "will get to enjoy the East and West Rooms."

"The Lincoln Bedroom?" Randal gasped. "Where Abraham Lincoln slept?"

Laura smiled. "Probably not. The room was his office before it was made into a bedroom. Some other presidents have slept in the room, though. The Queen's Bedroom has hosted several queens through the years, but others have stayed in there as well. People like Winston Churchill, for one. It used to be Anna Roosevelt's room. President Roosevelt's daughter.

"It's amazing to think I'm going to be sleeping in the same bed as Winston Churchill," Lacy sighed. She hesitated. "Wait, that didn't sound right."

Everyone laughed.

Laura headed toward the long hallway. "If you'll follow me through the Colonnade, I'll take you to your rooms."

Chapter Fourteen

Catching Up

Meg's jaw dropped as Laura opened the door to the Lincoln Bedroom. She felt Lacy pressing against her back trying to get a better view. Taking a few steps forward, she heard an audible sigh coming from her niece. Meg never gave the inside of the White House much thought, but this bedroom was unbelievable. True to its name, the room had a nineteenth century style to it. She could almost picture a tall, top hat-wearing man standing next to the oak chair at the desk.

The rosewood headboard went up the wall, and what resembled a crown capped the top. Burgundy drapery lined with a golden rope hung from the crown, and sheer, white lace fell from the drapery to the floor. Meg had never seen anything so elegant, even though the whole crown motif looked a little strange. *How am I going to be able to sleep in a museum?*

"The bed is so huge," Lacy whispered. She turned to Laura. "Are you sure Lincoln never slept in this bed? It looks like it was built for him."

Laura laughed. "I think everyone who's ever slept in this room has asked the same question. We're quite sure he didn't, but this room was his office. He signed the Emancipation Proclamation in here. Those slipper chairs over there were used by his administration."

Meg couldn't quite imagine Lincoln sitting on one of those chairs. It being his office, he probably hosted people

there she'd read about in history books. Standing in the
room was almost like being in church or a library. She didn't
feel right talking in her normal voice. Laura, however, didn't
seem to share her sentiment.

Laura's voice broke the reverence. "Shall I show you the
Queen's Bedroom?" she asked Lacy.

Jon nudged Lacy with his elbow. "I bet you've always
wanted to be queen for the day. Now's your chance."

Lacy grinned and followed Laura out the door and
across the hall. Meg noticed Kerrick grab Lacy's hand. Taking a personal tour of the private quarters in the White
House had probably never been on anyone's radar. The moment seemed surreal. Meg hurried after the group and heard
Jon close behind her.

"Oh Lacy," Meg gasped. "This room is so fitting for
you."

"For me?" Lacy seemed surprised.

"Yes. It's elegant yet confident. Doesn't that bed look
like it was made for a queen?"

"Actually," Laura said as she stepped forward, "it originally belonged to Andrew Jackson, and at one time, it was
used in the Lincoln Bedroom."

"I wouldn't have thought of that bed as belonging to a
man," Lacy said with a laugh.

"Well," Kerrick interjected, "Andrew Jackson had a
wife."

Meg didn't miss Lacy's sideways glance at Kerrick. *What
did that little look mean?* She glanced back at the bed and
thought even though the bed used to belong to Andrew

Jackson, the pink rose-colored drapery running around the top of all four of the corner posts must be a newer addition.

"I'm going to have a hard time going to sleep in here," Lacy said. "I'll want to sit up and stare at this decor instead."

Laura looked at Randal. "I'm sorry your room is not quite so monumental, other than the fact it used to be Ronald Reagan's gym. President Bush turned it back into a bedroom. Kerrick, you can stay in the East Bedroom. It's not exactly masculine. During Reagan's presidency, it was Nancy's office." She directed the group down the hall to show them the rest of the president's private residence.

"I'm assuming President Johnson's room is at the other end?" Lacy asked.

"Yes." Laura nodded. "President and Mrs. Johnson's room is down the hall on the left. I'll let them decide if they want to give you a peek. Why don't you take a few minutes to freshen up? Dinner will be served here in the private quarters at six thirty. Unfortunately, President Johnson will not be available to eat with you. He will join you at eight o'clock for a few minutes. He has a busy schedule tonight."

"We understand," Jon said. "I'm surprised he has any extra time at all."

Carla leaned forward, and Lacy grabbed the girl as if on cue. Meg smiled. Her little girl loved Lacy as if she were her big sister.

"I'll watch her for a bit," Lacy offered.

Jon and Meg walked back down the hall to the Lincoln Bedroom, and Meg heard the door close behind her as she went to take a closer look at the desk in the corner. She turned around in time to step into Jon's embrace.

"Well, Mrs. Davenport. Did you ever expect to spend the night in the Lincoln Bedroom?"

He kissed her gently, and Meg felt his hands slide down her back. She loved Jon so much and thanked God every day for bringing them together. Her life had gone into overdrive after meeting him, however. Somehow, marrying this wonderful man had put her in the crosshairs of danger.

Meg took a small step back. "Jon," she half whispered while looking down at the floor, "it feels a little funny to…you know…we're in the White House and all, and…"

Jon closed the distance and pulled her back against him with another long kiss. "Sweetheart, trust me. This room or this building is not a church, but I understand your reverence. I used to be a history professor. Remember? Even if it were a church, there's nothing more sacred than a man loving his wife."

He did love her. Meg had never been so cherished in her life. She leaned into her husband and enjoyed the security and peace she always felt in his arms. Their lips had just met for another kiss when a knock sounded at the door.

Jon opened the door to find a young woman standing with a port-a-crib. "Dr. Davenport? I'm Missy. Laura asked me to bring this crib to you. Will that meet your needs?"

"Thank you, Missy," Meg said, striding toward the open door. "It will work just fine. Thank you."

Jon took the crib, thanked Missy again, and closed the door. "Of course, this crib does remind us we will have company tonight."

"Not necessarily," Meg said with a grin. "I noticed the closet is as large as a small bedroom. I bet it would be perfect for our little sleeping beauty. Speaking of Carla, we should probably go find her."

"The job of a parent never ends," Jon said with a sigh.

Meg enjoyed dinner with Gina and couldn't help but think back to her first encounter with the First Lady. Of course, back then, she was the wife of a former governor who happened to be running for president of the United States. Meg learned just before meeting them that Randall and Gina Johnson were the parents of Jon's late wife. She'd almost gotten sick on the spot.

The Johnson's welcomed Meg right into the family as if she were their second daughter. Randall escorted her down the aisle at the wedding and gave her away to their son-in-law as his new bride. The whole wonderful event was like a dream, a fairy tale.

"So, Lacy," the First Lady said, turning in her seat toward the young coed, "being held by kidnappers this summer must have been terrifying. And then, you were taken again in Mexico? I can't imagine."

Lacy cleared her throat and placed her napkin on her empty plate. "I guess I was terrified this summer, but I was also angry. I suppose they could have killed me, but that thought never crossed my mind. By the time I knew it was Miguel in Mexico, I was almost unconscious. The doctor said he used chloroform or something like it."

"You were kidnapped again?" Randal said. "I didn't know that happened."

"Yes," Meg interjected. "We were in Mexico, and the same guy that took her in the Bahamas slipped into our house. Fortunately, he crossed paths with one of the Cartel leaders who ran him off the road."

"I'm not following," Gina said. "You better start at the beginning.

Jon took over the story telling and related all the events of the past few weeks. He told Gina of discovering the treasure in the cave under the island in the Bahamas and how Viking explorers had included a map on an animal skin scroll that probably held the location to an ancient city somewhere in Mexico.

"We went to Mexico for a short vacation," Meg interrupted. "We thought it would be good to try to get an idea of the history of the country, so we visited an old city north of Veracruz called El Tajin. The city we're looking for is sort of like El Tajin. At least, that's what we think. The scroll will probably help us find it, but we don't know what it says yet because the markings are almost illegible. One of Jon's friends is an expert with this kind of thing and is trying to decipher it now."

"It's all about this medallion," Lacy said, pulling the necklace out from inside her shirt. "This Miguel, drug lord guy, wants this medallion because it contains the clue that will help him find the treasure under Coral Cay. He doesn't know we've already found it."

Meg leaned in toward Gina. "We thought the cartel member who ran him off the road in Mexico killed him, but unfortunately, it was the other way around. Miguel is still alive. After the wreck and gruesome murder, Miguel ran off as the police arrived and pulled Lacy out of the trunk."

"Unbelievable," Gina whispered. "You are lucky to be alive, Lacy."

Jon laughed and said, "We think it's time for her to return to the boring life of being a college student. Biology 101 will be a piece of cake after her experiences these last few months."

"I'll tell you one thing this summer has done for me," Lacy said. "I don't think I'll ever look at history the same way. I'm now quite interested in studying Mexican history. I want to learn more about the Totonac, the Huastec, and the Olmec People. Did you know they actually played soccer in El Tajin?"

"I've read about that," Gina said, "except they hit the ball with their hips. Something about human sacrifices."

"That part of their history gives me the creeps," Lacy admitted. "Jon says we'll go back to Mexico sometime. Maybe soon."

"I doubt you'll be going anytime soon," Meg said. "Miguel is still around. It's just not safe, Lacy. Anyway, you have to go to school."

"I doubt we'll be having much school once this hurricane comes through," Kerrick said. "I turned on the T.V. in my room and saw it's now a five and heading for south Florida."

"Yes," Gina said. "It's going to be terrible. Randall has been working with FEMA personnel all day. He's meeting with them now, I suppose. It's really messed up Cuba and parts of the Bahamas."

"We're so concerned about Diego," Lacy said, "and Pirate's Cove. Diego stayed behind to watch over the compound."

"We have a storm cellar, and it's full of provisions," Jon said. "He'll be okay, but I'll be glad to get in touch with him."

"I'm sure Randall will have the latest," Gina said. "He always seems to know everything. I'll bet he already knows the details of your kidnapping, too, Lacy. Maybe he'll be able to tell us Miguel has been caught."

"Let's hope so," Meg said under her breath.

Chapter Fifteen

Presidential Conversation

"I hope I'm not too late for dessert," the president said as he walked into the dining room.

Randal's fork hit the floor and Lacy gasped. Kerrick pushed his chair back and stood up as if at attention. Jon grinned as the memory of meeting Randall Johnson for the first time flashed through his mind. At that time, Randall was just beginning his second term as governor of Virginia, and Julie had insisted he join her at the Governor's Mansion to meet her parents. He sweated bullets, but her father went out of his way to make Jon feel welcome and at home.

Losing his first wife had been difficult for Jon. Though they were married only a few years before cancer took her, Julie's family had welcomed him in as if Gina had been his birth mother. Randall and Gina were such role models to him. They greatly influenced Jon's view of marriage and of life.

Julie had been a special woman. She was so unlike most of the other women Jon met. After meeting her parents, Jon understood what made her stand out. She was just like her mother, and that was a good thing. Gina was classy, personable, authentic, compassionate, and discerning.

After Julie died, Randall and Gina insisted Jon would remain a part of their family no matter what. Gina urged him to date and even offered counsel for the kind of woman he should look for. That whole conversation had been strange, and Jon remembered not wanting to talk about remarriage. He thought he could never find another woman like Julie, but then he had a chance encounter with Meg Freeman.

He had known Meg since they were kids, but she'd been too young for a romantic relationship with him back then. She was more than three years younger than he and had been his best friend's little sister. He marveled at how the years shaped her life. She had become an amazing woman. She was beautiful and intelligent and had a heart of gold. She was deeply centered in things that mattered. He knew faith had been an important part of her survival after the sudden death of her husband in Afghanistan.

Meg wasn't Julie, but Julie wasn't Meg either. Meg was a take charge kind of person, but she also respected Jon in every way imaginable. Although she could dominate any situation, she never sought to dominate her husband.

A couple of years after Julie's death, Jon thought of whether or not he could ever remarry. The thought crossed his mind that if he did, he would lose his family—Randall and Gina. Although they often assured him that wouldn't be the case, he had a hard time believing them until he saw how they embraced Meg and welcomed her into their family. Their love was remarkable.

"Hello Randall," Jon said as he stood and shook the president's hand. "Great to see you again."

The president pulled Jon into a hug and then greeted Meg the same way. He walked toward Randal at the foot of the table and stuck out his hand.

"Allow me to introduce Randal Schmidt," Jon said. "He worked with us this summer on our salvage boat. He and his family live in South Kensington."

"Young man, it's a pleasure to meet you. Welcome to the White House."

"It's…it's…good to meet you, Mr. President."

"Please. Call me Randall. I'd like to be your friend, and since we share the same name, I can feel confident you won't forget mine."

"Yes, sir, Mr. President, ugh, Mr. Randall, sir."

The president laughed and turned toward Lacy.

"My dear, you get more beautiful every time I see you. It seems like the last time I saw you, you were just a kid. Now, you are a beautiful young woman." He hugged her.

Jon tried to remember how many times Randall had been around to meet Lacy. The only time that came to mind was the wedding in the Bahamas. It seemed as if Randall spotted Lacy's emotional needs back then and worked hard to help her feel special.

"It's great to see you again, too, Mr. Randall."

"I heard about your ordeal this summer and recently in Mexico. I'm so glad you're okay."

"Thank you, sir." Lacy's cheeks colored.

"And this must be Kerrick Daniels." The president shook Kerrick's hand. "I've heard so much about you, too, Kerrick, and I look forward to getting to know you."

"Thank you, sir. It's an honor to meet you and Mrs. Johnson."

"Please, call us Randall and Gina."

Everyone sat down, and Randall pulled up a chair beside his wife. An attendant brought him a cup of coffee and a small slice of pound cake.

"Lacy, tell me about Mexico," Randall said as he leaned back in his chair, taking a sip of coffee. "I've heard it from official channels, but I'd like to hear your take on the experience."

Lacy offered the president a play-by-play of their vacation to Mexico and subsequent run-in with Miguel. Here and there, Jon, Meg, or Kerrick shared their perspectives. President Johnson focused on every word and never interrupted. It was as if his mental computer was taking copious notes.

"So, this guy wants your medallion?"

"I'm sure of it," Lacy replied.

"We found a medallion two or three years ago," Jon said. "We were diving a reef near Conception Island."

"Isn't that where you hid out during the hurricane when that drug lord was searching for you? What was his name?"

"Lopez."

"Yes, Alvaro Lopez. I remember now. And he's related to this Miguel Martinez fellow who is after you now?"

"Yes," Jon agreed. "Lopez is Miguel's uncle. I think they worked separately, but they are related."

"We found a skeleton on Conception Island back in May," Lacy said, picking up the story. "He, or it, was holding a gold chain. We could tell one of the links was broken, as if someone pulled something from it."

"We discovered the hard way Miguel found the skeleton before we did," Kerrick stated. "He took a medallion from

the chain, one just like Lacy's. It turns out King Bluetooth…"

"Bluetooth?" the president queried.

"He was a Viking king in the tenth century," Jon offered.

"Oh, yes," Randall said. "Seems like I read about him
years ago."

"He created a treasure hunt for his children," Kerrick
continued. "He put clues on three different medallions that
would lead them to the treasure."

"Wow," Gina interjected. "What an amazing story. And
you obviously figured out where the treasure was hidden?"

"Lacy did," Meg said as she beamed at her niece. "We
found it, but we're not really sure what we've found. Hopefully, we'll figure that out soon. In the meantime, we've got
to do something to get Miguel off our backs."

"Just before coming upstairs," the president said,
"someone from Homeland Security called to tell me that a
Miguel Ramirez Martinez arrived in Houston from Veracruz
a couple of days ago. That has to be your man. There's no
indication he's left on another flight, so we are searching for
him."

"He's probably stuck in Texas because of the storm,"
Kerrick said. "After what happened with the Cartel, I bet he
figured it is safer in the States than it is in Mexico."

"I imagine you're right," Randall agreed. "We'll find him,
and when we do, we'll arrest him."

"Right now," Meg said, "I can't think of anything I'd rather hear."

"Agreed," Randall said. "What do you plan to do now? You're not going to be able to get back to the Bahamas for at least a week."

"I'm considering going back to Mexico," Jon said.

"Jon!" Meg said with such surprise Carla began to whimper.

"Meg, you heard that Miguel is in the U.S., so we wouldn't have anything to worry about. Mexico may be the safest place right now."

"Well, we could visit somewhere far away for a few days until Miguel is caught," Meg said. "I've never been to…to somewhere like Seattle."

"Seattle is a beautiful place," Randall said. "If you decide you want to go back to Mexico, I have a pretty good relationship with the president there. He has a home not too far out of Veracruz, and I bet he'd be happy to have you as guests."

"Not that he's suggesting you go to Mexico," Gina said. "Right, Dear?"

Randall smiled. "Of course, Sweetheart."

"Guests of the president of Mexico?" Lacy gasped. "You've got to be kidding."

"I bet his compound is guarded night and day," Kerrick added.

Jon saw Meg's arms cross her chest. She didn't do that often, so he knew she wasn't happy. He also knew she wouldn't say anything else about it until they were alone. Thankfully, Gina changed the subject. She understood body language well and decided another topic would be best.

They discussed the path of the hurricane, a recent conversation Randall had with the Queen of England, and the discovery of King Harold Bluetooth's treasure trove. Jon explained each of the pieces of the small pile of treasure and the scroll of animal skin they'd discovered.

"Miguel has no idea we've already found the treasure. We hope to hear from Cindy soon," Jon said. "She's a friend and language expert. She has connections, and we're hoping she'll be able to pull some information from the scroll."

President Johnson looked down at his watch. "I hate to leave such good company, but I have a video conference with the Prime Minister of Japan in fifteen minutes."

"We understand, Randall," Jon said. "We need to find a young lady here in the city, anyway. We're hoping she can give us a clue as to where to find Randal's brother. It seems he's somewhere in Mexico."

The president pushed back from the table. "Good luck with that. You sound almost as busy as I am. Let me know if I can help. Hopefully, I'll be able to see you in the morning for a few minutes before you leave."

"Excuse me," Gina said. "I need to see Randall off. I'll be right back."

Everyone stood as Randall and Gina left the table. Young Randal bent over to retrieve his fork from the floor. Jon suggested he, Kerrick, and Randal head down to 13th Street and find Logan Circle.

"Randal," Kerrick said. "What's Freddy's girlfriend's name?"

"Coco."

"Coco?" Lacy said. "Like the drink?"

"Yep. A shortened word, kinda like a nickname, from the name *Socorro* in Spanish. It means help."

Lacy grinned. "Interesting. So, you know some Spanish, like your brother.

"Yeah. When you live in the Projects, you learn stuff."

Kerrick laughed. "I bet you do."

"I like Coco—her name, I mean," Lacy said. "I'd like to go too, by the way. It's not fair just the guys get to go out on the town."

"We're not exactly going out on the town," Kerrick said. "Having a woman in the car might hinder our mission."

Lacy choked as she took a sip of water. Jon wondered if she was choking because Kerrick called her a woman or because she was incensed that he thought she shouldn't tag along. Probably both.

"Trust me," Lacy said coolly. "You'll be able to find a prostitute with or without a woman in the car."

The thought of what Lacy knew about prostitutes passed through Jon's mind, but he let it go. He was more concerned about all of their safety and wondered if it would be safer leaving Lacy at the White House. Of course, it would be safer. Then again, Lacy had proven herself in some challenging situations, so he didn't have the heart to make her stay back.

"She's right," Jon said. "I think it'll be okay. Let's go in fifteen minutes."

Everyone left the table, and Jon pulled Carla from her highchair. He watched Meg head toward the Lincoln bedroom. She seemed a little distracted, maybe even cool, and he figured he knew what was going through her mind.

Chapter Sixteen

White House Steam

"You know how I feel about going back to Mexico," Meg said just as Jon shut the door to the bedroom.

Meg couldn't believe Jon would even consider returning to the place where Lacy was almost killed. Going back to face the Cartel was insane, but Jon always tried to help even if it meant putting himself or others out. That quality was his weak spot.

"Honey," Jon began as he put Carla down onto the carpeted floor, "Mexico is safer than anywhere else right now. We know Miguel is in Houston."

"How do you know he's in Houston?" Meg shot back. "Just because a Miguel Ramirez Martinez went through customs doesn't mean it's the one we know. For all we know, our Miguel has the airport in Veracruz staked out awaiting your return."

"*Our* Miguel?"

"Don't make light of this, Jon. You know what I mean!" Meg stared back at her husband.

"I'm sorry, Sweetheart. You're right. 'Our Miguel' just sounded a little funny. I'm not making light of anything. Although all three of those names are common in Mexico, what are the odds two people with all three names would be coming through customs at this time? I'm not a statistics guy, but my guess is the odds are low."

Meg crossed her arms and dropped down onto one of the chairs. One of Abraham Lincoln's chairs. They should be enjoying the experience of sleeping in the room used as Lincoln's office, reliving the history that took place in this room. Instead, they were arguing about going back to Mexico.

"Jon, this is not about odds and statistics. This issue is about our lives. Carla's life. Lacy's life. Don't you see what's at stake? The Cartel is made up of ruthless killers. If Miguel doesn't kill you, they could. Going back there is just not worth the risk. Right now, we could go anywhere in the world we want to go. Literally! Why in heaven's name would we go back to Mexico?"

Jon sat down in the chair across from her and crossed his legs. He looked like he was about to reminisce over a fun memory from their childhood or tell a bedtime story. He could be infuriating without even knowing it.

"Honey, first of all, I don't plan on doing anything that puts us in danger. Secondly, the reason we would go back to Mexico is Freddy is there. He is in trouble and needs someone to help him. If we don't help get him out of this problem, who will?"

"I don't know who will, but are you really willing to risk your life and our lives by going back?"

"No, I'm not. But I don't think we're risking our lives if we go back. The Cartel is not after us. They want Miguel. Miguel *is* after us, but he's in Houston."

"You hope he's in Houston," Meg interrupted.

Jon uncrossed his legs and leaned forward on his elbows. Nothing rattled him. Now, he looked like he was about to negotiate some real estate deal.

"Meg, I'll get Randall to check with the customs people and find out if the Miguel Ramirez Martinez who came into Houston had a passport showing he's from the Bahamas, or Columbia. If he is, we can be sure he's our Miguel. Then, going to Mexico would be like going on another vacation."

"I don't care whether this guy is from the Bahamas or not," Meg blurted out. "Mexico is too dangerous for us right now. Surely you see this, Jon."

Jon leaned back in his seat and looked around the room. Meg waited on his reply and could have predicted he would have some calm counter comment to what seemed like reasonable logic. He appeared to be studying the paintings on the wall until Carla crawled over and pulled on his leg.

"You need a little attention, Sweetie?" Jon asked as he picked her up, kissed her, and sat her back down onto the floor. "I guess hearing me and Mama arguing is upsetting you?"

Meg uncrossed and crossed her arms again. She jerked one leg over the other. *We're not arguing. I'm arguing, and you are playing me. Playing me like a fiddle.*

"Think about it, Meg. I'm not going to do anything to put us in danger. If Miguel is in Houston, Mexico is probably the safest place to be. He knows the Cartel is after him, which means he knows he must get to safe territory. Texas is a safe place for a Spanish-speaking person to hang out for a while."

Jon was always logical, and Meg found it difficult arguing with him. She didn't want to be logical. She wanted to be safe.

"Look," Jon continued. "We don't have to decide anything right now. Let's just think about it. You have a nice, pleasant evening with Gina while I go out and find Coco."

"That's another thing," Meg said, her voice a little louder than she intended. "You're about to go out to Prostitute Row to pick up some half-naked girl who is basically owned by someone. You think that's not putting yourself in a dangerous position? You believe she will calmly get into your car and her pimp will just let her go with this knight in shining armor who has come to rescue her? Think again. You're putting yourself and our loved ones in danger in an attempt to help someone else."

"I'm going to ask a young lady a few questions and offer her a ride home. This is America, Meg. We're not in some communist country breaking the law. This woman deserves the chance to live a different life if she wants it. I can't leave her on the streets if she needs help getting off of them. I can't become someone I'm not."

Meg put her head in her hands and felt a tear rolling down her face. His last statement was right, and she knew it. He could not become someone different than God intended. She felt his hands on her shoulders, but the moment was interrupted by a knock on the door.

"Jon," Kerrick's muffled voice came through the thick wooden door. "We're ready when you are."

"Okay, Kerrick. I'll be out in a minute."

Jon pulled Meg to her feet and looked down into her teary, red eyes. "I love you, Honey. More than words can say. I'll be back in a little bit, and maybe I'll have some answers. Let's just start there. Okay?"

Meg leaned forward and rested her forehead against his chest. What could she say? He was going to find Coco whether Meg liked the idea or not. She was in the White House for heaven's sake, and the First Lady was probably sitting at the dining room table waiting for her to return.

"Whatever, Jon. Do whatever you feel you have to do."

Meg turned and walked into the bathroom to wash her face. She couldn't argue with him. Well, she could, and she did. She just never won.

@◆@◆@◆@◆

Jon pulled the bedroom door closed behind him and walked toward Kerrick and Lacy, who stood waiting near the elevator. He realized he should have Gina call ahead to make sure one of the Secret Service guys would have their car ready. He had no idea where they parked extra cars at the White House.

He took a few steps past the elevator and saw Gina sitting at the dining room table. "Meg will be back in a minute. What do I need to do to retrieve our car?"

Gina smiled and looked up at Jon. "I'll call down for you, Jon. It's no problem. Is everything okay with Meg?"

"She'll be fine, Gina. She's a little shaken about the Mexico thing. She's also having a little trouble with me going over to Logan Circle to talk to a prostitute. I understand her concerns."

Gina's eyebrows arched up. "You're going to find a prostitute?"

"Long story. We're trying to find Randal's brother. Little Randal, that is," Jon smiled. "Freddy is somewhere in Mexico, and his girlfriend was with him. It seems now she's working the streets in D.C. I'm just going to ask her a few questions."

"You always have a soft spot for people in trouble, Jon. Seems like you never would have met our Julie if her car hadn't broken down on I-75. You do understand why Meg is upset, don't you?"

"I do, Gina, but she'll be okay."

"For what it's worth, she has a point. That's not a safe place over there."

"I know, Gina. We'll be okay."

"Be careful, Jon. Please drive away if there's any sign of trouble."

Jon leaned forward and kissed her cheek. "Yes Ma'am."

As Jon walked toward the elevator, he realized Kerrick and Lacy had been watching and listening to his conversation with Gina.

"She is like your real mother, isn't she?" Lacy said.

Jon had a difficult time reading what was behind her question. Surprise? Envy?

"Yes. She is. You know, my mother died some years ago. Gina is the closest person I have to a mother on this earth. I love her like my mother."

"And she loves you," Lacy said as a statement and not a question.

"Yes, she does."

As the doors to the elevator were closing, Jon saw Meg walking toward the dining room. He would have liked being a fly on the wall listening to the conversation that was about to take place.

@◆@◆@◆@◆

Meg saw Gina's head turn toward her as she returned to the dining room. This sweet lady was so different than Meg's own mother. In the past, Meg felt free to talk with Gina about anything and everything. She was the kind of person Meg knew would hold a confidence, which meant whatever Meg had to say about Jon would never leave this room. At the same time, Meg made it a practice never to speak critically of her husband to others.

Although Meg's parents had been married for thirty-six years before her father died, their marriage had not been a model relationship. She knew they loved one another, but she also observed a number of things about their marriage she did not want to emulate. For one thing, her mother regularly criticized her father to other people, and Meg always thought that wasn't right.

Before she'd married the first time, she and Steve went through premarital counseling with her pastor. He confirmed her opinions, and Meg had vowed never to criticize her husband to other people. Pastor Chuck said if it were possible, couples should always solve their problems behind closed doors. Even though their marriage lasted only two years before Steve was killed in Afghanistan, she kept that vow. She also maintained that commitment in her second marriage to Jon.

A memory flashed through her mind from a few months earlier. Jon had said, "Meg. I love so many things about you. One thing I love is I know my name is always safe on your lips." It was actually quite easy because she knew her name was safe on his.

"Hey Gina. I'm sorry that took so long."

"No problem, Meg. The wait was nothing, and besides, I've become an expert waiter as First Lady."

Meg laughed. "I bet you've had to hone that skill a bit. I think I would."

"I think learning to wait is a lifelong process. I've come to believe waiting is sort of connected to trusting."

"Trusting?" Meg raised an eyebrow. "I've never thought of it as being connected to trust."

Gina always had wonderful insight on so many issues about life and relationships. She once told Meg a man's greatest need was respect. Meg remembered hearing about the importance of respecting her husband, but she always thought a man's greatest need was sex.

"If your husband knows you don't respect him," Gina once said, "sex is almost an insult. There's a reason why God commands a wife to respect her husband and a husband to love his wife. It has to do with the greatest needs of men and women."

It had always been easy to respect Steve and Jon. Meg never considered the whole respect issue a command. What if her husband didn't deserve respect? She would have to find at least one thing worthy of respect and focus on that issue. Thankfully, that was not her problem.

Meg sat across from Gina. An attendant appeared from nowhere and placed a fresh cup of coffee in front of Meg. *Gina must have a secret button under the table.*

"So how is waiting connected to trusting?" Meg asked.

"When I have to wait on Randall, I have to trust he is doing everything possible to come to me as quickly as he can. I have to trust he is putting my needs ahead of his own. If he's not, we talk about it during our staff meeting."

Meg leaned forward. "Your staff meeting?"

"Yep. In our fifth year of marriage, we started setting aside one night a week to talk about the state of our marriage, and we've been doing it ever since. We bring up issues that might help the other be a better spouse."

"Wow. Why did you start your fifth year?"

Gina grinned. "Because of the first four."

Both women laughed.

"Waiting on Randall also means I am trusting him to grow to become the best possible version of Randall Johnson. He typically makes good decisions, but not always. He would tell you that. However, even when his choice is wrong, I'm trusting him to always be learning and growing from each circumstance."

"So, you don't share your opinions about his bad ideas or decisions?"

"Oh, I don't mean to say that. He wants to hear my opinions. That's his expression of trust. We're supposed to be like iron sharpening iron. If I never shared my opinion or he never shared his, we wouldn't have the advantage of maximum personal growth. I think that's why God said it was not good for man to be alone. We grow better together. Even single people need community for maximum growth."

Meg pulled her coffee cup to her lips. Gina had such wisdom. Maybe that's what forty-two years of a strong marriage did for her. Meg wondered if she'd ever have that kind of wisdom to share with others. She hoped so. Her mind instantly went to Lacy. Her niece needed her to be wise, and Meg needed not to fail her.

Chapter Seventeen

Logan Circle

Kerrick watched out the window as Jon navigated the streets of downtown Washington, D.C. He couldn't believe so many people were out this late at night. Normal people were home with their families. Right? Did that make these people abnormal? Probably not. Some were immersed in the single scene and found moving from one bar to another covered the holes of loneliness in their hearts. Others may have been going to work third shift.

He watched a young boy run up to a man and swap a paper sack for a roll of cash. Not everyone on the streets tonight was honorable. He felt anger stirring in him as he thought about a drug dealer using a young kid as a runner. That boy would probably end up a dealer or be killed along the way.

So, Logan Circle is Prostitute Central. Who'd have thought? I bet ole General Logan is rolling over in his grave.

As Jon drove around the circle, Kerrick could see the darkened statue of General John Logan riding his horse. The General had been a hero during his lifetime and an important figure in the Civil War. Kerrick thought he remembered hearing in history that Logan had run for president, but he couldn't be sure. A girl wearing short shorts and a tube top stepped toward his widow, surprising Kerrick.

He felt Lacy's hands pulling his head around, and her lips connected with his.

When Lacy pulled away, Kerrick gasped for breath. "Wow! I—."

"Just marking my territory," Lacy said as the barely clothed teen retreated.

Kerrick laughed. "Trust me. You don't have a thing to worry about."

Randal turned around in the front seat and stared out the back window. "We're not in a horrible part of town, though bad stuff happens here."

"I'm amazed cops aren't running these girls off," Kerrick said, "or arresting them."

"They'd go somewhere else," Jon said, not taking his eyes from the road. "Most of these girls are probably homeless and drug addicts. Their handlers give them enough of a fix each night to make sure they won't run away. It's heartbreaking."

"Are they sex slaves?" Lacy asked.

"I have no doubt," Jon agreed. "Some were kidnapped or taken from the streets as young girls. The scum who takes these girls knows just how to get them addicted to cocaine and dependent on their pimps. After a few months, the girls are too afraid and too dependent to leave."

"It's crazy how this horrible lifestyle becomes their comfort zone," Lacy said.

"Jon!" Randal almost shouted. "Look over there." He pointed in the direction of the statue. "Beside the statue. Kind of near that tree. That's Coco. Gotta be."

Kerrick looked and saw a young girl who appeared to be about sixteen. However, from what Randal had told them, Kerrick knew she was nineteen. She didn't look her age, but she looked the part of a prostitute with high heels and a short skirt.

Jon pulled the car to the curb. "You guys stay here." He got out of the car and walked toward Coco.

Kerrick watched as Jon moved toward the young girl and noticed a man walking up from behind the statue. The man got to her first and said something. Coco replied and turned away from him, but he grabbed her arm. Kerrick could see Jon moving faster toward the pair.

I can't just sit here and watch Jon get attacked. Kerrick turned to Lacy. "Stay in the car and don't leave Randal. Lock the doors."

Before she could reply, he leapt from the car and ran toward what he knew would be an altercation. He thought he heard the doors lock behind him. Jon was now grabbing the man's wrist. The guy had to be Coco's pimp. Like a bolt of lightning, the man's right fist caught Jon in the jaw, and Jon staggered back. The pimp took two steps toward him, and Kerrick saw the flash of a blade.

The thug was so focused on Jon he didn't notice Kerrick coming up beside him. Kerrick's fist connected hard with flesh and bone, and something cracked under his knuckles. With blood spurting from his nose, the man lunged toward Kerrick. Although he had brute strength, he had no training. Kerrick had studied martial arts for years. His roundhouse kick plowed into the side of the man's face and dropped him to the pavement like a sack of rocks.

Jon regained his balance and had the girl by the arm. "Coco, I'm Jon Davenport, a friend of Randal's. He's in the car with me. Come with us."

The girl looked at her handler lying unconscious on the ground and nodded her head. The three hurried toward the car. Kerrick heard locks click again and the front and back doors facing the curb swung open. Jon had the car started by the time Kerrick and Coco jumped into the backseat. They sped off toward downtown.

Lacy grabbed Kerrick's hand and began inspecting his knuckles. "Are you okay? You could have been killed."

"Wow, Kerrick." Randal said. "You can fight."

"Coco, as I told you, I'm Jon. These two are Kerrick and Lacy, and you know Randal. We'd like to talk and help you, if you'll let us. Can we take you to get something to eat?"

Coco stared out the side window. Kerrick wondered why the girl had come with them, but he figured she knew she had no choice. Her handler would take out his anger on her. If the bruise on her cheek was any indication, he'd abused her before.

"Come on, Coco," Randal pleaded. "Let Mr. Jon help you."

"I ain't hungry," Coco said.

"I am," Jon said, but Kerrick couldn't imagine Jon being hungry after what they ate for dinner.

Jon maneuvered the car over to 14th Street and headed north. Within a few minutes, he turned into the parking lot of an IHOP restaurant.

Lacy reached over the back seat into the luggage area and pulled out her lightweight jacket. "Coco, it's usually freezing in these places. You want my jacket?"

Kerrick thought he noticed the girl smile as she took it. They piled out of the car and walked into the restaurant like a happy family going out for a late-night snack. He caught sight of Jon's face and remembered the blow he'd taken. Maybe happy family was a stretch.

❀❀❀❀❀❀❀

Lacy watched Coco dig into a pile of pancakes. So much for not being hungry. She was glad the girl let Jon buy her something to eat. She thought about her own life and decided she may not have it so bad after all. Watching Coco stuff another forkful into her mouth, Lacy felt a pang of sorrow. What would make a girl do what Coco did every night?

Everyone else ordered coffee and a fruit crepe. Lacy wasn't hungry, but she ate slowly as she watched Coco. She looked up at Jon and saw him wince as he opened his mouth for a bite. His jaw was turning a dark shade of blue.

"Uncle Jon, that's got to hurt."

"I've had worse," Jon said with a grin.

"Sorry Bo hit you," Coco said.

"Who is Bo?" Jon asked, though Lacy was sure he knew.

"He says he's my daddy, but he's a…" Coco paused and looked at Lacy.

"Are you using, Coco?" Jon interrupted.

"That's why Bo's mad. He told me to stay at the cat house tonight. They like to shoot us up, but I don't want it."

"Listen, Coco. I can help you out of whatever problem you're in."

"I ain't in no problem," Coco insisted.

Jon took a sip of his coffee and let Coco's reply hang in the air for a moment. "I think Bo was about to hit you, and it doesn't look like it would have been the first time."

"Don't mean I got a problem."

Trying to change the subject, Lacy asked, "Do you know where Freddy is?"

"I ain't seen him in over a month. Last time I saw him was in Xalapa."

"The capital of Veracruz?" Jon asked.

"Don't know about no capital, but it's in Veracruz."

Jon leaned forward on his elbows. "Is he a part of Los Unidos?"

"No, well, sort of. He wanted to be in Los Unidos, but he started hanging around Rafael. Rafael is acting like he's in Los Unidos, but he's about somethin' else. Maybe Jalisco."

"What is Jalisco?" Kerrick asked. "Another cartel?"

Coco answered with a mouthful of food. "Yeah." She chewed a minute before continuing. "Maybe. I mean, Jalisco New Generation is a cartel. Don't know if that's what Rafael is about or not. If he'd touched me one more time, I'd killed him. That's why I left."

"And Freddy stayed?" Jon asked.

"Yeah. I guess he's still there."

"Is he living in Xalapa?" Lacy asked. "We really want to help him. Do you think he'll let us help him?"

"He ain't in Xalapa. He's probably in Los Rios or some-where around there. That's bottom of Veracruz, Veracruz city I mean. Rafael was tryin to get him to go somewhere down near Catemaco."

"We've been to Catemaco," Lacy said. "It's beautiful."

"I say near, but maybe a couple of hours or so from the lake. I'm not sure. Freddy's a fool."

"What about you, Coco?" Jon asked. "Will you let me help you?"

"I don't need no help," the young girl said again. "You just made me miss a lot of tricks, and Bo ain't gonna be happy."

Jon reached into his pocket and pulled out several one-hundred-dollar bills. "See this, Coco? This would buy you a ticket to anywhere in the United States. I have friends near Atlanta who can help you find a new life. If you let me, I'll use this money to make sure you get to my friends. Otherwise, it stays in my pocket. I'm not going to fund your addiction and give Bo my money."

Coco snorted. "I ain't goin to Atlanta."

"Suit yourself," Jon said. He slipped the bills back into his pocket and pulled a business card out of his wallet. Sliding it across the table, he said. "Here's a card with my phone number on it. Call me if you change your mind."

Coco looked at the card and left it lying on the table. "I ain't changin my mind."

When they left the table to head for the car, Lacy noticed the business card was missing. She couldn't believe Coco wanted to go back to the streets when she had a chance to get away. Maybe she would call Jon later.

Coco directed Jon to drive to a corner on Florida Avenue where she got out of the car. She pulled Lacy's jacket from her shoulders, tossed it back into the car, and walked away into the night. Lacy felt such sorrow for this poor girl. Evidently drugs had such a hold on her she couldn't bear to leave her lifestyle for a new one.

"I can't believe it," Lacy said in the silence as Jon drove back toward the White House.

"It is hard to believe," Jon agreed. "Drugs are a powerful demon."

Lacy looked at her watch and saw it was past twelve thirty. "It's late. Is it bad that we're just now coming back?"

"Randall and Gina will understand," Jon said. "Gina probably warned the Secret Service we'd be out late."

No one said a word as they drove through the night and turned into the entry to the White House. Lacy thought it was sad the Secret Service had to surround the White House with such protection. A street ran in front of the mansion, but no one was allowed to drive or even walk on it. An agent searched the car and had each of them step through a metal detector before allowing them to drive toward the president's house.

Lacy felt numb. She didn't know what to say. She felt Kerrick's hand slip into hers as they walked through the quiet colonnade toward the central part of the White House. Their footsteps echoing off the walls of the building made the only sound of the night.

Standing at the door to the Queen's Bedroom, Lacy watched Jon ease into his bedroom. Kerrick took her hands in his, and she looked into his face.

"I'm sorry, Lace. I know tonight was difficult for you."

"I'm sorry, too. I'm so sad for Coco."

"Me too."

He leaned toward her and placed his lips on hers. "I love you, Lacy. Good night."

Lacy wrapped her arms around Kerrick and enjoyed the security of his heat and strength. "I love you, too, Kerrick," she whispered. "You were amazing tonight." She kissed him again. "I'll see you in the morning."

Chapter Eighteen

Friends in High Places

After getting ready for bed, Jon stood still listening to Meg breathe. The left side of his face pulsed with a dull ache every time his heart beat. He should have gotten some ice for his cheek or jaw. Fortunately, the guy had been a little off balance.

Meg wasn't asleep. He could tell. He'd listened to her breathe enough at night to know the difference. He eased the covers back and crawled into bed. He pulled his right arm up and put his wrist under his head as a yawn slipped from his mouth. He heard a rustling of the covers and felt Meg's hand on his bare chest.

She moved her cheek against his chest, and he could smell the freshness of her hair. He inhaled her scent and rubbed his left hand down her back. She slid up beside him, and he felt her lips on his. Tender. Soft.

"I love you Jon Davenport, and I trust you."

Interesting comment. I should hope you trust me. "I love you, too, Meg Davenport. Crawling into bed beside you always reminds me home is wherever you are."

He found her face with his hand and pushed her hair behind her ear. He figured her conversation with Gina had gone well or maybe spending the evening alone in Lincoln's old office had stirred her heart. Whatever. It didn't matter. Their lips met again. He was home.

❀❖❀❖❀❖❀

"Well, I'm glad you two lovebirds were able to leave the nest and join us for breakfast," Lacy said as Jon and Meg walked into the dining room. "Nice shiner, Uncle Jon."

Jon's hair stood straight up on one side, and his right cheek was black and blue just below his eye. His face was also swollen. Meg yawned as Carla pulled on her mother's hair.

"Excuse me," Meg said.

Gina stood to her feet. "Jon! What in the world happened?"

"Meg warned me not to talk back to her anymore," Jon said with a little grin. "I should have listened."

"Kerrick told me you found Coco, but he didn't tell me you had trouble," Gina said. "You should have awakened me last night so we could have put ice on it."

"I've already told him that," Meg said. "He came to bed last night in the dark, and I had no idea he'd been hurt."

"The guy Kerrick leveled is the one who's hurt," Lacy said as she looked up at Kerrick and rubbed his arm. Her eyes rested on his swollen knuckle. He should have gotten some ice last night, too.

Jon took Carla from Meg and put her into a highchair at the end of the table. He and Meg sat down and began serving their plates with eggs, grits, and bacon.

"I see you've brought grits back to the White House," Jon said with a grin.

"Of course," the president said with a laugh. "I had to teach these people about a real breakfast. So, what happened last night?" Randall asked.

Jon, Kerrick, Lacy, and Randal told their versions of the story. Lacy was so proud of Kerrick. She didn't know he could fight like that. He told her he took karate but taking karate and leveling a street thug are two different things.

"Unfortunately, there's a lot of crime in the city," the president said. "I'm glad you're okay and you found Freddy's girlfriend, or former girlfriend, I guess."

"I can't believe she wouldn't let you help her," Gina added. "Such a tragedy."

"So, where do you go from here?" President Johnson asked. "I checked on the Bahamas this morning. Great Exuma has suffered from the storm, and Miami is being hit hard as we speak. I'm afraid there will be considerable damage."

"I saw that on the news this morning," Jon said. "I was hoping the storm would miss us."

"I feel so bad for all of those people," Meg said as she placed a bowl of grits in front of Carla. "They're saying there's been a number of deaths in the Bahamas, and Miami has never faced a category five hurricane. Ever."

"It's going to be bad," Randall agreed. "I'll fly down later this week once the storm has passed. I'm sure the whole region will be devastated. You won't be able to land at the Great Exuma airport anytime soon. It's pretty messed up."

"I think we should take you up on your offer and return to Mexico," Meg said, looking over at Jon. "Randall, would it be too much of an imposition to call the president of Mexico and ask if we could stay in his Veracruz home? Or maybe he would have a better suggestion."

"I'm happy to call him, Meg."

Lacy looked over at Gina and saw a gleam in her eye. Something was up between Meg and the First Lady, but Lacy just couldn't figure out what. Meg acted weird about the Mexico thing last night, and now, she's suggesting they head south.

"Mama!" Carla cried out.

Lacy burst out laughing after looking at her little cousin. Grits dripped from the top of her head onto the tray of her highchair.

"Carla!" Meg said. "Why do you have to make such a mess?"

"It's called job security, Dear," Jon said. "It's Carla's way of saying she can't make it without her mama."

"I don't think mamas are the only ones who can clean up babies," Lacy said with a grin.

"No," Jon agreed, "but Meg is so good at it."

"You may want to be careful, or you'll have a matching bruise on the other cheek," Meg said over her shoulder.

The president laughed. "She's tough Jon. I've always known that."

"She's tough on the outside," Jon said with a smile in his voice, "but she's soft as butter on the inside. The truth is Randall, she's perfect."

Meg cleaned most of the grits off of Carla's head, and everyone finished their breakfast. Lacy wondered if they ate big meals like this every day. She decided they probably didn't, or President Randall would be a large man.

"Thank you, Randall and Gina for breakfast," Meg said. "I better get this little monster in the tub. Lacy, you and Kerrick make sure you're packed and ready to go."

"We've loved having you here," Gina said. "I've got an appointment in forty-five minutes myself, so I need to be excused. Hopefully, I can see you off before my meeting."

"Jon," Randall said as the others left the table. "I'll contact President Diaz and let you know what he says."

"Thank you, Randall. That will be wonderful."

"Will you be able to join us for Christmas? Christmas in the White House will be quite the treat."

"We'd love to."

"Bring Lacy and Kerrick along. They are a delight, and I have a feeling we will add a new member to our family before long."

Lacy felt her cheeks glowing as she turned to leave the dining room with Kerrick. As they walked toward the Queen's bedroom, she pretended not to be listening to Jon and the president, but she took in every word.

"We think so too," she heard Jon say. "We like him, Randall. He is a fine young man."

I like him too!

Jon and Randall remained at the table as everyone else left the dining room. Gina returned with a pot of coffee and refilled their cups before returning to the kitchen.

"Jon," Randall said. "Why don't we slip down to my office and give President Diaz a call? You'd probably enjoy seeing the Oval Office anyway."

"That sounds wonderful, Randall."

As they left the private residence on the second floor and headed to the West Wing, President Johnson asked Jon for his opinion on the Cartel in Mexico. Jon knew some about the Cartel but probably no more than what he gleaned from the news, which wasn't much. He knew they were causing a problem in the U. S. through drugs and human trafficking.

"I suppose the only good thing about our Cartel issue," Randall said as they approached the Oval Office, "is the different cartels are constantly fighting each other. Maybe they'll wipe each other out."

"That would certainly solve the problem," Jon agreed with a laugh.

"Good morning, Mr. President," a Secret Service agent said at the door of the office.

"Good morning, Phillip," Randall said. He turned toward the agent on the other side of the door. "Good morning George. Thank you for being here this morning."

"It's our pleasure, Mr. President," the stiff agent replied as he opened the door for the president and walked into the room first.

Randall and Jon followed George into the office. Jon assumed the president rarely, if ever, entered a room alone. The eagle-eyed agent scanned the room and returned to the hallway, closing the door behind him.

"It takes a little getting used to," Randall said. "You know, they check the office thoroughly when they know I'm coming down and then lead me in here to check it one more time. It's amazing these men and women sign up to serve knowing they're agreeing to give their lives for me. It's very humbling."

"I'm sure it is," Jon agreed.

The first thing that caught Jon's attention was the Resolute Desk. He'd heard so much about it through the years and seen the picture of John F. Kennedy's son peeking out from under it. Jon's father had insisted he watch George W. Bush address the nation from the Oval Office after the 9/11 attack, and he remembered seeing the desk.

He looked through the three large windows and could see the Rose Garden. Jon couldn't believe he was standing in the room that had been occupied by so many important people in history. He took in the two couches facing one another in front of the desk and the presidential seal in the center of the ceiling. He felt his feet sink into the plush rug that covered most of the floor.

"Jon, give me a second," Randall said as he reached for the phone on his desk. "Melony, good morning. Please see if you can get me President Diaz. Tell him I'm sorry to bother him without a prior arrangement, but I have a personal favor to ask." He listened for a moment. "Okay. Thank you. I'll be waiting."

Randall hung up the phone. Jon felt such pride in his father-in-law for serving as the president. It was hard to believe. The phone rang.

"Thank you, Melony," Randall said into the phone. "Mr. President. How are you this morning?" He listened. "Yes. I'm fine. I'm sorry to interrupt your morning, but I have a favor to ask. You may have heard about a little problem my son-in-law had in Veracruz recently…"

Jon walked around the office looking at the paintings on the wall. Abraham Lincoln was Randall's favorite president, so a large painting of Lincoln hung facing the desk. On the right side, he saw a painting he'd seen many times, at least in prints. George Washington knelt in the snow beside his horse, praying.

"It's all worked out, Jon," Randall said.

Jon hadn't realized the conversation was over.

"President Diaz suggested you use his private cottage near Catemaco just outside of San Andres Tuxtla. You mentioned Catemaco as well as Veracruz. The president has a vehicle you are welcome to use, and if you need one, there's a helicopter as well. He said you'll find a full-time staff, along with the normal security personnel."

"Wow, Randall. That is incredible. Thank you. Meg will feel better having security around.

"I'm so glad I could help. I just wish I could spend more time with you today."

"I know you have a million things to do," Jon said, "so we'll be heading on our way. I need to take Randal home and get to the airport. Thank you for your hospitality."

Don completed his final inspection of the airplane as Lacy, Kerrick, and the Davenports walked toward the small jet. He was the most thorough pilot Jon knew, just one of the reasons Jon liked him. As Jon handed their luggage to the attendant, his phone buzzed. When he pulled it out of his pocket, he recognized a Washington, D.C. phone number on the screen but had no idea who'd be calling.

"Jon Davenport," he said into his phone.

Meg raised an eyebrow as Jon lifted a finger and mouthed the word *police*. He walked away from the airplane. Something was up, and it didn't look good.

Chapter Nineteen

A Lost Girl

This particular bus didn't go to Catemaco, so Miguel was going to have to spend the night in San Andres Tuxtla. Catemaco was so close he could have walked the seven miles to the tourist hot spot, but he planned to catch a bus the next morning.

As the bus rolled into San Andres Tuxtla, Miguel marveled at its size. It was like heading to the county fair only to end up in Disney World. Except this city offered no fun rides. It did, however, offer many places a man could hide.

Stepping from the bus, he wondered if he should stay here or move on to Catemaco. He walked into the bus station and saw an attendant setting out luggage. His one small piece had been pulled off first. Two expensive looking suitcases sat next to his, and after looking around the bustling station, he grabbed all three and managed to get them out the door. Fortunately, his bag had a strap, so he was able to carry the larger suitcases and walk away from the city center.

After walking a few blocks, he took a taxi to the Hotel Isabel and was pleased to see masses of people crammed into the city. Taxicab drivers blew their horns and street merchants shouted about their wares. This place was already beginning to feel like an old pair of jeans—familiar, comfortable, and predictable.

Hotel Isabel was nice enough. The place offered adequate rooms and had a restaurant in the building. He paid for three nights. The desk attendant grabbed the two suitcases Miguel had taken at the bus station and followed him upstairs to his room.

The room wasn't bad. It had air conditioning, a couple of decent beds, and hot water. It even had cable television. Miguel paid the equivalent of about eighteen dollars a night, so he couldn't complain. The attendant left, disappointed Miguel had offered no tip, and Miguel studied the stolen luggage. The latches were locked and needed a combination. He hurried up the street from the hotel to a hardware store and purchased a small crowbar. *This better be worth it.*

Back in the room, he placed the crowbar against the lock and had visions of his first venture into a life of crime. His mother entertained a man the night of Miguel's twelfth birthday. The smiling man placed a suitcase down in the main room of the house before following Miguel's mother to the back of the house. Although young Miguel knew the bag was off limits, the lock on the top captured his imagination. What would be so valuable a man would secure it with a small lock?

After searching the house, Miguel found a short piece of rebar in the front yard. He got to work on the old lock. The rusty lock was no match for the rebar, and he was inside the luggage in just seconds. He didn't know what he expected to find. Candy or money? Instead, he found several plastic bags of powder mixed in with a bunch of clothes. He was disappointed. It was kind of like his first taste of coffee—disgusting.

Why would little bags of white powder be secured with a lock? He pocketed the bags and snapped the luggage back together, minus the lock. Maybe the grinning idiot wouldn't notice it. Miguel showed it to his friend's older brother who offered him $200 pesos for the bags.

Thinking back to how he had been stiffed still made him sore. That boy knew he would score thousands of dollars for those bags of cocaine. Once Miguel learned of his error, he vowed it would never happen again.

Miguel pried the suitcases open and saw one was filled with men's clothing, and the other with women's. He dumped the lady's suitcase out on his bed and found two necklaces and a couple of rings. They looked valuable, but they could be fake.

He rifled through the other suitcase and discovered a zipper hidden in the seam that went around the edge of the interior. *Your hidden compartment is not very hidden, my friend.*

Miguel pulled the zipper and reached into a small pocket. To his surprise, he pulled out a stack of $500 pesos bills. *Merry Christmas, Miguel! Why did this man carry cash in his luggage? His stupidity is my gain.*

Miguel found a jewelry store and told the owner his mother had passed away. He wanted to know the value of her jewelry. He nearly choked when the owner valued one necklace at nearly $2000 and one of the rings was worth close to $1500 in American dollars. Miguel sold both of them to the shop owner for $2500 and left the store. He decided the man was lying, and the jewelry was probably worth twice the amount quoted. He was satisfied, though. He had more than enough money to get him back to the Bahamas. If he needed more, he could always return to the jewelry store after closing.

He decided to stay in the big city, though he might visit Catemaco. He was going to make the best of this little vacation. No Cartel. If he could have Lacy with him, it would be a vacation indeed. This whole trip had been a disaster. He had to figure out how to get that medallion. With the storm hitting the Bahamas, the Davenports could be anywhere in the world. At least he would have time to come up with a better plan.

@◆@◆@◆@◆

"What is it, Jon?" Meg asked as her husband joined her in the airplane.

She had watched him walk across the tarmac and knew something wasn't right. Her husband was easier to read than the weather, and she found her forecasts about him were almost always one hundred percent accurate. He looked broken. Something bad had happened.

"She's…" he choked and stared down at the floor. He rubbed his eyes and dropped into the seat beside her. He didn't say anything for a long moment. She noticed he hadn't buckled his seatbelt. "She's dead," he finally managed.

Turning sideways in her seat, Lacy asked, "Who's dead?"

Meg saw a lone tear making its way down Jon's right cheek. She tried to remember when Jon had last cried. Carla's birth. Tears of joy when Carla was born. This tear had nothing to do with joy.

"Coco," Jon croaked. "The police found her body this morning in a dumpster."

Lacy couldn't hide her shock. Her hand clamped over her mouth. Although Meg hadn't met the girl, the impact was just as profound.

"What happened, Jon?" Meg whispered.

"They don't know. I feel sure it has to do with last night. Regardless, we can't leave, yet. I have to go to the police station and give a statement." Jon looked up at Lacy and Kerrick. "All three of us need to go. It shouldn't take long."

"Do I need to come?" Meg asked, unbuckling her seatbelt.

"No, you and Carla just wait in the private lounge. We should be heading south before lunch."

"That was my next question," Meg said. "Should we eat before taking off?"

"I think we'll be airborne in time to eat a late lunch in flight," Jon said. "I'll make sure Don knows that before we head toward the station."

Meg watched as Lacy pulled Carla from her seat and carried her down the steps. Meg followed Jon out of the plane and took his hand as they walked toward the private terminal.

Before entering the lounge, Meg stopped and pulled Jon toward her. "Are you going to be okay?"

"You know, I should have…"

"It's not your fault," Meg interrupted. "You can't blame yourself. You did everything you could to save that girl."

"Not everything."

"Jon, your only other option was to kidnap her and tie her up. She made her choice, and it was a bad one." Meg pulled his head down toward hers and placed her lips on his.

She knew his heart was breaking. He was the kindest man she knew. Somehow, he had to know he couldn't save the whole world. "It's not your fault," she said again.

"We'll be back as soon as possible," he mumbled.

Meg reached out to take Carla from Lacy and watched Jon, Lacy, and Kerrick walk out of the terminal. Carla jabbered on about something on the television screen inside the lounge. *Oh, to be able to enjoy the world of innocence.*

Two hours later, Meg looked up from Carla's coloring book to see Jon standing beside her. "Wow, that was quick."

"Yeah," Jon agreed. "The detectives interviewed us all separately at the same time. It's almost as if her death didn't matter too much. Just another prostitute killed in the city. Hazards of the job, I suppose."

"I'm really sorry, Jon."

"Me, too. Let's go."

Meg thought back to their conversation before breakfast. She couldn't believe they were going back to Mexico. She half figured Lacy would balk at the idea, but when they all discussed it after breakfast, Lacy was the first one to agree. She was so fascinated with finding Bluetooth's lost city that she was more than ready to go. Jon reminded her their trip would be more focused on Freddy than treasure, but maybe they would have time to familiarize themselves more with the culture and geography of the place.

"What about Cindy?" Lacy had asked. "Can you call her to see if she knows something?"

"She'll call me," Jon replied. "As soon as she knows something, we'll know something."

At least they would be flying to what had to be a small fortress. Surely, the president of Mexico would have top security at his compound. Maybe President Diaz would help them locate Freddy, and they could get the boy back to his family where he belonged.

The thought of having to tell him about Coco's death clouded her mind like a fast-moving thunderstorm. How would Freddy respond? Evidently, he and Coco must have had a falling out before she left. Tragic. Everything about Freddy and Coco's story was tragic. What would lead a young girl to enter the sex industry in the first place? Desperation? Drugs? Maybe she sold herself to someone in order to get out of Mexico and back to D.C.

Thinking of Coco made Meg realize her upbringing was so tame compared to some people. Meg's greatest worry had been pimples and arguments with her father about short dresses. Gratitude filled her heart as she considered the value of a father who cared about her clothing choices.

She gathered Carla up in her arms and followed everyone else toward the plane. Carla's hair smelled of baby shampoo, love, and hope. Meg knew her little girl would never have to decide between sex or security. She would always have a mother and father who loved her and took care of her. She would always be safe in the strong arms of parents who cared about every detail of her life.

Meg hurried to walk beside her husband. She reached out and placed her free arm around his waist as if she were rescuing a drowning victim. Maybe he wasn't drowning, but at the moment, he might be in a little over his head. But he had her, and she had him. That fact would never change.

Chapter Twenty

The Alligator's Snout

Lacy couldn't believe she was returning to the place of her most recent nightmare. She remembered seeing a picture of a bird standing on the snout of an alligator and thought she might be that bird. Then again, Miguel was probably somewhere in Texas or Oklahoma by now, so he would be her last concern. Thanks to Hurricane David, she knew the drug lord would not be in the Bahamas or in Florida, but thanks to the Cartel, he also wouldn't be in Mexico.

Their plane touched down at General Heriberto Jara International Airport outside of Veracruz City just before ten p.m. She marveled at being in Mexico only nine hours after leaving D.C. How did that happen? Having a private jet didn't hurt, and not having to wait long for the flight to Veracruz had been a bonus. *Having a rich uncle has its perks.*

As the plane taxied toward the terminal, she looked out and saw the rotor blades of a sleek, black helicopter slowing to a stop and armed soldiers running out to surround it. She saw more machine guns during her first visit to Mexico than she had seen her entire life. Mexico was both a strange and beautiful country.

The pilot's voice came over the intercom asking customers, in English, to remain in their seats as guests of the government deplaned. He then repeated the message in Spanish. Lacy looked around to see who the famous V.I.P.s were. She figured she wouldn't recognize them unless it happened to be Jenifer Lawrence or Angelina Jolie. It was probably some political figure she wouldn't know if she bumped into him.

A flight attendant came to stand beside her first-class seat. "Miss Henderson, Mr. Daniels, Dr. and Mrs. Davenport…please follow me."

Lacy's mouth fell open when it hit her. *We're the guests.* She couldn't have been more shocked if a large toad had jumped up and kissed her full on the lips. She finally responded to the kind woman's invitation and Kerrick's elbow in her side. She noticed a girl pointing at her and saying something to her mother. *She probably thinks I'm a movie star. Crazy.*

They hustled out of the plane and toward the helicopter she had seen earlier. Their helicopter. It seemed as if one hundred sets of eyes bore down on them, watching them make their privileged escape. They could have taken a cab. This extravagance seemed unnecessary and a little embarrassing.

The hour ride took them from the lights of the modern city of Veracruz and Boca del Rio over what Lacy figured must be dense jungle. She tried to remember what the terrain had been like when they drove south to Catemaco. It didn't seem that dense at the time, but now they were flying more inland.

The helicopter gained altitude as they cleared a mountain. Lacy wished it were daytime. She would have loved to see the colorful villages dotting the landscape. She remembered the coastal highway before it wound up into the mountains. It took them to some city that must have been built around that stone head carved by an Olmec Indian two or three thousand years ago. She couldn't believe she could remember that they were called Olmec people. Jon would be proud.

Off in the distance, she spotted the lights of a large compound that reached up into the sky like large, laser, octopus arms seeking to draw them earthward. It had to be the president's home, or more accurately, his vacation fortress. Lacy wondered what it would be like staying at the president's house.

The helicopter hovered over a spacious lawn before its slow descent. Lacy had never ridden in a helicopter before and found she was a bit disappointed it had to end so quickly. She thought of being at the fair when she was ten, wishing the Ferris wheel would never stop. The landing was cotton soft, and a soldier pulled open the door.

"*Buenas noches*," he said as he reached up for Meg's hand.

Meg moved toward the open door, and the man took her hand and motioned for her to duck as she stepped to the ground. One-by-one, they exited the helicopter. Lacy squinted against the blinding rooftop lights as she tried to take in the ancient fortress and the grounds surrounding it. Although the lights in her eyes made it difficult to see, she could make out enough to appreciate the beautiful flowers lining the immaculate lawn.

"Nicer than our last place in Mexico," Kerrick whispered into her ear as they approached the main structure. "That's for sure."

They walked through the main entrance, and Lacy saw right away that no expense had been spared to make the place modern while trying to maintain the old charm. Candles and lamps twinkled and cast a soft glow on the floor tiles. To Lacy, the place looked like what would happen if an ancient cathedral and large castle were remodeled by Chip and Joanna Gaines.

As they moved into the cavernous living area, a short, wide man stood to greet them. "*Bienvenidos.* Welcome to *Casa de las Montañas.*" Though heavily accented, his English was very good. "I hope your flight was pleasant. My name is Alejandro Morales, and I serve President Diaz as his special assistant. He sends his greetings and regrets he cannot be here to welcome you in person."

Extending his hand, Jon stepped forward. "It is a pleasure to meet you, Señor Morales, and we are grateful for the president's hospitality. His kindness is overwhelming, and your hospitality is also appreciated. This is my wife, Meg, and my daughter, Carla."

Señor Morales took Meg's hands and gave her the customary kiss on each cheek. "I was told, Señor Juan, you have a beautiful wife, and my informants were correct. *Mucho gusto* Señora Davenport. And what a beautiful little girl."

"Thank you, Señor Morales," Meg said.

Morales' eyes slid from Meg's face to her neck. "And your necklace is beautiful. You have magnificent taste."

Lacy watched Meg finger the diamond solitaire necklace. She knew it was her aunt's favorite, though she had others that were much more valuable. Meg once told her it was the first gift Jon had given her after proclaiming his love for her.

"Thank you, Señor Morales. It was a gift from my husband." Meg's eyes met Jon's, and she smiled tenderly. "Allow me to introduce my niece, Lacy Henderson, and her, or our intern, Kerrick Daniels."

Lacy noticed Meg's cheeks color a bit. Was her aunt embarrassed? She grinned as she thought about Kerrick being *her* intern. *He's my intern all right.*

"Señorita Henderson," the man said as he took her hands into his and repeated the cheek kissing. "You are as beautiful as your aunt. It is a pleasure. And Señor Daniels. It is a privilege to have you at *Casa de las Montañas.*"

Kerrick reached out to shake hands with his host. "Thank you, sir. It is an honor to meet you and to be in your home, or the president's home. Thank you for your hospitality."

"You are welcome to stay as long as you like," Alejandro said. "I will be here to serve you and assist in any way possible."

Lacy stared at the fake smile of their host.

❧❦❧❦❧❦❧

Lacy leaned against the door frame of her bedroom as a young woman led Jon and Meg down the hall. "Good night, Aunt Meg and Uncle Jon."

"Good night, Lacy and Kerrick," Meg said. "I know you are both exhausted and need some sleep."

"Yes, Ma'am," Kerrick said. "We're about to go to bed."

As the Davenports rounded the corner out of sight, Lacy pulled Kerrick into her bedroom. "So, we're going to bed?" She grinned up at Kerrick.

Kerrick wrapped her up and pulled her against his strong body. He tilted his head, and they shared a passionate kiss.

Kerrick finally pulled away. "I've been wanting to do that all day Señorita Henderson."

"Is that a fact Señor Daniels? I don't think I'm convinced." Lacy grinned.

He pulled her back into a tender but intense kiss that sent Lacy's head spinning and heart pounding. Every kiss with Kerrick was like their first—memorable, thrilling, and filled with promise.

Kerrick whispered into her ear. "I love you, Lace. We should get some sleep."

"I'm not sleepy," Lacy said.

"You are and just don't know it. I have no idea what we'll be doing tomorrow, but I'm sure we'll have a busy day."

On the flight from D.C. to Houston, Lacy wanted to talk with Jon about a strategy for finding Freddy, but he wasn't in the mood for talking. Everyone was shaken up over Coco's murder, and in the end, no one spoke much.

"How will we find him, Kerrick?"

"Good question. I guess we'll drive back toward Veracruz in the morning and find that place Coco told us about. Los Rios, I believe."

"Do you think he's still with Rafael."

"Probably," Kerrick said, pulling Lacy over to sit down on a small love seat.

"We know Freddy is staying in Los Rios with a guy named Rafael," Lacy said with a sigh. "But that's all. That won't help us find him. Los Rios has to be a big place."

Kerrick pulled out his phone and typed in the words Los Rios Veracruz Mexico into the search bar. A map came up showing a small area on the southwest side of Veracruz.

"It's not that big," Kerrick acknowledged. "It seems to me an American boy is going to stand out."

"True," Lacy agreed. "I guess we could go there, start asking people questions, and show Freddy's picture around."

"Seems like that would work. I don't know why people wouldn't be willing to help us."

"What about the lost city?" Lacy asked. "Did you hear Jon tell Meg he had a message from Cindy?"

"No. I didn't hear that."

"Evidently, Cindy called from Spain while we were flying to Veracruz. Maybe she's been able to read that scroll."

Lacy shivered as she thought back to their late-night dive at Coral Cay. It felt like years ago but was just a few weeks earlier. Finding King Harold Bluetooth's treasure trove seemed like an impossibility. At one point, she thought they'd be more likely to find a family of unicorns than the pot of gold at the end of the rainbow. It turned out not to be a rainbow but an underwater cave entrance.

The scroll of animal skin had been well preserved, but it was hundreds of years old. She didn't think there was much chance Cindy could find anything on the scroll, but stranger things had happened.

"Maybe I should text Jon and ask him what Cindy said," Lacy suggested.

Kerrick raised an eyebrow and stared at her. "I don't think that's a good idea. They're probably going to sleep about now."

"Or not," Lacy said with a grin.

"I think it can wait until morning," Kerrick said. "Speaking of sleep, you don't need beauty sleep, but I do."

He stood to his feet and pulled Lacy up. She stared into his blue eyes and felt she could fall into them and be lost. She could look into those eyes all night, all year, for the rest of her life. His eyes held such promise, such hope. The corners of his mouth began to rise into a smile.

"What?" Lacy asked. "What's funny?"

"Nothing's funny."

"Then why are you smiling?"

Kerrick's face lit up as his smile stretched from ear to ear. It was like the sun when it rose above the eastern horizon in the morning. "You just make my heart so happy it shows on my face."

Lacy laughed out loud. "Boy, you are after something."

"Just your heart, Lace. Just your heart."

The room stilled with a silence so deep and thick it could have been sliced open like hot bread out of the oven. Lacy looked down at their bodies pressed together and returned her eyes to his gaze.

"You've already got that."

Their lips met again before Kerrick pulled away and backed toward the door. He had his hands together like he was holding something inside. "I'll guard it with my life."

"You had better," Lacy said, all playfulness gone. "You about killed it the last time we were in Mexico, you know? The Hannah thing? You do something like that again, I'll punch your lights out."

"I'll keep that in mind *mi amor. Buenas noches.*"

"Good night," Lacy whispered.

Chapter Twenty-one

Clues at Last

Jon dialed Cindy's number for the second time and looked at his watch. Although it was after midnight in Mexico, it was past seven a.m. in Spain. That wouldn't be too early. Why hadn't she left a better message for him? He was dying to know more. All she said was she had important news he might find helpful. *What's the news?* He rubbed his hand through his hair and paced the room.

Cindy wouldn't want to leave a detailed message on his voice mail. Even talking on cell phones could be dangerous, but then again, who would be listening in on his calls in Mexico? The thoughts of having an actual clue that could point them to the lost city was mind boggling. Of course, he needed to remember they were back in Mexico for Freddy and not for lost treasures or ancient cities.

He still couldn't believe King Harold Bluetooth's envoy left the scroll with clues under Coral Cay. The odds of Vikings visiting the Bahamas seemed so remote, but now, it was a forgone conclusion.

Although she was an expert in ancient languages, the scroll had been so damaged it seemed nothing was legible. Reaching out to Cindy had been an act of desperation, but Jon still hoped it would pay off. He remembered one time when Cindy performed a miracle in deciphering a passage written on a scroll.

Jon growled his disappointment as he got Cindy's voice-mail again. He left another message telling her he was about to go to bed, but she could call him any time day or night.

"Nothing?" Meg said as Jon tossed his phone onto the bedside table.

"Nothing!" Jon confirmed. "I'm dying to know what she's found. Maybe she'll call before we go to sleep."

Meg scrolled on her phone. "Looks like Hurricane David is wreaking havoc on Miami. I don't think our place in Miami Beach is going to make it."

Jon found the article on his phone and scanned it. "Wow. Unbelievable. It's going to take weeks before we're going to be able to get in there to assess the damage."

"Have you heard from Diego? Is he okay?"

"I tried to call him again when we landed and still nothing.

Jon slipped into bed beside his wife and pulled her close. He thought back to the discussion he and Meg had in the Lincoln Bedroom. He couldn't call it an argument, though it felt like one at the time. She was against coming back to Mexico, but here they were. She hadn't complained.

"You know, Meg?"

"What, Sweetheart?" Meg mumbled.

"I was lying here thinking about what a blessing it is to have you as my wife."

"You were," Meg said a little more intelligibly and rolled over to face him.

Jon pulled her into an embrace and kissed her. "I'm just amazed how supportive of me you are. I know you didn't want to come back here. I appreciate your attitude about this whole thing."

Meg kissed him. "It's easy to love and respect you, Jon Davenport. We couldn't go back home yet, and Mexico seemed like the safest place. I was wrong not to trust you."

"That puts a lot of pressure on me, you know."

Meg laughed. "I don't trust you because you're always right."

"I'm not?" Jon asked with a smile in his voice.

Meg punched his chest. "I hate to burst your bubble, but you're not. I trust you because I know you love me and wouldn't purposely do anything to hurt me. Now, hurting yourself is a different story."

"I wouldn't do anything on purpose to hurt myself," Jon protested.

"I didn't say you would. You might hurt yourself while trying to help someone else, however. That's my big fear, but in the end, I trust you. If something bad happens, then not only do I trust you, but I trust God. He is the difference maker."

"That's for sure, and we're going to need His help if we're going to find Freddy."

Jon kissed her forehead, her cheek, and her lips. "I love you, Meg Davenport."

@◆@◆@◆@◆

Jon sat on the front row of his fifth period class looking at the clock above the teacher's desk. A yawn slipped from his mouth as Mrs. Pierce droned on about the Olmec People and Mesoamerican history of central and southern Mexico.

He had football practice after school, and the only thing that stood between him and the football field was a few more minutes of Mexican history. He thought he should probably take notes, but he couldn't get the scroll open on his desk. He tried to open the animal skin folds, but every time he did, it crumbled in his hands.

As the scroll kept crumbling and falling to the floor, the bell rang. Jon looked up and Mrs. Pierce was still talking and writing something on the board. The bell rang and rang.

Jon sat up in bed to the sound of his phone ringing. He looked at his watch and saw it was just a little after six in the morning. He smiled at his crazy dream. He hadn't thought about Mrs. Pierce in years. She didn't teach Mexican history, though. *Crazy dream.*

He grabbed his phone, slipped into the bathroom, and closed the door. He hoped the noise hadn't disturbed Meg.

"Hello," Jon croaked into the phone. He should have tested his voice first.

"Well, hello Sleepy," a familiar voice sounded on the other end. "Sleepy as in Snow White's seven dwarfs."

"Thanks for the commentary," Jon joked. "Snow White is the last thing on my mind, Cindy. I'm so glad you called back."

"Sorry to wake you. I always thought you were an early riser."

"We flew into Mexico yesterday and didn't get to sleep until late. No big deal. I'm dying to know what you've found."

"I told you I have good news. I hope you don't mind that I reached out to a colleague in Israel for help."

"Israel?"

"Yep. He is an expert with x-ray microtomorgraphy. It's a process discovered a few years ago. He was part of a team who read the En Gedi Bible with this technology. That scroll was dated around the first or second century, so I figured he could help me make sense of this one."

"So, did he? I mean, could he read it?"

"Well, the reason it's taken me so long to get back with you is I had to make a fast trip to Israel. Believe it or not, he could read it. That process is amazing. With his equipment, he made an x-ray of the scroll and created digital slices he somehow separated like they were pages. We could read it clearly on his computer."

"Cindy, that's incredible, but I'm dying to know what it says."

"For starters, someone damaged some of it by trying to open it, and the outer layers were probably messed up because of deterioration."

"Someone damaged it? That would probably be me. Without thinking, I tried to open the scroll when we first got it."

"Although some of the writing was no longer legible, we were able to recreate most of the message. Some of my translation comes from words I think are correct. In other words, when I couldn't make out a letter or word, I picked something that made sense."

"Sort of like buying a vowel on Wheel of Fortune."

Cindy laughed. "Cute, Jon. I'm just warning you some of my translation may not be right. When you see my translation, you'll notice some of the words are red. Those are words I added to help the translation make sense. Don't fully trust those words."

Jon knew Cindy was the most meticulous person he'd ever met. Watching her translate an ancient document was like watching a vascular surgeon reconstruct the smallest of veins. If she added a letter or a word to her translation, it was because she had a strong reason to believe it was the right choice.

"Cindy, you are the greatest. Is this something you can tell me over the phone?"

"I'll email you the translation, but I needed to tell you there are a few words in the translation that bother me."

"Like what?"

"Well, whoever wrote this message used a word several times, but you'll notice I also made it red in the translation. The Runic word could be a few different English words. My best guess is it's the word *breast*, but it doesn't fit the context."

"You're right. I wouldn't imagine that word to be in a scroll…" Jon stopped remembering he had vowed not to say anything someone could intercept. He didn't think anyone could be listening in on his phone call, but anything was possible.

"I just remembered I decided to be careful and not say anything too explicit over this cell phone," Jon said. "I've learned loose lips sink ships, even in the salvage business when the ship has already been sunk."

"Good point, Jon. I'll drop this message into my storage box online. I won't say the name of it, but it's the one we've used before. You have access to it."

"Got it. I'll pull it up. Cindy, you are amazing."

"Not really. I just know the right people. They are amazing."

"I can't thank you enough. I'll read it and call you back in a little bit. I may have some questions."

"I need to also tell you even by inserting words in certain places, the whole document is difficult to understand. Runic is not exactly English. It seems your Viking was writing a message to his king, and he knew his king would understand. It's almost like he's talking in code. Some of it was written in another ancient language called Nahuan."

"Interesting. What is Nahuan?"

Cindy cleared her throat, and Jon imagined her lecturing a class of students at the university. "The Nahuas were a part of an ancient indigenous civilization in central and southern Mexico. They were also in El Salvador and even Guatemala at one time. They were connected to the Aztecs. Many of them settled in the region where Mexico curves up to form the Yucatan peninsula."

"How about that!" Jon laughed. "Sounds like we're at least close to the right place."

"Really? Where are you?"

"Hold on a second, Cindy, and I'll tell you where we are. I have to confess when we flew in on the president's helicopter last night, I didn't know where we were being taken."

"The president's helicopter? Jon, you never cease to amaze me."

Jon pulled his phone down from his ear and tapped the maps app on his iPhone. He pressed the locate button.

"Looks like we're in the mountains just outside of Santiago Tuxtla. We're guests of the president of Mexico."

"President of Mexico? Wow. Isn't there an Olmec carved head in Santiago Tuxtla? I think I remember reading that somewhere along the way."

"Yes. We saw it on our last trip to Catemaco. The thing sits right in the center of town, but it's protected under a little shelter."

"I hope my translation of the scroll will help you, but I'm afraid a lot of it will be contextual."

"Contextual?"

"You know. You'll only understand it in the proper context. I had to work from Runic to Nahuan to English, but I think it's close to right."

"Well," Jon sighed. "It's better than nothing. It might at least point us in the right direction. Thanks so much, Cindy. I'll be in touch."

Chapter Twenty-two

Message from Antiquity

Meg reached over to discover the other side of the bed was empty and cold. Where was Jon? She lay still trying to orient herself to her surroundings. Mexico. President Diaz. *Casa de las Montañas.* She sat up and looked around the dim room. Everything was made of dark wood that must have been at least a hundred years old. She saw the glow of a computer in the corner of the room and her husband bent over it reading.

Her feet touched the cold, stone floor, and a shiver ran through her like she was stepping on a block of ice. She hadn't thought about needing bedroom shoes, but maybe they could find some in town, assuming they were near a town. If whoever designed this monstrosity of a house had wanted it to feel like a castle, they had succeeded.

Meg thought of her home near George Town on Great Exuma. Thinking of Hurricane David, she wondered if she still had a home at Pirate's Cove. What a contrast her home was to this medieval, dark feeling place. She preferred sunshine and bright colors to this Viking-looking stronghold.

As Meg placed her warm hands on Jon's bare shoulders, he flinched but kept his eyes on the computer screen. She saw the words to a document. Some of them were red.

"What are you looking at, Hon?"

Jon turned his face toward her, and she leaned down for a kiss.

"Cindy called a while ago and told me how to get a copy of the translation of the scroll. This is it."

"What does the red mean?"

"It means she's not one hundred percent sure about the word, but it's her best guess."

Meg leaned over and peered at the screen. Nothing on the page looked like complete sentences. It appeared more like history lesson notes than clues for lost treasure.

Jon motioned toward the screen. "This first part is telling the history of the Nahuatl people and how they settled in the region under the mountain's shade. That's what they called it."

"The region under the mountain's shade?" Meg raised an eyebrow. "That narrows our search down. There are only about a million mountains in Mexico."

Jon laughed. "True. Although the Nahuatl people moved around a bit, they settled mostly in this region of the state of Veracruz."

"At least we're in the right place," Meg said.

"That's what I told Cindy."

"What's this about a goddess? Of course, it's red, so maybe it's not a goddess."

"Cindy thinks the word goddess makes sense. It seems Bluetooth's man wrote about this people group and the goddess of the mountains. After explaining some about these people, he talked specifically about the lost city. He calls it the City of Gold."

"El Dorado?"

"Maybe, though I'm not sure it's the same place we've heard about in folklore. He says it has golden streets and silver statues. At least, Cindy thinks the comments about silver refer to statues. They have gold ones as well. He described a carved head with golden eyes and mouth, insinuating the interior of the head is solid gold."

Meg remembered seeing the Olmec head in the square of Santiago Tuxtla. The thing was huge—four feet tall, or more. If a head like that was filled with gold, it would be worth a fortune. After their previous visit to Catemaco, they stopped in Santiago Tuxtla on the way back to Veracruz to see the famous carved head. She marveled that an Olmec artist had carved the thing around the time David had been king of Israel.

"This scroll even describes seeing a lake of gold, though Cindy questions whether or not the word should be lake."

"What about clues as to where this place is located? Wasn't that the real purpose of the scroll?"

"I'm sure it was. Evidently, this explorer thought it important to inform Bluetooth about these people and their religion. Remember that Harold Bluetooth was the king who brought Christianity to Denmark. He was an evangelist of sorts. His man knew the king's passion, so he wanted to inform Bluetooth of their pagan religion."

"Maybe, he was letting Bluetooth know these people needed God."

"Maybe. Can you imagine King Bluetooth, a Viking, launching a missionary venture to southern Mexico in the 10th century?"

Meg tried to imagine that possibility. She remembered visiting Denmark and seeing the Jelling Stone. King Bluetooth had become a Christian and had the remains of his father disinterred in order to give him a Christian burial. Evidently, they followed some pagan ritual when he died, and Bluetooth thought it would help his father get into heaven if they'd bury him properly, in a way he thought might honor God. Reading the history had saddened her. Bluetooth's actions would have done nothing for his father's soul, but the King didn't realize it.

"On the other hand, the history could have been for the purpose of a warning. It seems this goddess of the mountains sent out soldiers to kill intruders."

"That's not very comforting," Meg said and felt something dark pull on her mind. "I'm having a hard time connecting this scroll to Bluetooth's intent. I thought the treasure was about uniting his family. They all hated each other and would have to work together to find the lost city."

"He schemed that up after his man returned with the news," Jon added. "By that time, his son was trying to spark a rebellion against his father, and his daughter had married someone from a clan in Norway. They all hated each other. I think Bluetooth was desperate and knew the promise of a lost city would tempt his kids to work together. It's not a great scheme, but it seems like that was his last effort. The next thing we know is his son, Swen, either killed him or had him killed."

"So, what about the clues?"

Jon scrolled through the document to the last page. Meg saw a number of red words and wondered how they would ever find the place. If Cindy wasn't sure about the translation, the odds of them finding it now a thousand years later were pretty slim.

Meg leaned toward the computer to get a better view. "Breast? Does that say the breasts of the mountain?"

"That's Cindy's best guess," Jon said. "It makes sense, in a way. Notice that the word *heart,* as in *heart of the goddess*, is in black. Of course, 'goddess' is still in red. If we're talking about a goddess, it makes sense she'd have breasts."

"Sounds to me like he was a man who'd been away from home too long," Meg quipped.

"Maybe, but wherever he was, he could see the ocean. That narrows it down. I just don't know what to do with some of this. It says something about a mermaid covered in rubies and a trail of gold. It sounds more like a fantasy novel than actual clues."

"Interesting. I'd like to read the whole thing, and I'll give you my thoughts. Maybe we should read it aloud to Lacy and Kerrick, too. They are eager to know about the translation. On a different note, what are we going to do to find Freddy?"

"Let's get some breakfast and talk with Kerrick and Lacy. We'll figure out a plan."

@♦@♦@♦@♦

As Meg and Jon walked into the dining room with Carla in tow, Jon inhaled the smells of bacon and fresh bread. Surprisingly, Lacy and Kerrick were sitting at the table. Lacy was dipping honey from a small clay pot on the table and dripping it onto a tortilla.

The dining area was huge and could have accommodated a couple more tables just like the one where Lacy and Kerrick sat. The walls looked like a dark colored plaster with large wooden beams going up the wall over ten feet. The tall ceilings looked like a continuation of the walls with a large chandelier hanging over the table.

"Lala," Carla said as they approached the table.

"Did she just say 'Lala'?" Lacy gasped, jumping to her feet. "Carla just called me Lala."

Meg laughed. "It seems like her understandable vocabulary has grown to four words: Mama, Dada, Unc A, and Lala."

Lacy grabbed her cousin and smothered her with kisses. Carla giggled uncontrollably.

"You are the most precious little girl in the world," Lacy said as she planted a light kiss on the little girl's cheek.

A noise erupted in the room causing everyone at the table to freeze. Lacy pulled away from Carla and wrinkled her nose. "Was that what I think it was?"

"If you're thinking what I'm thinking," Meg said, "then you are correct. If you take a deep whiff, your assumptions will be confirmed."

Lacy carefully held Carla out toward Meg. "I think she wants her mother."

"What happened to all of the sweet kisses and hugs?" Meg laughed before grabbing Carla. "I thought she was precious. Come on Pumpkin. Why did you pick now for a diaper change? If you had done that five minutes ago, it would have been a lot more convenient."

Meg carried Carla back toward their bedroom, and Jon pulled out a chair at the dining room table. An attendant appeared with a cup of coffee and set it on the table in front of him.

"*Buenos días!*" the woman said.

"Good morning, uh…*Buenos días!*" Jon stuttered. "*Gracias.*"

"Did you sleep well Uncle Jon?" Lacy asked after receiving a cup of coffee from the attendant.

"I slept okay, but I was a little apprehensive."

"Really?" Kerrick leaned forward in his seat. "About what? Is everything okay?"

Jon grinned. "I got a text from Cindy last night and was dying to know what she had on her mind. I called her several times, but she didn't answer my calls."

"What?" Lacy nearly shouted. "I can't stand it."

"We probably shouldn't talk so loudly," Jon counseled.

"Oh. Sorry," Lacy said.

"I finally talked to her this morning, and I have the translation."

Lacy made a sound like she was about to burst. "What did it say?"

"Let's finish breakfast and then go to our bedroom. I'd rather keep this bit of information to ourselves."

"Sounds wise," Kerrick said. "Lacy and I have been talking about our plan to find Freddy."

"Do you have a plan?" Jon asked.

Lacy cleared her throat. "Well, you remember Coco said the last time she saw him was in Xalapa, the capital city of Veracruz."

"But," Kerrick interrupted, "she said they were probably in Los Rios. Lacy and I looked at Los Rios on the maps app on my phone. It's not a big place, and it's not terribly far from here. Maybe a couple of hours."

"We thought if we could get a car, we could search the whole area in an hour or two," Lacy interjected. "Is there a way to get a car?"

"I remember Randall saying they'd have a car for us. If not, we can rent one in town. We're not too far from Santiago Tuxtla."

"Isn't that where the head is?" Lacy asked. "You know, the stone head?"

"Sure is," Jon agreed. "Let's eat breakfast and find some transportation."

"*Disculpe*," the young woman said when she returned with a cup of coffee for Kerrick. "Señor Morales call and offer car. He no come a hora, ummm…now. He come…" she motioned with her finger as if sliding it over the top of a ball.

"¿*Vendrá esta noche*?" Lacy said.

"*Sí, Señorita. Esta noche.*" The young woman said several more words in Spanish before walking back into the kitchen.

Lacy turned to Jon. "He's coming tonight and wants to meet us for dinner, but he's left a car here for our use."

"Perfect," Kerrick said. "We may find Freddy today and then start looking for something else exciting to do."

Chapter Twenty-three

Search

Kerrick looked out the window as Jon pulled the Land Rover to a stop in front of what looked like a small store. The street wasn't nearly as full as those in Veracruz, but a number of people walked up and down both sides. One older man stood behind a cart of freshly killed chickens while other people stood behind tables of cloth, leather goods, children's clothes, cell phone covers, and other products. They saw a fancy car pull up and hoped to sell their day's quota to one rich customer.

Jon disappointed Kerrick and Lacy by suggesting they wait until returning to *Casa de las Montañas* to discuss the scroll. Kerrick thought they'd spend the ride talking about the scroll, but Jon said he wanted to read them the translation word for word. He said it could wait until that night.

"We stand out," Lacy said, "don't ya think? I mean, I don't see too many brand-new Land Rovers driving up and down the street."

"We do indeed," Jon agreed. "But this thing sure did drive smoothly over what would have been a bumpy ride."

A small Volkswagen Jetta drove by, and Kerrick tried to imagine it going over some of the speed bumps they'd crossed on their drive to Los Rios. "What did you say those speed bumps are called?"

"Tope," Lacy said. "Think toupée, as in wig, but change the first vowel to a long o and put the accent on the first syllable. It sounds like toepay."

"Got it," Kerrick said and laughed. "If we stay here for another ten years, I might get this language down."

"You'll be surprised how many words you'll start picking up," Meg said from the front seat. "Again, what's our strategy?"

"We split into two groups," Lacy said. "Kerrick and I will start on the south side of Los Rios, and you guys start on the north side. We stop at every house and business asking about Freddy and showing his picture. We should all have pictures of him on our phones."

"Fortunately," Jon said. "Los Rios is not very big. Hopefully we can cover it shortly. If you find something, call us, and we'll do the same."

Lacy and Kerrick crawled out of the Land Rover and watched them drive off toward the other side of town. Kerrick scanned their surroundings. Other than the little shopping area, he noticed what looked like residences down the street.

"I suppose we need to start asking around," Lacy said as she pulled out her cell phone.

They wound their way through the small market area lining one side of the street. Everyone was eager to talk, but they wanted to sell products, not offer information. Kerrick made the mistake of buying a new cover for his iPhone, which made everyone see the American couple as shoppers instead of information seekers.

Two hours later, Kerrick guided Lacy into a small, open-air restaurant called *La Cabañita*. He suggested Lacy order them lunch.

"I wonder how Jon and Meg are doing," Lacy said. "I bet Carla is not happy."

"At least they had a stroller—thanks to Señor Morales."

A cute little girl came up to their table with several hand-made necklaces around her neck and a ring on every finger. Her dark hair was pulled into a braid that ran down her back, and her eyes sparkled with excitement. She pulled a necklace off and held it out to Lacy.

"How do you say the word 'ring' in Spanish?" Kerrick asked Lacy.

Lacy shook her head and turned to the little girl. "*¿Cómo se dice?*" Lacy pointed to the ring on the girl's finger.

"*Anillo. Muy bonito*," the little girl said.

"She says very pretty."

"Ask her how much it costs."

"*¿Cuanto cuesta?*"

"*Treinta y cinco pesos.*"

"Thirty-five pesos," Lacy repeated.

Kerrick reached over and looked at the rings before digging coins out of his pocket. He dropped some into the smiling girl's outstretched hand. "*Te gusta*," he said and pointed to one of the rings.

"Not *te gusta*," Lacy corrected. "I like it is *me gusta*. *Te gusta* means *you* like, as in the girl likes."

Kerrick looked at the grinning girl. "She knew what I meant."

The little girl held out the ring to Kerrick. *"Gracias Señor."* She held up a necklace for Kerrick to inspect.

"No, gracias."

Once the girl left, Kerrick took Lacy's hand and slipped the ring on her finger. He had noticed men staring at Lacy. He didn't blame them. She was a knockout. He wanted to declare she was not available, though he wondered if they'd even notice the ring.

Lacy had pulled her blond hair into a ponytail and slipped it through the hole in the back of her cap that said Veracruz across the front. Although she said she'd dressed down for the occasion, her yellow tank top and white shorts drew admiring glances.

Kerrick's eyes roamed over Lacy's body from head to toe. *The problem is you can't hide beautiful.* Their eyes locked. Kerrick leaned forward and placed a quick kiss on her lips. "I think we better hurry up and eat and get busy trying to find Freddy."

They dove into their barbecue lunch like they hadn't eaten in a couple of days. It was good, and they were both full when they finished. Kerrick downed the final swallow of his soda.

"Let's get back to our search," Kerrick said as he stood to his feet. He turned just in time to step in front of a waitress carrying tacos and sodas. Food and drink spilled everywhere, and the poor, surprised girl fell on her backside. His wallet and cell phone skidded across the floor to the feet of a young woman at a nearby table.

Kerrick helped the waitress to stand. He reached in his pocket and handed her fifty pesos. "I'm so sorry. Hopefully, this money will cover the food I made you drop."

Lacy translated what he said to the waitress who smiled sheepishly and nodded before bending to clean up the mess.

The young woman at the other table picked up Kerrick's wallet and phone and returned them to Kerrick. Before handing over the phone, she noticed the picture on the screen. Kerrick didn't remember having Freddy's picture open on his phone, but his phone must have unlocked before he collided with the waitress.

Lacy saw the woman looking at the picture. "Do you know him? Uh, I mean…*Lo conoces?*"

"*Sí. Lo he visto.*"

"What did she say?" Kerrick asked.

"Kerrick, this girl knows Freddy and has seen him," Lacy said with a grin spreading across her face.

"You've got to be kidding. Ask her where we can find him."

Though her Spanish was limited, Lacy did her best to engage the young woman. She finally understood the woman to say Freddy lived near her, and she would be willing to take them to his house.

Ten minutes later, they stood in front of a small, block house that appeared empty. The young woman knocked on the door, but no one came. The lady next door walked over and explained the American boy left with Rafael a week or two ago, and she had no idea where they went. She thought the American was going back to the States or moving to another city because he had luggage with him.

Lacy thanked both of the women for their help, and she and Kerrick walked away from them. "It looks like we're at a dead end."

"I suppose it's possible he's on his way back to D.C.," Kerrick suggested.

"Could be," Lacy agreed. "Let's call Jon."

Kerrick pulled out his phone and passed along the news to Jon before disconnecting the call. "Jon said to walk out to the main road, and they will pick us up."

Lacy looked at her watch. "At least we should be able to get back to Señor Morales in time for dinner, but I was hoping for good news about Freddy."

"Yeah. This stinks. We know where he was but still have no clue where he is."

◎◆◎◆◎◆◎◆

Lacy towel-dried her hair and let it drop down her back. Meg told her dinner would be more formal, but Lacy didn't have anything formal to wear. Clean jeans and the light blue blouse she'd purchased in Miami would have to do. She leaned in toward the bathroom mirror and inspected her face. A little blush, maybe some eyeliner. *No. Scratch the eyeliner.*

Lacy pulled on the jeans as her mind raced over the dizzying events of the last few months. She had agreed to help Jon and Meg with at risk teens so she could get away from her mother. A summer scuba diving in the Bahamas and living on a boat had also sounded exciting. Turns out, it was the best three months of her life.

Lacy lay back on the bed and pictured the girl walking through the airport and meeting up with Meg. She was no longer that girl. Maybe the summer had changed those boys, but it had certainly changed her. For one thing, she rarely cursed anymore. Now, if a word slipped that made Meg flinch, Lacy was embarrassed. Somehow, her summer in the Bahamas made her want to be more…respectable. Likable.

Meg had a big influence on her, but Kerrick was the difference maker. He brought out the best in her. She wanted to please him. She wanted him to be proud of her. Maybe she was pathetic, but these feelings were true. The fact he loved her was stunning, unbelievable.

Watching Jon and Meg had been a big deal for her, too. They were so perfect. Ever since their wedding on Great Exuma a few years earlier, she wondered how they were when no one was around. Were they always so loving and happily married? The summer months answered that question. They were the real deal. She wondered if marriage could be that way for her?

She thought of her parents arguing and living disgusting lives. For the last few years, the idea of marriage had been far from her plans. She was sure she would rather remain single the rest of her life than to endure what she saw in her own home. It was amazing how that opinion had all changed over the course of the summer.

The floorboard creaked outside her door as someone walked down the hall. Lacy looked at her watch and sat up. She had to finish dressing and get downstairs to the dining room. She wondered if Alejandro Morales was a good man simply hosting them, or was he like everyone else who had an agenda?

For some reason, she didn't trust the man. Oh well. How many girls got to vacation at the Mexican president's *Casa de las Montañas*? Not many. She would enjoy the dinner and her time with Kerrick. Maybe they could figure out the location of this lost city. Jon had suggested they gather in his bedroom after dinner to talk about the scroll. That would be interesting.

Chapter Twenty-four

No Swimming

Sitting at a table in the only decent club in San Andres Tuxtla, Miguel felt bored and ready to move on. He could think of a thousand cities where he'd rather be imprisoned, but he got stuck in this place. The street outside the club was filled with noisy buses climbing up the hills toward the city center. He considered heading to Mexico City. It was louder but filled with greater possibilities. That region, however, was closer to the Los Unidos Cartel's base of operations.

He thought of his narrow escape a week earlier and his fists clinched. *They're all insane.* Miguel grinned as he thought about the pitiful weakling who begged him for mercy. *Did he think I was a priest?*

The man deserved to die. Besides, he had to send a message to all of Los Unidos. *You don't mess with Miguel Ramirez Martinez and live to tell about it.*

He considered the murder that made Los Unidos want him in the first place. *So, I killed El Capitan's son. It was a mistake. That's what he gets for being with a married woman.*

Miguel wasn't usually so careless, and he couldn't make those kinds of mistakes again. Of course, it's not like he could have turned on the bedroom light to make sure he had the right girl. She had looked like Lacy from the bedroom window. It was unfortunate Pedro Escobar's son happened to be in the wrong place at the wrong time.

He looked up at a television screen in the bar and watched a breaking news story about the hurricane. He sure wasn't going back to the Bahamas for a while. Those pictures on the screen made what were once houses look like match sticks. He may never be able to go back.

The two men across from him were getting louder and beginning to irritate him. More than a little drunk, the idiots were now arguing. Miguel stood and was about to tell the losers to shut up when one of them said something about a fat wallet. He froze and listened carefully.

"Fat wallet…Diamond…Rich Aussie…The Reserve."

Miguel sat back down to process what these guys were talking about. It seemed some rich couple from Australia was staying at The Reserve. *What's The Reserve?* One of them mentioned a lake. *It must be somewhere around Catemaco.* He thought about his dwindling stack of cash. He still had plenty, but it never hurt to have more.

He dropped money on the table for his drinks and left the club. Once he returned to the lobby of his hotel, he found a bunch of brochures for tourists and located one for La Reserva de Lago Catemaco. That had to be it. He flipped through the brochure and saw huts on stilts built along the side of the lake. The beauty of it was most of the huts were spread apart and sat alone. Breaking into them would be like fishing in an aquarium. Finding the right hut might be more challenging. He saw the resort offered hot tubs, hiking tours, massages, and a five-star restaurant. Would a trip to this place be worth it?

The idiots said fat wallet and diamond. If the woman had one diamond, she probably had several. He decided to check out of his room in the morning and head to Catemaco, the City of Witches. He grinned at the thought. Witches. It was just a few miles away. He could spend a few days in the resort, find the couple, and drop in for a brief visit. It wouldn't have to be messy, unless they wanted it that way. His smile broadened as he thought about his prospects.

Catemaco was abuzz with activity when Miguel arrived the following morning. He got off the bus in front of the Basilica of Our Lady of Mount Carmel. The old church was ornate, and the front plaza had become a veritable shopping mall where people from the community sold small trinkets.

One old woman tried to sell him a green branch he could use in his prayers to the Virgin. He laughed at the thought of paying money for a branch he could wave at some statue. What a rip off. Besides, the only prayer he needed answered was that this rich Australian's wallet was fatter than he imagined.

He turned to walk toward the lake and bumped into a man, knocking him to the ground. A basket of pineapples spilled and rolled down the street. Miguel cursed at the man and stepped over his sprawled body. He noticed a man dressed in black leaning against the wall of a building watching the whole affair.

The man had an eerie smile and seemed to stare without blinking. "*Buenos dias, Señor.*"

Buenos dias? As far as Miguel was concerned, the only thing good about this morning was the fact he was closer to pocketing some cash and diamonds. He ignored the man's greeting and stepped onto the street to walk around him.

"You seem to need help, Señor," the man said.

Miguel didn't want to give him the time of day. Who knew what this guy was peddling? He probably wanted money. Didn't everyone?

"I have friends who can get you anything you want," the man continued.

Miguel stopped and processed what he just heard. Friends who could give him anything he wants? What did this man mean? "Who are these friends?" Miguel finally asked, turning toward the man.

"Let's say they have talents and connections," the man said.

"Are you saying they are witches?"

The thin man laughed. "The church would banish you for saying such a thing."

"Isn't this the City of Witches?" Miguel asked. "What does the church have to do with them?"

The man spat into the street. "It seems talking about witches and sorcerers made the church leaders uncomfortable. We had to change the name of our annual festival."

Miguel finally took a few steps back to where the man stood leaning against the side of a building. "What are you talking about?"

"I'm talking about the annual National Congress of Sorcerers. The church put pressure on the city leaders, and we had to change the name to *Magical Rituals, Ceremonies and Handicrafts*."

"So, what do you do at these meetings?"

"We cast spells. We've done a lot of things for a lot of people. We've even gotten a few people elected to office. The former governor of Veracruz tried to create a school for sorcerers here in Catemaco, but it got voted down. It doesn't matter. We still do our work."

"You said you can get me anything I want."

"Yes. If you're willing to pay, anything is possible."

Miguel imagined sitting down with some emaciated woman revealing his plan to murder a couple and steal their money and diamonds. Talking to anyone about it would not be a good idea. Getting anything he wanted, however, was appealing. He could ask for Lacy's medallion or all of the Davenports' wealth. Getting anything he wanted was tempting, but involving others in his scheme would be a bad move.

"I could use some luck," Miguel began. "Luck with a current…well, let's just call it a venture."

"If all you need is luck, you have come to the right place." The man reached into a bag hanging over his shoulder and pulled out a round, silver object. "I have this talisman that comes from deep inside the mountains. It carries powerful magic."

Miguel eyed the round piece of metal with a stone of some kind resting in the center. It also had a chain attached and functioned as a necklace.

"This talisman carries deep, dark mysteries that only those who practice black magic can understand. It has been in my family since the Olmecs settled this region. I will sell it to you for a good price."

The Olmecs? Miguel couldn't remember hearing about the Olmecs. This necklace probably came from a pile of trinkets the old man had stored somewhere waiting for the next gullible tourist.

"Keep your trinket, old man. I'm not a fool."

"If you want what you came here for, you'd be a fool to leave without buying this talisman."

Miguel eyed the necklace again and thought about Lacy Henderson. He'd never seen her medallion, but as far as he knew, it was priceless. Maybe it would be worth buying the talisman. "How much?"

"It's easily worth five thousand pesos, maybe more. I'll sell it to you for a thousand pesos."

"One thousand? You're kidding, right?" Miguel turned to leave.

"Eight hundred, and that's my lowest price. This talisman has great power. It will get you the girl."

The girl? What did this old man know about Lacy? Miguel felt something in his gut. Of course, the old man could just be guessing Miguel had come for a girl, but then again, he seemed to know something. He reached into his pocket and gave the man eight one hundred peso bills. He pocketed the necklace and walked toward the lake.

Tourists and people selling seats on boats used for tours of Lake Catemaco covered the dock. Miguel stared at a sign that explained the tour and saw one of the stops was The Reserve. One hundred pesos? This place was such a tourist trap. He reached into his pocket and pulled out the money. Within thirty minutes, he rested inside a boat waiting to pull out.

Unfortunately, he had to endure the nonstop speaking of the tour guide and a sales presentation of mud from the lake at one of their stops. *Mud from the gods? Who believes this nonsense?* Obviously, some people did because he saw several women forking over money for the mud.

The boat stopped at The Reserve, and everyone climbed onto the dock. The driver told the group they could eat lunch here, and they would head for Monkey Island once everyone returned. Miguel heard a couple ask if they could wait and catch another boat later in the day, and he stepped up beside them. The driver looked over the three and agreed. He said he would be back by three o'clock that afternoon, and if they weren't on the docks, they'd have to find their own way back.

Miguel noticed movement in the water as the head of a large alligator surfaced. He hadn't thought of it before, but an alligator could be useful.

The guide noticed Miguel looking at the creature and grinned. "If you were thinking about taking a swim, I wouldn't suggest it."

"For sure," Miguel agreed.

"The lake is full of them—especially on this side. Sure messes up our fishing."

The Australian couple Miguel had heard about was easy to find. Their accent unmistakable, he heard them before he saw them. They appeared to be in their late thirties and were well dressed. The woman was stunning.

No doubt they had money. They stood out like coal in the snow. He listened as they talked to another tourist about their hut and the hike they planned for the next day. A trail began at The Reserve and would take them to a village in the mountains where hikers could spend the night.

Miguel fingered the talisman. *Maybe this thing is for real. I couldn't ask for a better setup.* He wondered if they would leave the money and the diamonds in the hut while they hiked. Not likely.

A better plan might be to have a chance encounter on the trail where the couple would have an unfortunate accident. He could take anything of value before disposing of the bodies and going back to their hut. Piece of cake. Maybe the talisman would turn out to be the best investment he'd ever made.

Chapter Twenty-five

Fodder

"So, Doctor Davenport," Alejandro Morales said between mouthfuls of grilled fish, "are you a medical doctor?"

"No, Señor Morales. I was a professor at a university. My doctorate is in history."

"History is a wonderful subject. We have a lot of amazing history here in Mexico."

"We visited El Tajin on our last trip," Jon said. "It was interesting. I was especially intrigued by the ballcourts."

"Ah, the ballcourts. Human sacrifice would have given the players a great incentive to win. Yes?" Morales laughed like he'd just heard the funniest joke ever told.

Jon felt a little disgusted. Many cultures throughout history practiced human sacrifice, which had always disturbed him. In this case, it was even worse.

"I have a feeling if you were captured by the chief of El Tajin, you would have been sacrificed whether you won or lost the game," Jon suggested.

"I came to the same conclusion," Kerrick interjected. "Seems like I remember reading someone was supposed to be sacrificed every day. At some point, they would have run out of losers."

"You are right," Morales said. "The Totonac people were ruthless and desperate. I'm sure they put the bird head mask on whoever happened to be imprisoned in their cells and brought them out to lose their heads—game or no game."

"Bird masks?" Meg asked.

"The prisoner wore a beaked helmet covered with feathers," Warming to his audience, Morales continued. "It was as if the sacrifice would be food for the gods. They escorted the prisoner to the altar, laid his masked head on the chopping block, and decapitated him with a machete. I'm sure the crowd would have erupted in applause. Just like a football match—or you call soccer. Yes?"

Jon noticed Lacy's face draining of color as she put her fork down. Human sacrifice was not a great topic for dinner conversation. Images of the altar at El Tajin flashed through his mind, and he felt a shiver run down his back. *No telling how many innocent people died in that place.*

"This region must have a rich history," Jon sought to change the subject, "though I'm not as familiar with it. I know a little about the Olmec people, and I've heard of the Nahua people."

"Yes," Morales beamed. "The Nahuas lived all through this region, and you can still meet their descendants in villages today. Many rich stories, myths actually, about the people of the mountains cover this area like morning dew. A lot of artifacts have been discovered in the mountains east of Catemaco. The indigenous groups were often afraid to go into the mountains because of the folklore, which means many hidden artifacts have yet to be found."

"What folklore is that?" Meg asked as she reached for her napkin.

"The goddess. The Nahuas believed if you ventured into her mountains, the goddess would send out soldiers to kill you. A lot of the people in that region today still believe the stories to be true, and they stay out of the mountains."

"Where does the story of the goddess come from?" Lacy asked.

Morales beamed. "Do you really want to know? If you have two hours to spare tomorrow, I can show you. We can take a short ride in the helicopter. You will enjoy some of the greatest beauty of the region and maybe all of Mexico."

"We'd love to take a tour," Jon said. "What time should we be prepared to leave?"

"How about eight o'clock in the morning? I have an appointment at noon, so that would give us plenty of time to fly over the area."

Jon's mind went back to the translation of the scroll. Flying over the region would give them a bird's eye view of where the lost city might be.

"We can't wait to see it," Jon said.

Lacy followed Kerrick into Jon and Meg's bedroom and felt like she was about to burst. At the conclusion of dinner, Jon leaned toward her and suggested she and Kerrick come to their room for a bedtime story. She knew he meant the scroll.

Lacy had a memory of waiting on her father to come to her room one night when she was little. He promised to read her a bedtime story. The anticipation of her father's attention had been like waiting on a sunrise or for a rose to bloom on her neighbor's fence. She waited and waited. She woke the next morning with the book in her hands. Just one of many broken promises.

"Lala?" Carla jabbered as she toddled over to Lacy.

"Carla, give everyone hugs," Meg said. "It's bedtime."

The little girl went from Lacy to Kerrick to Jon giving hugs and sloppy, wet kisses. Lacy's heart swelled with joy. How could one little girl bring her such happiness? She represented hope. Possibilities. A life not yet lived.

"Get ready for bed, sweet bug," Jon said as he kissed his little girl. "I'll be in for prayers in a minute."

Lacy watched her uncle's eyes follow Meg and Carla into a small room that connected to the larger bedroom. His eyes shifted from the little girl to Meg. Was it admiration? No, it was more than that.

"I'll make us some coffee," Jon said. "You guys will have to wait for your story until after we get Carla down."

Lacy leaned back and rested her head on the couch. *You have got to be kidding. I've been dying to know about this scroll, and now I have to wait?*

"Jon, I'll make coffee for me and Lacy," Kerrick suggested. "You go on back with Meg."

A few minutes later, Kerrick returned with a cup of coffee that had just the right amount of cream. He knew her. Her heart felt as warm as her cup. He sat beside her, holding his cup in his right hand while his left hand rested on her knee.

"Isn't she the sweetest thing?" Kerrick said. "How many like her do you want?"

The room seemed to get hotter. Lacy cleared her throat. "Uh, you mean babies? I once thought I wouldn't have children."

"You've got to be kidding. I told you you'll be a great mother."

"Wrong. I don't know anything about being a mother."

"Just because you haven't had a good role model doesn't mean you are naturally doomed to be a crummy mother. You can learn from any circumstance. If your mom was bad, then she taught you what not to do. Besides, I'd say Meg is a great mom and a perfect role model."

"You're right about my mom, and Meg is the greatest. I don't think I can ever be like her."

Kerrick took Lacy's cup from her hand and set both of their cups onto the coffee table. He took her hands and stared into her eyes. They felt like laser beams going deep into her soul. His beautiful blue eyes softened. *Are his eyes wet?*

"Lacy."

She leaned forward.

"I've only known you a little over three months. I've watched you deal with unbelievable circumstances. One thing I've learned about you is you can be anything you want. Your past or present doesn't have to shape your future. Besides, you're not the same girl I met in May on the dock in Pirate's Cove." Kerrick smiled. "You've changed."

Lacy reached deep, trying to find her voice. She cleared her throat. "How have I changed?"

"For one thing, your language has changed. When we met, you probably said ten curse words in the first three minutes of our conversation."

"I did not!"

Kerrick smiled again. "You did. When I saw you walking down the dock, you took my breath away. You are drop dead gorgeous. Lacy, you are the most beautiful woman I've ever seen."

Lacy squirmed and felt as if she'd pass out. She wanted him to stop and to continue. Something deep in her stomach began to fly like dandelion seeds blown in the wind.

"Your language, however, turned me off. I was stunned. I wondered how such a beautiful girl could talk like that."

The dandelion seeds crashed to the bottom of her stomach. Lacy dropped her head. She had hung around a bad crowd in high school, and her language had been shameful.

Kerrick took her chin in his hand and raised her head until she looked back into his smiling eyes. "That's one way you've changed. You don't talk like that anymore. It's amazing. Over the last three months, you've gotten even more beautiful."

Lacy felt heat cover her neck and face. Kerrick knew just how to get to her.

He leaned forward and touched his lips to hers. "I know it's only been three months, but I have fallen so deeply in love with you I'm drowning. No, not drowning. Soaring."

Lacy's eyes moved down to the stain on her shorts she'd been meaning to get out. The summer had changed her. He and Meg had changed her. She would never go back to the old Lacy. If anything, she wanted more change. She wanted to be like Meg. Her patience. Her tenderness. Her…faith? Maybe.

The bedroom door opened, breaking her trance. Lacy stood and hurried to the kitchenette to get a paper towel. She blew her nose and sounded like a goose. *Now, that was drop dead gorgeous.*

"All right, boys and girls," Jon said as he walked toward the Keurig. "Let me get coffee for me and my sweet bride, and I'll read you something that will give you fodder to chew on."

Lacy returned to the couch and sat beside Kerrick. She didn't know if she was glad or sad Jon interrupted the moment. Meg stepped into the room and pulled Carla's door closed. She appeared a little flushed. Lacy smiled. Meg and Jon were so in love. Lacy felt her heart quicken as she imagined what happened behind the closed door. A kiss? A whispered promise? Whatever it was, it was marriage the way marriage was supposed to be, unlike anything she had seen her entire life. They had a love that would last a lifetime. Was that possible for her?

The bedroom was as large as the living room and kitchen of her old house. A living area was across from the kitchenette, and a large, oak bed covered most of the other end of the room. Jon retrieved his computer from the desk.

"I told you Cindy sent us the translation, and I thought I would read it to you. Some of the translation is questionable, but Cindy said she used context and did her best. I'll tell you she's the most brilliant translator of antiquities I know, so I have no doubt her translation is the best we'll ever get."

He sat down on a small love seat next to the couch, and Meg sat beside him. He made a few clicks on his mouse pad and cleared his throat.

"The first part tells the history of the Nahua people, and then, this guy offers clues that tell Bluetooth how to find the city. One clue you'll hear right away is he says the city sits in the region under the mountain's shade. I'll read the history first."

Jon began reading the history of an ancient people that was fascinating and surprising. The longer he read, the more reverent Lacy felt. It was almost as if she were sitting at the feet of the old Viking listening to his tales of an exotic land.

The Nahuas had strange beliefs and fears. They were polytheistic and animists, and it seemed like they offered sacrifices to every god imaginable, except for Jon and Meg's God. The group began a southern migration, and most of them settled beyond the lake in the region under the mountain's shade. The area was rich with game, but they hunted sparingly for fear of the goddess of the mountain. If outsiders came in and destroyed the land or hunted unnecessarily, she sent out warriors who killed them with lightning and fire.

They found great mineral deposits and unearthed gems and priceless treasures. The Viking said they even had a lake of gold, and he discovered ruby and diamond-covered silver statues throughout their city. One was in the shape of a mermaid and others were carved heads the size of boulders. The heads had golden eyes and mouths, and the Viking surmised the carving was hollow inside and full of gold.

"Sounds like a pumpkin at Halloween," Lacy said, "except this one had more than just a candle inside."

Kerrick laughed. "I wouldn't mind having a pumpkin like that," he said.

"He says we can find it by going to the breast of the goddess where you can look out to sea. Look for her heart and the stone symbol."

"The breast of the goddess?" Kerrick raised an eyebrow. "What is that? I mean, I know but not really."

Jon laughed. "Remember he also said he could see the ocean from the breast of the goddess, so I assume he's talking about the peak of a mountain."

"Maybe, two peaks." Lacy chuckled. "And the stone symbol? What do you suppose that is?"

"He doesn't say, but he says Bluetooth will know it. Cindy says the entrance to the city will be found in the heart of the goddess, deep in the earth."

Lacy crossed her arms. "Heart of the goddess? That's clear as mud. We ought to be able to find it tomorrow. Hope we have room in our luggage for a stone head filled with gold."

Meg laughed. "There's a reason why this place hasn't been found in all of these years."

Jon closed his computer and sat it on the coffee table. "At least we can fly over what could be the region tomorrow. You never know."

"What about Freddy?" Lacy asked.

"I don't know what to say about him," Jon admitted. "It seems like we're at a dead end. I suppose because of the hurricane, we have plenty of time to look for him. Have you seen any of the news reports on the storm?"

"Lacy and I kept up with it some," Kerrick said. "I've got a news app on my phone. It looks like Miami was hit hard. Have you heard from Diego about Pirate's Cove?"

"Not a word," Jon said. "I did hear from José. I think he's missing us."

"He wants to fly down and join us and thinks he can convince Ann to forego a trip north to visit relatives," Meg added.

"Typical man," Lacy said and laughed.

Jon stood up and stretched. "He said they would try to get here sometime tonight or early in the morning."

"Sounds like they're coming," Lacy said. "I thought Ann was still trying to make up her mind."

Jon sipped from his coffee and laughed. "José can be very convincing. Alejandro said he could fly into a small airport in San Andres Tuxtla, and we can pick them up in the helicopter."

"Maybe they'll be here in time for our adventure tomorrow," Lacy said. "I can't believe what's happening in Miami, but it looks like we won't have to worry about school for the rest of this week."

"Not for a month or more," Jon said. "I don't know what the university will do. As soon as we're allowed back on Great Exuma, we'll have to fly home."

"In the meantime," Meg said as she stood by Jon, "the adventure awaits."

Chapter Twenty-six

The Goddess

The H175 super-medium airbus helicopter took off from the grassy field near the villa. Jon had seen a helicopter like this before, but it had been outfitted for the military. This machine was definitely not for combat. It was plush and roomy. The seven passenger seats in the main cabin were leather and the picture of luxury.

He stared down at the compound and marveled at its size. Of course, it was the vacation home of the Mexican president, so he figured it would be large and well guarded. Jon spotted gun turrets in several hidden places along the walls surrounding the home, and he figured more sharp-shooters were positioned around the area.

Amazingly, José and Ann had arrived in Veracruz during the night, and Alejandro had a plane fly them to San Andres Tuxtla. Once they picked them up, Alejandro promised they'd see some of the most pristine, beautiful jungle regions of Mexico. Jon smiled as he thought about José and Ann joining them. José had become his best friend, and Jon valued his insight. The thought of being confronted by the Cartel or any other group also made him grateful to have his friend by his side.

José was a skilled fighter. Meg told with great detail how he had rescued her in Spain, and he fought beside Jon as they raided Miguel's compound on Coral Cay to find Lacy. He was fierce and focused. Jon remembered the all-business look his friend assumed when he went into mission mode. This trip, of course, wouldn't put them in any danger. They had access to the protection resources of the Mexican government, so they ought to be as safe as anyone in the country.

As the helicopter dropped toward the runway of a local airport, Jon saw two lone figures standing beside a small, twin-engine Cessna. As soon as the airbus touched down, Alejandro jumped out of the front seat and hurried to meet José and Ann, and the three of them rushed back toward the helicopter.

"So, you couldn't bear to miss out on the fun?" Jon teased as José sat beside him and Ann settled in across from Meg.

"You know I love Ann's family." José winked. "I was just worried about you guys hiking through the jungles of Mexico without me."

"I didn't realize we were going hiking," Jon said, still smiling. "What gave you that idea?"

"I know you, Jon Davenport. You won't be satisfied with just a fly-over of this area."

Jon leaned toward his friend. "You know me too well. I'll catch you up later on our search for Freddy and what we've discovered."

José nodded as the helicopter took off and headed east. Jon instantly saw the vast lake stretching east and south, and Alejandro's voice came over a speaker.

"Below us is Laguna de Catemaco," he said. "It is the third largest lake in Mexico covering an area of seventy-two square kilometers."

"Twenty-eight square miles," Jon heard Kerrick say to Lacy.

They had spent two days in Catemaco about a week earlier. It was a beautiful place on the edge of a large lake surrounded by mountains. Jon had read it was called "The City of Witches," but he hadn't seen anything that would explain the moniker. Someone had told them a number of witches and sorcerers lived in the area, and Catemaco had been the seat of black and white magic for hundreds of years. The city hosted an annual conference for sorcerers in March of each year, but their last trip had given no indication of such evil.

"You can see The Alligator in the lake below," Alejandro's voice sang through the helicopter, and everyone looked out the window.

"I don't see an alligator," Ann said. "We're too high up."

Jon remembered the guide's comments from their boat tour of the lake. He said one of the islands was called *The Alligator* because of its shape. "It's the island. Remember? See it just ahead of us? It's in the shape of an alligator."

"Oh, yeah," Lacy said. "I see it."

"If you'll look toward the edge of the lake," Alejandro said through his microphone, "you'll see La Reserva de Catemaco. It is a very popular tourist place. Trails lead from the back of the visitor's center toward several villages of indigenous people. They are the Nahuatl people I mentioned last night."

Jon watched the little huts along the side of the lake come and go as they passed over The Reserve. As the foliage thickened into dense jungle on the other side of the resort, he strained to see the trail Alejandro had mentioned. Every now and then, he made out what might be a trail, but he wasn't sure. Fifteen minutes later, an open village appeared at the foothills of the mountains. Most of the huts had thatched roofs, though he spotted a few concrete houses.

"Now," Alejandro announced, "we rise. The elevation begins to grow to over 1700 meters as we head toward Sierra de Santa Marta. This region has several volcanoes, but none are active. The Indians speak of smoke and fire, but scientists have studied this region for years and have declared the volcanoes to be inactive. The Nahuas say the smoke and fire is the breath of the gods."

As the helicopter raced toward the top of the volcano, Jon noticed a black animal leap from the branches of a tree.

"Did you see that?" Lacy asked from behind Jon. "I just saw a flash of black. It was an animal."

"I did," Jon said. "Maybe a panther. I imagine panthers live in this area."

"If you look to your left," Alejandro said through the speakers, "you'll see Sierra de Santa Marta. To the right, off in the distance, is the Goddess of the Mountains. I don't know how the ancients could have seen it, but if you are creative, you can see the goddess lying on her back."

Everyone peered out the windows and tried to make out the shape of a woman. The first thing Jon saw were the twin mountain peaks. He pulled his phone out and snapped pictures.

"They may have seen her profile from atop Santa Marta," Alejandro continued. "The myth says a great warrior became an eagle and saw the goddess lying on her back."

Morales laughed. "I'm not sure how the eagle communicated what he saw, but somehow, we know the goddess is here."

"I think I see her," Meg said. "Her breasts are obvious. I think I see her head."

"I see it," Lacy said. "There's her nose."

"Look toward the sea and you can make out her knees," Alejandro said. "Can you see them? Her knees are pulled up like she's about to get up."

The helicopter flew right over the top of the goddess, and Jon noticed the small gorge dip down between the two prominent peaks. He snapped more pictures as the helicopter began circling back toward Catemaco.

"This area was hit hard by an earthquake a few years ago that made the whole area unstable," Alejandro informed them. "We've had numerous tremors and rockslides in the region. Fortunately, once you get past the village of Santa Marta, no one lives in the area for at least 160 kilometers."

❀❖❀❖❀❖❀❖

Miguel cleaned the blade of his knife and stuck it inside his pack. Though it was a bit dull, it had been a good find in the market in Catemaco. He sat down under a tree and checked again to make sure he couldn't be seen from the trail. Even though the lake wasn't far from where he'd encountered the couple, it took him two trips to finish the task. It would have been easier if the man hadn't been so large.

He thumbed through the guy's worn wallet and saw it was indeed fat with cash. Tourists were so stupid. They practically begged to be robbed. He also found several useful credit cards, and the woman's ring glimmered in the sunlight.

He had been focused and efficient. He couldn't botch this part of the plan like he'd done in Veracruz. He decided one way or another, he was going to Mexico City, and he couldn't let a misstep cause him to spend another minute than was needed in this area. He'd recently heard over twenty million people lived in Mexico City. Surely, he could blend in. After a couple of weeks, he could fly back to the States. He might try Chicago for a while.

Images of The Reserve raced through his mind, and he wondered how he'd know which hut belonged to the couple. He had their key, but it had no numbers on it. He realized if he waited until nightfall, he could go to the hut that didn't have any lights. Simple. He could hang out here in the jungle for a while before hiking back.

He'd spent the previous night sleeping in a shed at the back of the property, so he wanted a bed tonight. He might just borrow the Aussie's hut. One of the last things the woman had said was he could have anything, so he'd take them up on it. They wouldn't be needing it. He could slip out in the morning before daylight and find the road back to town.

Miguel lay back in the grass and decided he could take a nap. The sun filtering through the trees indicated it would be a hot day, but the shade of the tree he was under offered protection from the heat.

Thinking about alligators, he sat up and looked around. They were ruthless creatures. He wondered how far inland they might travel to find food and decided to move farther away from the lake. He could find another perfect spot. Of course, he knew of at least two alligators who shouldn't be hungry for a while.

@◆@◆@◆@◆

Jon left the dining room where he'd been talking with Alejandro and climbed the stairs. He thought of the goddess as his mind mulled over the possibilities of what they should do next.

"What did Alejandro say, Jon?" Meg asked as Jon stepped into the bedroom and closed the door. Carla toddled over to him and wrapped her arms around his leg.

Jon bent down and picked up his little girl. "He said lunch would be ready in twenty minutes."

"Not that, Silly," Meg playfully slapped his shoulder and Jon grabbed her wrist and pulled her toward him. A little giggle slipped from her mouth as she felt his arms encircle her body. Her heart pounded in her chest. "You're going to…" His lips were on hers for a brief but promising kiss.

"I'm going to what?" Jon asked while looking into her blue eyes. He would swear that her eyes changed colors from green to blue.

Meg grinned as she looked down at Carla who was reaching for her stuffed bear lying on the floor. "I was going to say you're going to squish Carla."

She saw Carla bend over and pick up a silver chain. Her hand went to her neck. "My necklace!"

Jon reached out and Carla dropped the small diamond necklace into his hand. He slipped it into his pocket and pulled Meg back into his embrace.

Meg noticed her little girl went back to playing with her bear. She placed her hands around Jon's neck and pulled his face back down until their lips met again for a long, deep, satisfying kiss. Kissing was one of his strong points. The truth was he had a lot of strong points.

When they pulled away, Meg looked into the eyes of her husband. "Lunch is the last thing on my mind."

Jon's thumb traced her bottom lip. "Me, too."

Meg turned her head and eyed her daughter. "Maybe we should be thinking about lunch and not what we're thinking about. Little eyes and all that." She took a step back but continued to hold Jon's hands. "A moment ago, I was talking about what I heard you say to Alejandro. You said something about The Reserve."

"Ohhhh," Jon said, exaggerating the word. "I talked to him about the hiking trail that can take us up to Sierra de Santa Marta. He suggested we stay at The Reserve tomorrow night and then hike to a little community called San Antonio the following day. It would be about a seven-mile hike. We could make it to Santa Marta the next day, but we might need to camp out before hiking back the following day."

"Sounds like fun. What about Ann? Do you think hiking will be too much for her? Will it be too much for Carla?"

"Ann's tough, and she won't have to carry a pack. I'm sure Alejandro can find us a child carrier for Carla. You know, a backpack she can ride in."

"Where will we stay in San Antonio?"

"The people who own The Reserve own some huts they rent out. A lot of tourists hike to this village from the lake. Alejandro said we could rent backpacking gear at The

Reserve. Getting atop Sierra de Santa Marta is a little more challenging than the hike to San Antonio, so most tourists don't attempt it."

"But of course, we're not most tourists?"

Jon pulled her into his arms again and leaned in toward her. His scent engulfed her, pulling her in, and his lips were inches from hers. "You're right. You're not a tourist. You're a goddess. That makes you the Goddess of the Mountain." His lips gently pressed against hers.

As Jon eventually pulled back, Meg hummed as if thinking aloud. "If Carla's taking a nap, we're not going to have anything to do. It would be a shame to be bored in such a romantic place."

"It would be a shame indeed. I've got a few ideas."

"Mmmm…" Meg stood on her tiptoes and kissed him again. "I've got a few myself."

"Mama," Carla began pounding on Meg's leg.

"We have a little audience," Meg said.

"I remind her as often as I can that her mother is the joy of my heart."

Meg was still smiling as she picked up Carla. "You want some lunch, Munchkin?" Carla babbled something, and Meg kissed her fat cheek. "I think that means she's hungry."

Jon walked to the door and pulled it open. "I'm hungry myself."

Heat rose up Meg's neck as she walked out past her husband. Her free hand slid across his chiseled chest as she turned toward the dining room.

Chapter Twenty-seven

Catemaco

Jon rolled over in bed and draped his arm over Meg. They needed to get their day started so they could get to The Reserve, but he hated to miss this time with his beautiful wife. He could never get over the blessing Meg had been. He knew if he got what he deserved, it would be…well, misery, sorrow, and loneliness. It was because of grace that he had life, hope, joy, and Meg.

Her breathing was gentle and measured. She didn't sound like someone in a deep sleep. He knew she was awake and probably processing her day: taking care of Carla, packing for a few days of hiking in the jungle, and putting up with a crazy husband.

He lay behind her thinking of the possibilities. Her body was like a magnet drawing steel as he slid closer to her. He felt her warmth and inhaled her scent. Everything about her sent him over the edge.

His hand slid down her arm and waist as he reveled in the joy of knowing this woman better than any other person on earth. He found joy not only in knowing her, but in being known by her and loved by her. What a treasure! She leaned back against him as his lips found her neck.

He slipped his hand around her body as she rolled over to face him. As their lips met, the morning quiet split wide open with a wail from the adjoining room.

Meg's body tensed. "Carla? Something's wrong."

"I'll check on her," Jon said as he pulled the covers off them.

Meg was already sliding out of bed. "I'll do it." She rushed to see what was wrong.

"Oh, no." Jon heard Meg's voice float through the open door.

"What's wrong, Honey?" Jon asked as he moved toward the door.

He stepped into the room and was greeted by a strong, sickening smell.

"She's vomited all over the place," Meg said as she reached into the crib.

"Let me get a wet rag, Meg. You'll get it all over you."

Jon hurried into the bathroom and put two washrags under warm water. He returned just as Meg was pulling Carla's pajamas over her head. The bed was a mess, and Carla had been lying in the center of it all.

"Oh, Baby," Meg said. "What's the matter?"

Jon looked at her heavy diaper. "This isn't good."

"Let's get you in the tub, Sweetheart."

Jon began running water into the tub as Meg removed a messy diaper. She brought their naked daughter into the bathroom and sat her down in the tub as Carla cried and clung to her.

"Jon, go on to breakfast. Tell everyone Carla's sick. It's probably a stomach bug. Maybe, I'll come down to get something to eat in a bit."

"I'll stay and help you," Jon insisted.

"No sense in that. I can handle it. On second thought, maybe you could bring me a bagel and coffee after you eat. Really, Jon. I'm fine. Go ahead."

"Ok. I'll get you some coffee now and bring something else back in a bit."

Ten minutes later, Jon returned to the room and placed a cup of coffee on the dresser as Meg dried Carla off with a fluffy, white towel. He pulled out a diaper and laid a clean set of pajamas beside his wife. "Well, I guess I'll tell the group we'll have to postpone our hike. I don't think it would be good to take Carla out now."

"I was just thinking about that. Why don't you and the others go ahead? I'll stay here. There's no reason for everyone to miss out. I bet Ann would rather stay here, anyway. It will give her an excuse to skip out on the hike."

Jon chuckled. "You think Ann is looking for an excuse?"

"I'm not sure she's looking, but I have a feeling she'll jump at the opportunity."

"I hate the thought of leaving you and Carla here."

Meg looked around the plush room. "I can think of worse places. We'll be fine. It's probably just a twenty-four-hour bug. Once she's better, we'll go shopping and have some fun. Ann would love going to the market." Meg secured the diaper and pulled on Carla's pajamas. When she picked her up and held her close, she smiled and looked at Jon. "I'll miss being with you when you find the lost city, but wouldn't that be a wonderful way to top off this trip? Go ahead. Really, Jon. We'll be fine."

@◆@◆@◆@◆

Miguel rounded the curve in the dirt road, cursing as he stubbed his toe on another rock. He was not going to walk fourteen miles all the way back to Catemaco. He could either find a ride or steal one. The thought of someone remembering his face was troubling, but the possibility of spending all day on this God-forsaken road made the risk worth it.

He noticed a wide trail off to his left. He'd passed a few of those and knew the path would lead to another poverty-stricken house. He needed to keep walking. It would be night soon, and he still had a long way to go.

Not finding more diamonds or money the night before at the Australian's hut had been disappointing, but the stack of cash, the diamond ring, and the credit cards would serve him well. No one would miss this couple for a long time. He made sure of it. He removed all their belongings and dragged everything into the jungle where he buried it. When it came time for them to check out, management at The Reserve would assume they had left. This would buy him a lot of time, maybe weeks. So, he had spent half of the night going through all their things before ditching them.

He'd messed up when he discovered their stash of alcohol. He convinced himself a little celebration wouldn't hurt, so he downed several bottles of some off-brand liquor after he had managed to get rid of the rest of their belongings. When he awakened that morning, the sun shone brightly through the windows of the hut. He was fortunate no one noticed him slip out and walk around The Reserve before heading around the lake.

As he passed the trail, something stopped him. He paused and listened. It was a loud, bold laugh that sounded familiar. He turned down the path and approached the back of a house. This place didn't look as run down as the two houses he'd spotted earlier.

From the side of the house, Miguel observed people sitting in a circle. He'd been to this place the previous day when the boat stopped for a sales pitch. What a crock! That woman was pushing mineral water and magical mud. He looked at the group of gullible tourists and recognized right away they were Americans.

Laughter rang out again as the woman giving the presentation spread more mud on the girl's face. Miguel edged forward to get a better view. He saw her. Long, blond hair. Perfect body. He felt the blood drain from his face and something in his gut flipped. Lacy Henderson. He couldn't believe it. Jon, Kerrick, and the Spaniard stood off to the side. He knew them all like they were family. The wrong side of the family.

Miguel grinned. If Lacy were his, she'd be entertaining him, too. He watched in silence feeling something churning deep inside. *She will be mine. I will not be this close and let her get away again. I wonder where Meg is. I hate for her to miss the party.*

He knew the boat would take Lacy to The Reserve. Going back there would be risky. He'd have to somehow discover whether they were spending the night or just taking the lake cruise. If they were going back to Catemaco, he'd have to get back fast. If they were spending the night at The Reserve, he'd have to stay the night as well.

He limped back to the grounds of The Reserve an hour later and saw several boats tied up at the dock. The Davenports had to be here already. He looked across the small lagoon and saw Jon leading the group up the trail to the huts that bordered the lake. They were staying. It looked like they would be staying in the last two huts. He had to learn their plans. He remembered seeing a straw hat in the shed where he'd slept his first night. He'd at least get his hands on that hat. Any disguise would be better than none at all.

Once Miguel had the hat, he purchased a few snacks and a pair of sunglasses at the gift shop. Surely, Lacy wouldn't recognize him as long as he wore the glasses. As he turned to leave, Lacy and Kerrick walked through the door of the small shop. Miguel pivoted and began looking at a map on the wall.

He listened as Lacy tried to ask for a map of the region. They were looking for hiking trails. *So, they want to go on a hike. This situation is getting better and better.* He rubbed the talisman hanging from his neck.

They wouldn't be hiking toward the mountains this afternoon, so they would be going out in the morning. He couldn't have asked for a better scenario. He could kill Jon, José, and Kerrick. Then, he'd have Lacy for as long as he wanted.

This wild goose chase had gone on long enough, and it was about to be over. He'd still have to deal with Meg. A grin spread across his face as he considered the possibilities. With the Davenports out of the way, he could get the medallion, find the treasure, and help himself to anything of value at the compound in the Bahamas.

How would he kill them? He remembered seeing the manager of The Reserve shooting a large snake with a pistol. Miguel would have to find that pistol.

Chapter Twenty-eight

Jungle Hike

Lacy stepped onto the porch of the hut and approached Kerrick, who sat looking out at the lake. It was beautiful. He was beautiful. The sun spread across the calm waters as if someone were slowly raising a curtain to an enchanting sunrise. Several fishermen were already at work casting their nets. She hated Meg was missing all of this beauty. Her aunt loved sunrises.

She thought back to the morning at the president's villa when Jon told them Carla was throwing up and had a fever. Meg had insisted everyone go on with their plans, and she and Carla would stay behind. Of course, Ann wouldn't think of leaving her friend. Lacy thought Ann may have been a little relieved at missing the hike through the jungle.

Lacy walked up behind Kerrick and wrapped her arms around his neck. He flinched at first, not expecting her presence.

"Penny for your thoughts," Lacy ventured.

"I'd think what's going through my mind right now is worth a lot more than a penny."

"Oh, my. Now, I'm intrigued."

"You really want to know?" Kerrick paused and turned his head to look at Lacy. "I was sitting here watching the sun creep across the water, and it made me think about my life. I'll be graduating from college soon, assuming we still have a college to graduate from, and I've got to figure out what I'm going to do with my life."

"That is a heavy thought," Lacy agreed. "What have you decided?"

"Well, I have a lot of moving parts. Like, should I be a marine biologist? Just because I'll have the degree doesn't mean I should pursue the career. Jon offered me a job. Maybe I should take him up on it."

"Am I one of the moving parts?"

Kerrick turned sideways in the chair and pulled her down onto his lap. "It depends on whether or not you're moving. You are definitely one of the parts. I'd say my favorite part."

She looked into his blue eyes and touched his shadowed face. He hadn't shaved in a couple of days, and the growing stubble was sexy. The soap from his morning shower penetrated her senses. He could somehow make Ivory soap smell masculine.

What did she think about being one of his moving parts? She liked the thought and was stunned at its appeal. How in the world had she made such a turnaround in three months? The thought of sitting in a guy's lap considering the possibility of marriage would have been as strange as her becoming a sumo wrestler. Lacy wasn't old enough to be thinking about marriage, and she hated guys. Right? Not this one.

Lacy didn't know what to say, so she leaned in and kissed him. His lips were soft and tender. Was this a kiss that could last a lifetime? Could any kiss last a lifetime? The kiss deepened and grew more urgent, passionate. They finally separated, and she felt his chest rise and fall. Was he panting?

"You are my sunrise, Lacy Henderson. I can't imagine not having that moving part in my life."

He looked into her eyes, and she looked into his soul. He was kind, honest, and real. How had she stumbled into the arms of this amazing guy? The screen door of the hut slammed behind them breaking the spell. Lacy heard feet hurrying down the steps.

"Jon's going to get our breakfast," Kerrick said as if reading her mind. "He worked out a deal with the restaurant to give us breakfast and lunch to go so we can get on the trail. They also have backpacks and tents for us to use."

"So, we're really going to spend the night in the jungle?"

"Yep. We'll hike to Santa Marta today and spend tomorrow night somewhere around the peak of the goddess."

Lacy looked at her watch. "Is the restaurant open this early?"

"I don't think they open until seven o'clock, so I guess they're doing him a favor. They will have the gear there for us to pick up on our way out."

Lacy grinned. "I bet a few pesos encouraged them to be extra gracious. He told me last night he wanted us to be hiking by seven o'clock. Can we make it to that first village by lunch? What was it called?"

"San Antonio. We should be there before lunch. It's only seven miles. He talked about dropping our stuff at the place where we'll spend the night and doing a little exploring before dark. Thankfully, we can leave most of our luggage here at our huts.

"Yeah. I saw Jon pay for four nights when we arrived yesterday.

"He said he told the guy at the desk if we didn't show back up in four days, he could keep charging his card until we returned."

"Crazy," Lacy said. "A few months ago, I'd been out of Georgia only once in my life, and that was to attend Jon and Meg's wedding. Now, I'm about to go exploring the jungles of Mexico."

Fifteen minutes later, they heard footsteps coming up the path toward the hut. They stood to their feet as Jon stepped onto the porch.

"Good morning, you two," Jon said as he held out two paper sacks. "Breakfast."

Lacy looked inside one of the bags. "Are those breakfast burritos?"

"Yep, except better than the ones you eat at McDonald's. I've also got bottles of orange juice. Fortunately, the cook spoke pretty good English. She said if we'll come by the kitchen on our way out, she'd give us coffee and our sack lunches."

"I could definitely use coffee," Lacy said.

"She also told me she has a cousin who lives in Santa Marta, which is a village a little northeast of San Antonio. She told me about a trail connecting the villages. Her cousin has some rooms she rents out to hikers, so I thought we might try to get there by tonight."

"Sounds good," Kerrick said as he stood up.

"I just talked to Meg," Jon said, "and Carla is better. I'd still rather not be away from them for too long."

"How far are we going to hike today?" Lacy asked.

"About twelve miles." Jon put his hands into his pockets and looked surprised when he pulled out a gold chain.

"Is that Meg's necklace?" Lacy asked

"Yep. She dropped it, and I put it in my pocket. I forgot all about it. She'll kill me if I don't bring it back to her in one piece."

Lacy held her hand out. "Want me to keep it?"

"I'm good." Jon slipped the necklace back into his pocket. "Would you get José? Let's eat and get going."

@◆@◆@◆@◆

The waitress refilled Miguel's coffee cup for the fourth time. He looked out the window toward the Davenports' huts, but no one stirred. He was surprised they weren't up yet. He'd been the first to arrive at the restaurant just so he could follow them into the jungle after breakfast.

He twisted his cup around and looked at his watch. Nearly eight o'clock. Of course, they were rich people who didn't have to get up early. Jon Davenport, however, wasn't lazy. He and his friend were in good shape, so Miguel figured they were used to getting up early to work out. He'd heard José speak enough to know he was not from Central America. He had to be from Spain. He hated the guy.

Memories flooded his mind of returning to the house on Coral Cay to find that José and Jon had attacked his men and taken back Lacy. If it hadn't been for the ex-military jerk, Miguel would already have Lacy's medallion and the treasure. Jon was tough, but he couldn't have masterminded that escape. That was José. *I'm going to love watching him squirm as I slowly end his life.*

A group of tourists entered the restaurant, but still no sign of the Davenports. This was not right. Would he have to kill them in their huts? No, nothing stupid like that. They would start their hike eventually.

He heard the boat motor start up. *Could they be on the boat going back to Catemaco?* He bolted from the table and tried to get through the group crowding the door. By the time he'd made it to the dock, a boat full of people was far out into the lake. He couldn't tell whether the Davenports were aboard.

He slammed his hand against the tree and cursed. He saw Lacy buying the map in the gift shop yesterday. Surely, they weren't going back on the boat this morning.

"Señor?" Miguel looked up to see the waitress waving toward him and calling. He hadn't paid for breakfast. He cursed. Nothing like making sure someone remembered his face.

He waved and started back to the restaurant. He'd tell the girl he was trying to catch his friends before they left. No big deal. He decided to pay his bill and go back to talk with some of the guys on the dock. Maybe they could tell him if the Americans were on the boat.

Once he paid for breakfast, Miguel hurried back to the dock and found a couple of guys messing around, waiting on the next boat.

"Hey. You been here all morning?" Miguel asked.

"Si. We work the dock for Señor Burgos."

"I was supposed to meet some friends here, and I can't find them. I'm thinking they already left."

"We've only had one launch leave this morning, but it was full."

"My friends were Americans."

"Yes. There were some Americans aboard. If you're after that blond girl, she'd be worth going after." He shared a grin with his friend.

Miguel hurried off the dock trying to figure out how he could beat the boat to Catemaco. If he just had a car. He looked back at the office building and grinned. *Or a motorcycle!*

Thirty minutes later, the motorcycle left the bumpy gravel road and glided across the smooth pavement. Miguel looked out into the water and could see the boat heading toward the main docks. It looked like he would get there in time to watch them tie up. Perfect.

His motorcycle dipped into a pothole, and Miguel struggled to keep the machine upright. Some teenagers standing on the side of the road laughed. Miguel considered stopping to shut their stupid mouths, but he didn't have time. He motored on toward the main docks.

He stood in a cluster of people as the boat pulled up to the dock. He saw the blond hair of the girl catching the morning sun. *Lacy!* The group appeared to be gathering up luggage, and Miguel lost sight of Lacy. *There she is. Bent over in the front of the boat.*

He watched as she grabbed some luggage and turned to get off the boat. Heat slid up his back, and he thought his face might explode. *That's…not…Lacy.*

The men at The Reserve weren't wrong. The woman was a looker, but she was close to thirty, or older. Not his Lacy.

He couldn't believe it. He had lost them. How could that have happened? They must have left for their hike without eating, or maybe they ate back at the huts before the restaurant opened. He had to think. If they had taken the trail, they'd be hours ahead of him. He could drive the motorcycle back, but by now, the owner would be missing it.

Miguel pointed the bike back toward the dirt road that would take him around the lake. When he came to the last house before The Reserve, he drove the bike into the trees and parked it. He returned to the road and walked the final quarter of a mile to the resort. He was hungry now, so he headed back to the restaurant. Maybe he could ask a few questions. Surely someone knew something.

As he sat down at the table, a cute waitress took his order. He had seen her earlier that morning but hadn't spoken to her. He ordered the beef tacos.

She turned to walk away, but Miguel called out, "Señorita? I'm trying to find some friends. I met them in Catemaco a few days ago and was supposed to meet them here. We were going hiking together. Americans?"

The girl started to shake her head but stopped. "One moment." She disappeared into the kitchen. A bit later she returned with his tacos. "Was your friend Señor Juan?"

"Yes. Jon Davenport."

"My friend who works in the store talked to them yesterday and sold them a map." She nodded across the restaurant to the same guy Miguel had seen the day before. "The cook in the back said Señor Juan and his family left early this morning for a hike. They're going to stay in San Antonio, a few kilometers to the east. We have rooms in San Antonio.

A lot of people hike from here, spend the night, and return the next day. You could catch them, maybe, or you could wait for them to return."

"Too bad I missed them. I'll wait for them to return. Gracias." Miguel watched the girl walk back into the kitchen. She wasn't bad, but she wasn't Lacy or Meg.

He'd sounded convincing. Maybe the waitress thought he would wait on the Davenports. No way. He'd find them in San Antonio and set up a little party for them. He'd have to figure out how he'd take out three men. Taking out the Spaniard might be a problem.

After finishing lunch, he left money on the table and got up to leave. As he turned toward the door, he remembered the manager's pistol.

Chapter Twenty-nine

San Antonio

Lacy saw José turn and look back at their small group. She wiped sweat from her forehead and looked at her watch. It was a little after eight o'clock, which meant they'd been walking for an hour and a half.

"We're making good time," José said when they stopped to take a break. "At this rate, we'll be at San Antonio in about two more hours." He looked around at everyone sitting down. "Well, maybe not at this rate, but at the rate we were walking before you all got lazy."

"I'd say that after walking three miles since six forty-five, we deserve a break," Lacy said.

José laughed. "I'm not complaining. The harder part is still ahead. The map shows the trail from San Antonio to Santa Marta is going to be a bit of a climb."

The hike so far had been relaxing and enjoyable. Lacy wondered why she'd never hiked like this back in Georgia. She'd heard the Georgia mountains were beautiful and offered many trails, but she'd never been interested in the outdoors in the past. This hiking experience had been not only refreshing but also cathartic. She could almost feel her struggles falling from her shoulders like the sweat from her brow.

Lacy pulled out her water bottle. The lady at the restaurant was so kind. She packed sack lunches for them with extra bottles of water. The morning was beautiful, and the jungle was full of life. She was excited to be searching for the lost city. Well, maybe they weren't really searching, but their efforts to find Freddy were at a standstill. They may as well get a feel for this region. It's possible this was the location Bluetooth's scroll described.

The damp morning air made her wonder if rain was in the forecast. Vegetation along the sides of the path was thick, and a canopy of branches covered the path like the tunnel of plants at Six Flags Over Georgia. She grinned as thoughts of Mowgli and Baloo from *Jungle Book* came to mind. *That was India, Dummy. Wasn't it? Maybe Africa. No, India.*"

"All right, gang," Jon said as he stood and grabbed his pack. "Daylight's burning. Let's get going. I want to be in Santa Marta for dinner."

Two hours later they walked through the small village of San Antonio. Jon asked Lacy to help him talk to a lady in Spanish, and they walked toward a house that appeared to have a store set up in their front room. They came out with drinks for everyone, and Jon suggested they get to the other side of the village before stopping for lunch.

"It's early," Kerrick said as Jon handed out drinks. "I mean early for lunch. Not that I'm complaining."

"We ate breakfast early, and I don't want to have to carry these glass bottles with us once we empty them."

"True," Kerrick agreed.

Lunch consisted of refried beans inside tortillas, along with fresh pineapple. Lacy had already eaten more pineapple in the last two weeks than she'd ever eaten in her life, but she'd never tire of it. As she ate, she looked up the trail and marveled at how big the mountains were.

The climb to the village of Santa Marta was challenging but incredibly beautiful. Lacy examined the thick jungle growth and noted, high in the trees, a thick plant with tendrils hanging down toward the ground. She remembered reading once about an air plant. Maybe that was one.

She looked to the right at a beautiful pink orchid surrounded by lush green leaves. Lacy gasped when she saw the colorful bill of a toucan sitting on a branch near the flower. It was the most beautiful sight she'd ever seen. She reached for her camera. *Carla will love this.*

"Keel-billed toucan," José whispered just before she snapped the shot.

Lacy jumped at his voice, hitting a branch as her finger involuntarily took a picture. The bird flew away. She growled and managed to stop a word that used to be her favorite go to curse word when she was angry. She stared at the out-of-focus picture of leaves.

"Sorry," José said; he sounded sincere. "I'm sure you'll see more before we return."

She thought of the incredible shot she'd missed—rich jungle, pink orchid, and the rainbow-colored beak of the toucan. *Oh well. I'll have to watch for more.*

Lacy turned to José. "What happens if we don't make it to the village before nightfall?"

"We will. We should make it with plenty of time to spare unless you start slacking off on us."

"Me, slacking?" Lacy said as she imagined herself lying out by the pool at the president's villa. She'd eyed that pool lustfully while getting aboard the helicopter. *I'd much rather be hiking through the jungle taking pictures of toucans.*

A little after four o'clock, the trail intersected a small, dirt road that dropped down into a valley. Lacy could make out small houses dotting the sides of the road. "Is that Santa Marta?"

"Looks like it," Jon said. "The cook at The Reserve told me to go into the center of the village and ask for Señora Lubi. She has several small, thatched roof huts she rents out to hikers. She'll also fix dinner for us."

"Sounds great," Kerrick said. "I could eat an alligator."

"Don't think you'll have the chance to have alligator up here," José said with a grin. "You should have grabbed one back at the lake."

Jon looked down at his phone and back at the group. "You guys want to take a break and let me climb that hill so I can get a cell signal? I'd like to call Meg and check on Carla. I'll feel better if I know she's completely over her stomach issue."

"Sure," Lacy said. "It sounded like she was doing okay this morning, didn't it?"

"Yeah. I think it was just a twenty-four-hour thing. Too bad. Meg would have loved this experience."

José laughed. "Ann wouldn't have, not the hiking part."

Fifteen minutes later, Jon returned to the group with a smile on his face. Lacy loved her uncle, and she loved the fact his wife put a smile on his face he couldn't wipe away. She looked over at Kerrick and wondered if he'd be grinning like a loon while thinking about her.

"They were shopping," Jon said. "Carla's fine. Sounds like they're having a good time."

Finding Lubi was easy, and in no time, they dropped their packs inside a clean hut with concrete floors and sparse walls. Hammocks drooped from the ceiling but were tied up with a small rope making the room seem more spacious. They decided they'd all share one hut. Lubi had an outdoor shower at the back of the hut and an outhouse about one hundred feet further down a trail.

Lacy walked around the hut and eyed the shower. One knob and no curtain. *Fat chance. Cold water and public display—not in this lifetime.*

Leaving their packs behind, they climbed to an overlook on the trail to the Santa Marta peak. They weren't far away from the peak. Lacy looked south and saw what had to be the goddess far off in the distance. With a little creativity, she could make out the nose and a breast. The knees were a little suspect, but maybe it looked different from higher up.

Jon looked in the same direction. "That's where we want to go. The village is down in that valley to our right."

"I bet a trail leads from the village toward the mountain peak," José said. "If not, we'll have to make our own way."

"Lubi will know," Kerrick said.

By the time they returned to the village of Santa Marta, Lubi had prepared a dinner of chicken in molé sauce with rice and tortillas. It was delicious. Lacy couldn't help but think of Meg again. Hopefully she, Carla, and Ann were having fun.

"You going to take a shower tonight?" Kerrick said in a whisper as he leaned toward her.

"Don't you wish," she said before bumping her shoulder against his.

"I was serious. I'll stand guard at the corner of the house, with my back turned."

"And what about the other corner and the jungle behind the house? No, thank you. Girls don't sweat anyway. We glisten."

"Yeah," Kerrick said with a laugh. "You were glistening a lot on that last climb."

The thoughts of getting clean sounded better and better as the evening wore on. In the pitch black of the night, Lacy walked around the house and inspected the shower. She could barely see her hand in front of her face. Kerrick had already showered in the frigid water, so maybe she could endure it. She went back inside to get him.

Ten minutes later, Lacy looked over her shoulder toward the corner of the house where Kerrick stood facing the other way, and José stood at the other corner looking toward the road. She took a deep breath and gasped as she stepped under the ice-cold water. Her body jerked in revolt as the frigid water numbed her skin. In less than five minutes, she was toweling off and stepping into clean clothes.

Kerrick did a double take when Lacy walked past him. "I think you just set a new world record."

"Probably." Lacy called over to José. "Hey, José. I'm done. Thanks so much."

"So, if we only have cold water when we get married," Kerrick said with a grin, "our utilities will be cheaper, and we'll save a lot of time."

"We're getting married? News to me."

Kerrick pulled her chilled body next to his. He was warm and masculine. "Are you being coy with me?"

Lacy could feel his heart beating in her own chest as his arms wrapped around her. Her towel fell from her shoulders to the ground. "Coy?"

His warm lips were on her frozen ones in seconds. She decided a cold shower wasn't so bad after all. An incredible hike, wonderful meal, cold shower, and sweet embrace of this wonderful man made for an awesome day. Now, she just had to try to get a good night's sleep while swinging several feet above the floor in a cloth hammock. Not likely.

Chapter Thirty

Discovery

Meg walked through the warm pool water holding Carla. She and Ann spent the morning shopping at the market and came back for a quick dip in the pool and lunch before Carla's nap. The villa was the perfect place for rest and relaxation. Being practically related to the president of the United States sure had its perks. She missed having Jon around, but she knew he was having a great adventure. He was in his element.

Carla kicked as if trying to swim out of her mother's arms.

"You're going to be a little fish."

Carla splashed water into Meg's open eyes and giggled.

Ann lay on a lounge chair, and Meg noticed her friend appeared to be watching her. Ann had been melancholy since José took off with Jon for Catemaco, but Meg also knew how being pregnant could affect a lot of things, especially emotions.

"Okay, tadpole, time to get out." Meg carried Carla up the stairs at the end of the pool and grabbed her towel.

She looked at Ann. "You've been awfully quiet. What's on your mind?"

"Oh, I guess I've just been thinking a lot about being a mother and having a family. What will it be like? Will José like being a father, and will it affect our marriage?"

"I remember having those same thoughts. Jon and I loved being married so much, and I couldn't help but wonder if having a child would affect our marriage in a negative way. I can tell you being parents has made our marriage stronger. I love watching Jon with Carla. It's different—in a good way."

"Have you heard from Jon today? José hasn't called."

"No. He told me yesterday they didn't have a good signal where they were staying. He said they were in a little village called Santa Marta between the Santa Marta peak and the two peaks he's calling The Goddess. I think they're going to hike one of the goddess mountains. He'll call as soon as they have signal, but he told me not to worry."

"Not to worry about them? You mean we're supposed to sit here like good little wives and not worry about our husbands traipsing through the jungles of Mexico searching for a lost city? Right."

"They're having the time of their lives," Meg said. "You know that. Our men are like little boys at Christmas when it comes to stuff like this."

"True. So, you think they'll be back tomorrow?"

"Jon figured they'd be back within cell signal by then, but he made me promise we wouldn't worry."

"And you promised?"

Meg reflected on the nearly three years they'd been married. Not everything was simple or safe. From the beginning, they'd stumbled into drug lords, terrorists, and thugs. It was like Jon was a magnet for bad guys.

"I guess I lied," Meg said. "Well, I didn't exactly lie. I told him I knew he had an angel on his shoulder. I believe that."

"You can say that again," Ann said with a laugh. "I think Jon and José have a whole army of angels. In the meantime, we'll have to go shopping again. It's a tough sacrifice, but someone has to do it."

Meg laughed. Ann could shop all day every day, but Meg couldn't find the same joy in it. She liked going to the Mexican markets; however, everything had its limits.

"I would have enjoyed being with the group," Meg said. "I think you would have too, but all that walking may have been a challenge. I just hope Jon stays out of trouble."

"Trouble?"

Meg laughed. "You know how he is. He's always trying to help someone, and sometimes it backfires."

"He's got such a good heart. At least they're hiking in the middle of nowhere, so there shouldn't be anything that can backfire."

"Let's hope so."

@◆@◆@◆@◆

Lacy landed on the floor with a loud thump. She'd never slept in a hammock before, and 'sleep' didn't describe what she'd been doing the last seven hours. Getting into the contraption had been a challenge but making her early morning dismount proved hazardous.

Jon stood back trying to hold in a laugh, but José didn't bother trying to be discreet. Kerrick appeared at her side and helped her up.

"I'm glad I can provide comic relief for the trip," she huffed before finally starting to laugh.

Walking into the large room at the end of the house, they found Lubi up and working on breakfast. Lacy marveled at how hard this sweet lady worked to serve her guests. Working hard seemed to be part of the Mexican culture. Lubi motioned for them to sit and offered each a plate of scrambled eggs, refried beans, cooked plantain, and sweet bread she called pan.

José spoke with Lubi about a trail that would lead them to The Goddess. Though a trail led east out of the village, they'd have to hike cross-country to get to their destination. They had a topographical map, and someone included a compass with their backpacking equipment. The only problem they might encounter was washed out areas from recent storms. The rainy season this year had been bad. Also, significant rockslides occurred a few years earlier when an earthquake struck the region. Cross-country hiking might prove difficult.

Trekking through the misty dawn, they navigated a trail that snaked out of the east side of the village. The world awakened and Lacy began hearing the sounds of the jungle. In less than an hour, they left the trail and began a steep climb through thick brush that grabbed at their clothing.

They spent all day climbing up and down mountains as they pushed their way south. Though the terrain was challenging, Lacy found the jungle beautiful, even intoxicating. Cross-country backpacking, however, was not a walk in the park. Lacy sustained several scrapes and scratches.

She had never spent the night in a tent before, but that night she slept like a rock. The combination of being worn out and listening to the constant flow of a mountain stream lulled her into a deep sleep.

When they pulled on their backpacks the next morning, she felt refreshed and ready for another long day of hiking. Their goal was to get to the top of the next mountain, The Goddess, and then head back to the village of Santa Marta.

Lacy slipped more than once on the muddy slope of the mountain but made it to what appeared to be a ridge. Though no trail was visible, the climb was easier as they continued toward the peak. She enjoyed the cool morning air and decided she would take future backpacking trips. She looked back at Kerrick and noticed he wasn't even winded.

The top didn't offer a great overlook, so Jon climbed a tree to see if he could get a better view. "We're on The Goddess," he shouted down. "I can see the other peak to the south, and the gorge drops down between the two."

He climbed down the tree and dropped to the ground. "I want to show you something I discovered while looking at pictures I took from the helicopter."

Jon pulled out his phone and pressed his photo app. He scrolled through several pictures before finding the one of the gorge. "Look at this," he said while holding the phone out for everyone to see. "What does that look like to you?"

Lacy gasped. "A heart. Just like the scroll said—the heart of the goddess."

"That means if we drop down the mountain on the south side, that gorge is the heart," Kerrick said. "What did the scroll say about her heart?"

"It just said to find the heart of the goddess," Jon said. "Seems to me we've found it."

Lacy felt an exhilaration as if she were about to scratch off the numbers of a winning lottery ticket, but she knew in advance she was a winner. She followed Jon as he led them down toward the gorge. If the lost city were in the gorge, wouldn't someone have discovered it years ago? There had to be more to finding this place than just hiking to the bottom.

At one point, they came to a series of rocks jutting out from the side of the mountain, and Lacy could see a large stream flowing toward the gorge. It made sense. Gorges had streams or rivers running through the bottom. As they came to the edge of a small cliff, the mountain dropped straight down about fifty feet to a rock that stuck out like a shelf.

A shadow passed overhead, and she looked up to see another large toucan flying toward a nearby tree branch. She thought about her missed opportunity the day before, jerked her small pack around, and fished for her camera. Pulling the Nikon toward her face, she took several steps toward the tree. Her right foot stepped on a loose rock, and the rock slid a little sending Lacy sprawling toward the edge of the cliff. She caught herself before doing a face plant, but her camera flew from her hand.

A short scream slipped from her lips as she felt a stab of pain on her hands and knees. *My camera!* She watched in horror as her Nikon dropped out of sight. She imagined it smashing on rocks below the cliff.

Kerrick hurried to her side. "Lacy! Are you okay?"

"My camera! I can't believe I dropped my camera."

Lacy lay on the ground staring at the last place she saw one of the few things she cherished. She felt Kerrick's strong arms slip around her.

"We might can find it," Kerrick said. "We just need to make sure you haven't broken anything."

"I'm fine," Lacy said as Jon and José hurried toward her. She looked at her knee and saw blood oozing out, and her hands were scraped and bleeding a little. "It's no big deal." She got up and stepped cautiously toward the edge. Looking over, she only saw the tops of the trees below.

"I can't believe I did that!" Lacy moaned. "It took me over a year to save up for that camera."

"It may not be lost," Jon said.

"Yeah, but what are the odds it didn't break into a thousand pieces?"

"It depends," Kerrick said. "If it didn't land on rocks, it might be okay. Let's see if we can get around to the bottom of the cliff."

José reached into his small pack for a first aid kit. "Let me clean your wounds first."

A few minutes later, the group walked along the rock shelf looking for the best way to descend. They came to a "V" shaped notch in the cliff and climbed slowly down.

Lacy skirted the bottom of the cliff where she imagined the camera might have dropped. Kerrick, Jon, and José weren't far behind.

"Do you see it?" Kerrick asked.

Lacy looked to the top of the cliff and tried to visualize the angle at which it may have fallen. She knew the camera came out of her hand with some force. Almost as if she'd thrown it. Lacy heard laughter and turned.

"Would you look at that?" José called from several feet below them.

Lacy looked a little further down the mountain to where José stood. The camera dangled from a tree branch about ten feet off the ground.

"Looks like God wants you to have a camera," José said with a grin. "He just doesn't want you taking pictures of His toucans."

"I doubt God cares if I take pictures of birds," Lacy said as she made her way toward the swaying camera.

José squatted down. "Get on my shoulders. Just don't lean out too far or we'll fall down the mountain."

Lacy obeyed, and within a few minutes she cradled her camera in her hands. José reached back and held her arms as she slid down his back.

"Hey!" Kerrick's voice came down through the trees from the near bottom of the cliff. "Come look at this."

"What is it?" Lacy called.

"Just come see. You'll never believe what I've found."

Chapter Thirty-one

The Heart of the Goddess

Jon climbed back up toward Kerrick, and the others followed. He found Kerrick kneeling near the base of the cliff clearing away leaves and dirt.

José came up behind him and squatted to get a better look. "What is it?"

"That's right," Jon said. "You weren't with us. We saw that design at El Tajin."

"Look at that," Lacy said as she came up behind the group. She pulled out her camera and snapped a picture. "It's one of the upside-down nines."

Jon laughed. "I guess I never thought of it as a nine." He looked at the stacked stone design that almost appeared to be a part of the cliff. They saw a number of these designs around the ancient Mesoamerican city north of Veracruz they visited on their last trip to Mexico. "It looks like it was covered with dirt. How did you find it, Kerrick?"

Kerrick laughed. "I slipped and tried to catch myself. My hand slid down, and I felt a stack of stones. I was curious, so I started clearing away the dirt."

"I wonder if anyone else has ever seen it," Lacy said.

"Lubi said there's been a lot of heavy rain lately," Kerrick pointed out. "Maybe this area used to be covered with more dirt and plants."

Jon tried to remember if the symbol had any significance in El Tajin. It was a part of the design of the ancient city, almost as if it was a cornerstone of a structure. He looked up at the cliff and noted there was nothing about what he was staring at that resembled a corner. He scanned the base of the cliff wondering if any more symbols were further down.

"I found an article about it a few days ago," Lacy said, as if she were reading Jon's mind. "I was looking through the pictures I took while we were at El Tajin, and I got curious about all those upside-down looking nines."

"What did you discover?" Jon asked.

"The symbols are kind of a mystery, but some archeologists think it has something to do with spirit travel."

"Spirit travel?" Kerrick asked.

"Yep. It seems they were like road signs showing spirits how to be released into the afterlife."

"Weird. I wonder whose spirit was supposed to come floating by this place. Why would there be something like this in the middle of nowhere?"

Jon knelt and inspected the rock. "Maybe it wasn't the middle of nowhere 2,000 years ago."

Kerrick pointed down the slope of the mountain. "We are looking toward the heart of the goddess. Didn't the scroll say something about the heart? Maybe this cliff will direct us to Bluetooth's city."

Jon couldn't help but feel excitement as he considered the possibilities. The scroll they found in the cave under Coral Cay definitely said something about the shade of the mountain and the heart of the goddess. He led the group along the base of the cliff thinking about the hopelessness of finding another symbol. It would be covered with dirt and growth, just like the last one.

Fifteen minutes later, a bird flew past the group. Jon jerked back in surprise.

"Where did that bird come from?" José asked. "I thought you were going to jump out of your skin."

"It about gave me a heart attack," Jon said. "It looked like it flew right out of the ground."

José stepped forward and knelt to inspect the ground. He removed loose vines and peered into a hole. After rummaging through his backpack, he pulled out a flashlight and pointed it into the hole.

"What do you see, José?" Lacy asked, trying to look over his shoulder.

"It looks like a cave, but this is a small opening."

"Like an air shaft," Kerrick said.

"I suppose we may find an opening further down the mountain," Jon suggested. He turned and began walking and sliding down the slope, holding onto small tree trunks as he descended. The others followed. He stopped at the edge of another drop off that fell eight feet before the mountain returned to a gradual slope.

José lowered himself down the rock to the ground below. He walked several feet to the right, stopped at the edge of a boulder and whistled. Jon saw his friend aim the flashlight at something and disappear. It took a few minutes, but the group worked their way down the rock and over to where they'd last seen José.

"It's a cave, all right," Lacy said as she peered around the boulder into the darkness. "José?"

Jon looked at the boulder and saw a slit behind it big enough for someone to slip through. He couldn't believe José stepped into a cave like that without a second thought. His friend had guts.

A beam of light reflected off the cave wall, and José's face appeared in the opening behind the rock. Spider webs covered his hair.

"Guess what's in this tunnel," José said, unable to hide his smile.

"A mermaid covered in rubies?" Jon joked.

"Don't you wish? It is interesting, however. You'll need your flashlights, and don't forget to duck a little. I don't think this passageway was made for tall Americans."

Kerrick and Lacy dropped their packs to the ground and dug for their lights as Jon slipped behind the boulder and stuck his head back out.

"It should be okay to leave your packs by the rock," Jon suggested. "We won't be long."

Jon, Kerrick, and Lacy stooped and followed behind José as they crept through the darkness. Jon flashed his light on ancient marks revealing someone's great effort in creating the tunnel. José suddenly stopped, and Jon bumped into his back.

"Sorry about that. I didn't see your brake lights."

"Look," José said as he lit the floor of the tunnel.

Jon followed the beam to a set of steps winding down into the darkness. On the left side of the first step was the same stone symbol they'd seen earlier. *Spirit travel?* "How far down did you go, José?"

"Just a few steps. I figured you'd want in on the discovery."

Lacy squeezed beside Jon and looked down at the steps. "They look pretty steep to me. And no handrails."

Jon laughed. "We'll go slow. José, if anything looks dangerous, we'll turn back."

Though the steps were made for smaller feet, they were expertly carved into the stone. The tunnel had been protected from rain and the steps showed no signs of erosion. Jon noticed places in the wall that had probably held torches for the Nahuas. This cave had to be the place Bluetooth's guy had written about. They wound down through the darkness with only the light from their flashlights. The air was damp, but they could breathe easily.

The thought of climbing back up the stairs did not appeal to Jon. He had no idea how far they'd come, but the stairs continued down. José stopped when a path split off to the right. Everyone stood in silence staring at the steps below them.

Lacy cleared her throat and whispered, "Gold."

"I think we've found Bluetooth's city," Kerrick said in a reverent whisper.

"El Dorado," José muttered.

"Is it okay to keep going down the steps?" Lacy asked. "I've got to know what's at the bottom."

Jon slipped past José and stood on the first golden step. He could tell the tunnel turned to the left. "I'm sure people walked this way two thousand years ago. Just stay close, and let's go slowly."

They descended another ten feet or so, and the tunnel opened to what seemed to be a large room. The others came and stood beside Jon as their flashlight beams danced across the surface of water. A lake.

"Is that really…" Lacy stalled unable to continue.

"It looks like a golden lake," José said. "I read something about this phenomenon deep inside volcanoes. Something about water being forced up through geothermal energy sites pushing gold and silver into pools deep under the ground."

Lacy found her voice. "Is that really gold?" She motioned to the water where mist rose into the air, like steam from a hot bath.

Jon knelt and touched the water. "It feels like my bath water, and it looks like the water is clear." He scooped some water and let it drain from his hand. "The gold is on the bottom, so it makes the water look gold. I see silver in there, too."

"Unbelievable," Kerrick said. "The scroll said something about a lake of gold. Didn't it?"

"It did," Jon agreed.

Lacy reached into the hot water and picked up a golden nugget. "We've found it. The city of gold. So, that means all of the other things we read about in the scroll are here?"

"I suppose we can assume that to be true," Jon agreed. "I'm for exploring, but it makes me a little nervous walking through these tunnels with only flashlights. We should at least have rope."

"I've read stories about people dying in caves like this just because they got lost and turned around," Kerrick added.

"I've got a short rope in my pack, and if we need it, we can probably find a longer rope back at Santa Marta," Jon said. "I hate to stop exploring, but I don't want us to have regrets later."

"I won't call it a regret, but I'm dreading the climb back up to our packs," Kerrick said, "I'm starving, though, so lunch will be a good motivator."

Lacy stood and dropped the gold nugget into Kerrick's hand. "You mean to tell me we are standing at the edge of a golden city that's been lost for 2000 years, and all you can think about is food?"

"I've got one or two other things on my mind," he said staring into her eyes.

The light was dim, but Jon thought he could see Lacy blush. She dipped her head, and Jon grinned. Kerrick was good. He knew how to change the conversation with a few well-placed words.

"Okay." Jon stood and cleared his throat. "We can survive a little while without lunch, but it's foolish to proceed without rope. We shouldn't have come down the steps without it. I just wasn't thinking."

Lacy started climbing the stairs. "I'll get your pack."

"We'll go back up," Jon insisted. "We should probably get all of our packs. I'd hate for an animal to get into our stuff."

Though Lacy was several steps ahead, they trudged up the stairs, with Jon bringing up the rear. It made Jon think of climbing the steps of the Washington Monument when he was a child. This climb, however, was more like three or

four Washington Monuments stacked on top of one another.

He watched Lacy climb into the darkness. She seemed
determined to beat them all to the top. Jon's heart was
pounding. He didn't know how she could scamper up the
stairs. It was like she had something to prove. How could he
convince her she didn't have to prove anything?

As Jon rounded the last corner, he heard Lacy scream.

Chapter Thirty-two

Coatepec

Lacy screamed and struggled as she felt strong hands grab her. The man pinned her arms to her side and pulled her back from the mouth of the cave. Why had she been in such a hurry to make it back outside first? Stupid.

"Hello, Lacy," a voice said into her ear. "Nice to run into you again."

She knew that voice too well. He was supposed to be in Houston. How had he found them here?

She felt sick as Miguel's lips pressed against her cheek. She moved her head forward and brought it back with as much force as she could muster. The crack was sickening, and she knew his nose was broken.

He screamed in pain, but Miguel managed to hold onto her. She felt his grip tighten on her arm. As Kerrick, Jon, and José barreled out from the cave, he jerked a pistol from his pocket.

"Well, well," Miguel sneered. "Dr. Davenport. What a privilege. Too bad you won't live long enough to enjoy the party."

They were sitting ducks. She wanted to scream and run, but she knew she had to fight. Miguel leveled the pistol at them, which loosened his grip on Lacy. She stomped on his foot and wrestled to get out of his grasp. She elbowed his arm just as a shot rang out. *Did he miss?* She turned toward Kerrick, but Miguel's strong hand wrapped around her arm.

He threw her to the ground, but his fingernails still dug into her flesh.

Something zipped past her and pierced Miguel's chest. *A dart?* In the next instant, he was covered with them. One stuck deep into his neck.

Reaching for his neck, Miguel loosened his grip on Lacy. The pistol dropped from his hand as he fell to his knees, clawing at the darts.

Kerrick hurried to Lacy and pulled her away from Miguel. José reached for the pistol, but a well-thrown spear stuck in the ground mere inches from his hand. No one moved as a large group of men surrounded them.

Lacy stared in disbelief. She felt as if she'd stepped back in time. The men, clad only in loin cloths, held long, hollow tubes in their hands. *A blowgun? For darts?* The tan-skinned men stared silently at them.

Eyeing them, Lacy wondered if she would die next. *Nahuas?*

"Are you okay?" Kerrick whispered, as he wiped dirt from her arms.

She looked around the group to see men armed with blowguns, spears, and knives. "I'm okay." She looked down at Miguel lying on the ground. His body twitched as he stared sightless toward the sky. "Is he…"

Kerrick nodded. "Those must be poison darts."

Kerrick turned to face the men, and Lacy scanned the group of Nahua warriors. Eighteen. Her eyes landed on José and Jon. She wondered if they were formulating a plan to save them from these men, but what could they do? These warriors were dangerous and deadly. No one in her group had more than a knife, and that would be no match for poisonous darts and spears.

The men prattled on in a language Lacy didn't recognize. She looked at José to see if he was able to understand, but he also seemed clueless. *What was it Alejandro said about the warriors of the goddess? Didn't they kill trespassers?* She looked down at Miguel's unmoving body. He was dead. No doubt this time.

One of the Nahuas appeared to be in charge and gave instructions to the others. Two warriors walked toward her and Kerrick. They tied their hands and covered their eyes with blindfolds. Fortunately, Lacy could wiggle her nose and get the blindfold to slide up enough so she could see the ground at her feet. A warrior pushed her forward, and she stumbled and fell to her knees. She managed to get to her feet and started walking. She heard more grunts and sounds that had to be Jon, Kerrick, and José being pushed along the path.

She expected to slip back through the entrance to the cave, but they descended the mountain in a different direction. She fell numerous times only to be jerked back up and forced to continue. They eventually stepped onto a worn path, and it seemed as if everything became darker. *Is the jungle so deep here it blots out the sun?*

In time, the path became easy, and Lacy could tell they were walking beside the smooth rock walls of possibly another cliff face. Another smooth rock appeared on her right, and she realized they were walking into a cave. The leader called out something, and the group stopped. Through the opening at the bottom of her blindfold, Lacy saw a rock formation and tilted her head back. She gasped. *A mermaid. I can't believe it. And jewels. Oh, my God. That must be priceless.*

Someone pushed her forward, and they marched deeper into the cave. She bumped into Kerrick and realized everyone had stopped. Someone up front talked in that strange language, and another voice responded. He sounded angry, and Lacy figured he was the person in charge. Though he spoke the language, his accent didn't sound like the others.

They stood still for a while, but Lacy could hear something going on not too far away. Men grunted as if laboring or lifting something heavy. She heard the crackle of wood and smelled smoke wafting past her. She cringed and gagged as the smell changed from wood to something else. Something horrible.

She doubled over, ready to lose what remained in her stomach, but someone pulled her up straight and untied her blindfold. She blinked several times to let her eyes adjust before focusing on a most unbelievable sight.

A rock terrace wall rose behind her reminding her of the pyramids she'd seen at El Tajin. To her right was a flat altar stone, and she saw what was making her nauseous. Something burned on the altar, and Nahua men and women surrounded it kneeling and bowing. Everyone was topless. The men's loin cloths did little good as they bowed on the ground. The women wore what looked like skirts.

Trying to figure out what was burning, Lacy inspected the fire and noticed the Nahuas had removed Jon's, José's, and Kerrick's blindfolds. She felt queasy again as she saw a foot sticking out of the fire. The shoe was familiar. She'd stomped on it a little earlier. *Miguel.*

"Are you all right?" Kerrick whispered.

"Yeah. Other than being a little sick," She turned away from the grotesque funeral pyre. "I guess we now know he's finally dead."

"I'm not grieving," Kerrick said with a scoff. "He deserves whatever he's getting."

Lacy shivered as a chill ran down her back. Was it okay to wish someone were in hell? Probably not. She'd have to ask Meg. Assuming she got to see her again. "I can't believe this place. Are we going to get out of here alive?"

"We're alive so far," Kerrick said. "Let's focus on that. This place makes me think of El Tajin."

Lacy looked up and saw that though they were in a cave, the ground gradually rose to a large open area. Structures lined each side of a passageway that resembled an ancient road, and she noticed a courtyard ahead on the left. *A ballcourt. Just like at El Tajin.*

She wondered how this place had remained hidden for so long. Maybe the jungle growth kept it hidden. Of course, warriors killing anyone who got close would not make it a tourist hotspot. She remembered the earthquake and the comment Alejandro had made about rockslides. *Maybe this place has been uncovered for only a year or two.*

Lacy scanned the ancient city again, and her eyes landed on the ballcourt. Her stomach clinched as a thought entered her mind. The Nahuas had killed Miguel, but they had spared everyone in her group. *Why?*

@◆@◆@◆@◆

Jon eyed his surroundings and noted one light-skinned young man in the group. All the warriors who surrounded them were Nahuas or some other indigenous group, but this guy was taller and looked Caucasian. The warriors appeared to have stepped out of the pages of National Geographic. Strong, almost naked, standing and poised with blowguns and spears.

The white kid was different. He looked like he could have been from anywhere in Georgia. Even from a distance away, Jon thought he seemed awkward. *Maybe he's new?* Jon hoped he'd have the opportunity to meet this young man.

He figured out the head guy wasn't really Nahua either. He spoke the language, but his accent gave him away. The leader of this group was taller than the rest, though he still appeared to be a Mexican or maybe from Spain. Even from a distance, Jon could tell his skin was lighter, and his hair was jet black. The man began walking toward the spot where Jon and the others stood.

"You trespass in Coatepec," the man said in broken, accented English. "I am Patli Ilhuicamina, Chief of the Coatepec. You trespass and must pay."

"We didn't trespass into your city," Jon protested. "You brought us here blindfolded."

"You enter the most holy place. Penalty is death."

Patli said something to the warriors in the strange language, and Jon felt strong hands grip his arms. He wasn't sure what to do. Were these men about to kill them? He saw fear in Lacy's eyes as Kerrick reached for her.

Jon wondered how he led his friends—his family—into this trap? He'd been careless. He hadn't considered Miguel might still be around to cause them trouble. He hadn't imagined the possibility of this kind of danger from the native people.

Out of the corner of his eye, he saw José jump and land a roundhouse kick to the face of one of the men. In just seconds, two more men lay on the ground, and José moved toward Patli.

Jon jabbed the warrior's face behind him with his elbow and managed to disable the man standing beside him by kicking his knee. He turned toward José only to see a blow-gun pressed to a warrior's lips. "No," he yelled as he saw José reach for his neck before collapsing to the ground. *The darts. They've shot him.* Jon punched another man in the gut and reached for the neck of another, but a crushing blow to the back of his head turned his world black.

Chapter Thirty-three

Violated

Lacy watched in horror as Jon collapsed to the ground, and an army of warriors surrounded her and Kerrick. Before she knew what was happening, their hands and feet were bound with rope. She felt the hands of the warriors all over her as they hoisted her above their heads and began moving down the road away from the Chief.

"Kerrick?"

Fear and anger raced through Lacy's heart. They may kill her, but she wasn't going down without a fight. She squirmed and turned, trying to gain leverage, and they almost dropped her. She pounded one of the men in the head with her foot so hard that he stumbled, but another one took his place and grabbed both of her ankles.

She twisted her head and could see Kerrick being carried behind her. They passed by stone structures on each side of the road, and she spotted the ballcourt she'd noticed earlier. It looked like a miniature soccer field. A shiver ran down her spine.

The warriors entered a building and took them into a damp room that felt like a cave. They threw Kerrick onto the floor but carefully laid Lacy on the ground. They stood above her, staring, and she forced herself to return their looks. Their heads turned at the sound of a man's voice at the entry. Although Lacy had no clue what he said, she heard two thumps and was sure what they were—the bodies of Jon and José. *Are they alive?*

The men backed away from Lacy, and she heard a door close. The room went pitch black and the next sound she heard gave her hope.

"Lacy? Are you okay?"

"Kerrick!" she gasped. "Oh, Kerrick."

She heard him sliding toward her. "Kerrick?"

"Keep talking so I can find you."

"I'm here, Kerrick. I'm here." She felt his body bump into hers.

"Did they hurt you?" Kerrick asked.

"No. I thought they were…no, I'm fine."

"My hands are tied behind my back," Kerrick said. "Are yours?"

"Yes. They tied my hands and feet."

A sound reverberated through the room, and light shot through a crack in the door. The door scraped open, and light from a torch flooded the room. Chief Patli entered with several warriors. He stepped over the crumpled body of José and walked toward her.

She couldn't ever remember feeling such hatred toward a person. She wanted to claw his face and spit in his eyes. Her rage was growing like a volcano. She had no doubt Patli would kill them all.

Patli pulled her to her feet and brushed hair from her face allowing his finger to graze her cheek. Smiling at her, he slid his finger down her cheek to her chin. Lacy thought she might be sick. He ogled her from head to toe, like a slab of beef being inspected in the market. Wishing her hands were free to hit the creep, she turned her head away. The chief grabbed her chin and turned her head back toward him. He squeezed her chin so hard she whimpered in pain. When Kerrick tried to get up, one of the men held a spear down at his throat.

After one last leering appraisal, the chief turned and left. Helpless, Lacy stared in the dark at the closed door. She felt violated. A chill ran down her back as she lowered herself to the ground.

"I'm going to kill that man," Kerrick breathed with such hatred Lacy could almost feel it radiating from him.

"I'm fine, Kerrick. He didn't do anything."

"That man will never touch you again."

"If he does," Lacy said between clinched teeth, "I'll kill him first."

"We've got to get these ropes off. I'm going to try to get my hands onto yours. See if you can untie my ropes."

Lacy heard Kerrick grunting and wiggling into place. "I feel your hands," she said, "and I'm holding the knot. Be still."

She struggled to loosen the knot but couldn't get it to budge. Too bad she didn't have long fingernails like her friend Laura back in Georgia. She imagined clawing the eyes of Chief Patli with those fingernails.

"I can't get the knot to move at all. I'm going to use my mouth." She rolled over and moved her cheek slowly down his arms until she felt the rope. She bit down on the knot and started working it with her teeth.

Within minutes, Lacy's mouth ached, and the rope was covered with her saliva. *Did it move or was that my tooth?* She tugged on the rope again and again. She felt it give. She turned around and took hold of the knot with her hands. She pushed and pulled until Kerrick's wrists were free.

"Great job, Lace. Let me get yours loose."

As Kerrick worked on the rope binding her wrists, Lacy heard a noise coming from the other side of the room. *Is that Jon or José?* She thought José had been shot with a poison dart. She had heard two bodies dropped onto the floor of their little prison, but why would they have brought José to the prison if he were dead?

"Got it," Kerrick said, as Lacy felt the rope drop from her hands. "Untie the rope at your feet."

Lacy rubbed her wrists before focusing on her feet. When her legs were free, she stumbled across the room to where she'd seen Jon when the Chief entered with the torch. She tripped over Jon's body and fell. *Stupid. What are you thinking?* She felt around and touched his face. "Jon? Are you okay?"

She touched his neck and felt the unmistakable beat of his pulse. His hair was matted together with something sticky. *Blood. Oh, God, he's bleeding.*

Her breath caught, and she choked back tears. He was alive, but he was hurt. She stroked his face as tears rolled down her cheek. Her uncle was the finest man she'd ever known. She could honestly say the day he married her Aunt Meg was one of the best days of her life.

He had saved her life in more ways than one. It was probably because of him that she was willing to risk loving Kerrick.

"Uncle Jon? Can you hear me?"

Jon groaned and moved his head. Lacy pulled him to her and propped his head in her lap. She heard Kerrick moving around the room, looking for José, but she focused on Jon. She placed her hand against his cheek.

"Lacy?" Jon wheezed. "Are you hurt?"

"Oh, Uncle Jon." She leaned over and hugged him. Lacy loved her uncle, but she'd not hugged him many times before. That would change. "I was so afraid. Uh, yes, I'm okay. They've brought us to a room or prison of some kind. Are you all right?"

Jon lay silent for a moment. "My head's killing me. Can't see anything." It was like he was taking inventory.

"The room is pitch black, and I felt blood on your head. I saw one of those men hit you with a club."

"I can't remember."

"You tried to fight, and one of the guys clobbered you. At least they didn't hit you with one of those poison darts. They shot José."

"Where is he?"

"He's in here," Lacy said. "Kerrick? Have you found José?"

"He's over here," Kerrick's voice floated through the darkness. "He has a pulse, but it's slow."

"Those darts killed Miguel," Lacy said. "Is José going to die?"

Jon moved, trying to sit up. "Miguel was shot with a bunch of those darts. I just saw one of them go into José."

Lacy helped him sit up before moving away from him to find Kerrick and José. She could hear Kerrick breathing and got down on her hands and knees so she wouldn't trip over him. She had taken a CPR class once. Did José need that kind of help? She felt Kerrick kneeling on the ground and reached for José's wrist to check his pulse. There it is. Slow. Steady. Like he was sleeping.

As if reading her mind, Kerrick said, "Maybe the dart just put him to sleep."

"I was just thinking that."

"Here," Kerrick said. "Take my shirt. Put it under his head for a pillow."

Lacy maneuvered around José's body, lifted his head, and placed the balled-up, makeshift pillow under him.

"What are we going to do?" Lacy finally asked.

"I wish I knew." Kerrick got up and shuffled across the room. "The door won't budge. I guess I knew it would be locked."

Lacy heard Kerrick moving around the room. She knew he was checking for another way out, but she doubted he'd find one.

He plopped down beside her, accidentally sitting on her hand. "Sorry. There's no other way out."

"Just rest," Jon said from the other side of the room. "We don't know what's going to happen. We may need our energy."

Less than thirty minutes later, keys jangled in the door. Guards entered the room, one with a torch, the other with a large knife. Lacy gasped as the guy with the knife pulled her to her feet. She took a swing at him, and though a bit surprised, the guard sidestepped her fists of fury with no problem.

Someone else placed a jug of water into the room, along with a bowl of tortillas. The guards left as quickly as they had entered.

"I was afraid he was going to…" Lacy paused and sucked in air.

"He came in to cut our ropes," Jon said.

Kerrick got up and moved toward the door. "Evidently, they don't want us to starve."

Lacy, Kerrick, and Jon ate tortillas and drank water before finding a place to lie down on the floor. Kerrick pulled Lacy next to him, and she rested her head on his shoulder. She had a memory of sleeping with him in the lighthouse back at Florida Cape State Park. She'd give anything to be back there now.

Chapter Thirty-four

Brainwashed

At the sound of the door scraping on the floor, Jon jerked awake. As light filled the room, he rubbed his eyes and noticed José sitting against the wall.

He saw a lone figure standing near the door with a torch. It was the kid he'd seen when they came into Coatepec. The first thing Jon noticed was he didn't wear a loin cloth like the other men in the group. He wore jeans. This inconsistency confirmed Jon's earlier suspicion this guy was new.

"Freddy!" Lacy blurted out and jumped to her feet.

Jon stared at the young man and immediately saw Lacy was right. They'd seen the picture of Randal's brother while visiting Randal and his mother in South Kensington and had shown it to at least a hundred people since returning to Mexico.

Freddy's head jerked around as if someone had slapped him. "Who are you?"

"We came to Mexico to find you," Jon answered. He got up, wavered, but walked toward Freddy with outstretched hand. "I'm Jon Davenport. Randal worked with us this summer in the Bahamas."

Freddy looked like he'd seen a ghost, or maybe as if someone had caught him in the act of doing something wrong. His hand felt cold and wet. *Is he's nervous?*

Freddy cleared his throat. "You looking for me? Why?"

"Your mother is worried about you," Jon said. "She thinks you've joined the Cartel. Is that what this group is? Part of the Cartel?"

"No, man. This ain't no Cartel. She needs to forget about me."

Jon inspected Freddy for the first time. He couldn't remember his age, but it seemed like Betty had said twenty-something. Maybe twenty-two. He was skinny. Maybe even malnourished. He was dirty and unkempt.

If this group wasn't the Cartel, what was it? Hadn't Chief what's his name called the people Coate something?

"Where are we, Freddy?" Lacy asked.

"You are at the true center of the world. This is the capital city of Coatepec, and we are the Coatepec people, the supreme tribe of the Popoluca of Mexico. Mexico belongs to us."

His words sounded like a line from a delusional lunatic. Jon started to say Freddy was a Virginian, not Coatepec, but he decided to keep that thought to himself. Playing along, Jon said, "I've never heard of the Coatepec, and what does Popoluca mean? I didn't realize Mexico belongs to them."

"Oh, yes. The Popoluca are the true tribes of the world. We are the original tribe. Mexico was stolen from us. Chief Patli says in due time the gods will return the land to us."

"The gods?" Jon replied. "What gods?"

"Coatilcue, for one. She's the goddess of the mountain."

"I'm sorry, Freddy," Kerrick said as he got to his feet, "but I'm as much a Coatepec as you. What the heck are you talking about?"

Freddy stared at the ground before speaking. "I've not been here long enough, but I'll soon be a Coatepec warrior, which is why I came to see you. To deliver a message and work as the Chief's interpreter."

"He seemed to speak good English," Jon said. "Why does he need an interpreter?"

"Nahuatl is his native language, and he's fluent in Spanish. Since I also speak Spanish, I will speak for him."

Jon stared at Freddy, knowing the kid was misled. Jon knew for a fact Nahuatl was not Patli's native language. The man was a liar. He probably was not the true chief either.

Freddy's eyes went around the room and landed on Lacy. "Chief Patli says your coming has been prophesied."

"Me?" Lacy asked with surprise.

"Yes. He told me the prophecy states the offspring of the goddess Coatlicue will be born, and through you will come the deliverer of our people."

Lacy stared in disbelief. "Through...Wait, what?"

"Your child will be the promised one."

Lacy said through clenched teeth, "You can tell your chief he's full of..." Catching herself, she stopped in midsentence.

Her breath came out in short spurts, and Jon wondered if he should calm her down. The last thing they needed was for her to be going off on the guy who could be their one ally.

She took a deep, calming breath. "You can tell him if he's waiting on me to have a child, he's going to have a long wait. Like maybe ten years, if ever. Got that? And if Chief

Pervert thinks otherwise, tell him he's got another thing coming."

Silence enveloped them as Freddy appeared to be inspecting the dirt floor. He finally looked at Lacy and opened his mouth but shut it before any words came out.

Jon watched in silence, his emotions warring inside him. His anger near the boiling point, he had to figure out how to get everyone out of this place. He assumed a calm he didn't feel. He needed more information.

"What is this place?" Jon asked. "I mean, this room? I know we're in some ancient Mesoamerican city, but why are we locked up here?"

"This is the preparation room," Freddy replied.

"Preparation?" Kerrick asked.

"Yes. Preparation for the consummation festival." Freddy's eyes landed on Lacy again before looking back at Jon. "Before the consummation, there must be a proper sacrifice."

"What does that mean, Freddy?" Jon asked.

Freddy's gaze floated around the room before stopping on José. Jon noticed José's eyes were open. He was okay. Maybe.

"I don't know all of the details, but it has to do with the ballcourt. Chief Patli will be coming by later. I'm just to deliver the message and tell you to eat the meal provided in a little while. You'll need the strength."

Freddy placed the torch in a sconce on the wall and walked out of the room. Jon heard something drop into place, and he knew the door was secured. He imagined metal sleeves on each side of the door holding a wooden plank securing the door.

As soon as the door closed, Jon turned toward José. He noticed his friend's eyes following his movement. "How are you feeling?"

"Like I've been hit by a bull."

"José!" Lacy cried. "We were so afraid for you."

"I'm okay. I've been shot before with worse than jungle tree frog poison."

"Frog poison?" Kerrick's voice raised a bit. "I wondered what was in those darts."

"I'm guessing that's what it was," José said. "That's what was used hundreds of years ago. If this group of people is trying to play some Mesoamerican game, I assume they're using poison in those darts."

"So, you think this is a Mesoamerican game?" Lacy asked.

"Seems that way to me," José replied. "If I were a betting man, I'd say Patli has started a cult connected to the history of these people."

"I agree," Jon said. "A lot of things don't add up. For one thing, if Nahuatl is Patli's native language, I'm the King of England."

"True," José said. "His accent is not right."

"Why does Freddy need to serve as a Spanish interpreter?" Jon asked. "You speak Spanish, José."

"It's all part of the game. It's beneath the exalted chief to speak to lowly prisoners."

"Maybe. José, I guess you're fortunate you only got one dart," Jon said. "I'm thinking from the way Freddy looked at you, they want you alive for something else."

José agreed. "I had the same thought."

"What do you mean?" Lacy asked as she knelt beside José.

"Freddy said this is the preparation room," José said. "Two words caught my attention: Consummation and sacrifice."

Jon's eyes moved from José to Lacy. "He's right. There's only one of us who will need to avoid consummation. The rest of us will have to outsmart sacrifice."

Kerrick sat down beside Lacy and clasped her hand. "He said something about the ballcourts. They must have other prisoners in the place, and we're going to have to play them in one of those ancient soccer games."

Jon thought back to their trip to El Tajin. Prisoners were brought to the city and made to play the game, and the losers were sacrificed to the gods. He shivered at the thought of trying to defeat someone so he and his friends could stay alive.

"So, we win, and someone else dies," Lacy said. "Wow."

"We need to come up with a way to get out of here before any game starts," Jon said. "Freddy said *before* the consummation festival there had to be a sacrifice. That means nothing will happen to Lacy until after the game. We'll be out of here by then."

"How are we getting out?" Lacy asked.

"I haven't figured that part out yet," Jon said, "but I will."

"Uncle Jon, I need to check your head," Lacy said. "Your injury." Jon sat on the floor as Lacy cleaned his wound with water from the jug. "It's not too bad. The blood made it look worse than it is."

Jon heard a commotion at the door. Voices? A wooden latch. The door opened and Patli walked in, followed by Freddy and four more bare-chested men with spears. Lacy sat the jug down and turned while Kerrick helped José stand.

Patli's eyes roamed up and down Lacy's body. "*Bonita. Muy bonita.*"

Kerrick moved toward the chief, but José grabbed his arm as two of the warriors stepped forward.

"I know what *bonita* means, Creep," Kerrick said. "If you touch her, I'll kill you," Kerrick growled.

Patli glanced at Kerrick and laughed out loud. In defiance, he reached out to stroke Lacy's cheek. Her right fist shot out toward his face, but Patli moved like lightning and grabbed her wrist.

"Not smart," Patli said and squeezed her wrist until she cried out.

Kerrick jerked out of José's grasp and moved toward Patli, but two spears poked his chest before he could get close. Kerrick froze.

"Kerrick!" Lacy shrieked.

Patli glared at Kerrick and rattled something off in Spanish. Jon saw José's jaw clinch as he processed Patli's words. Freddy translated, "He says all he has to do is give the word, and those spears will go through you."

Jon noted Freddy's face was as white as a sheet. He was scared to death, but of whom?

"Patli spoke again in Spanish to Kerrick and laughed. Freddy translated, "Do you not think she's beautiful?"

Jon didn't know Spanish, but he knew the word *bonita* meant beautiful. Patli was making fun of Kerrick.

Everyone in the room stared at the point of the two spears. Jon knew stopping this murderous lot from killing them would take patience and discipline. He caught Kerrick's eye and silently pleaded with him to stand down.

Jon couldn't remember ever being in such a tight spot. It seemed death was imminent, but every moment they lived gave them more time to work out a plan to escape. The Chief was not going to hurt Lacy, at least not right now. Somehow, they would find a way out.

Jon thought about Meg and Carla and felt a pang of regret. He loved them so much. He had to get out of this situation for their sakes.

He looked over at José. His dear friend. They had spent most of their time together over the last couple of years, and Jon considered him closer than a brother. He loved him and knew if anyone could get them out of this situation, José could.

Patli gently cupped Lacy's cheek. He said in English, "All our little…differences will work out soon. You'll see."

Lacy spit at him, but he took a step back, and her saliva fell to the ground. He said something in Nahuatl, and four more men moved into the room. Jon didn't realize anyone else was in the hallway. The men grabbed their hands and bound them again.

Patli said something else, and Jon and José were jerked from the room. Jon knew José had the skills to take out these men. He also knew José would want to assess the situation completely before doing anything.

At the moment, the odds were stacked against them.

Chapter Thirty-five

La Elegida

Lacy couldn't believe what was happening. The Coatepec warriors pushed Jon and José out of the little room and slammed the door. Where were they being taken? Were they going to be killed?

The door opened again, and several men stepped into the room. One of them grabbed her, but she elbowed him in the gut and sent him to the ground in pain with a well-placed knee.

Kerrick punched one of the men before Lacy saw Kerrick grab his neck. She turned and saw one of the warriors with a blow gun against his lips. "No! Kerrick!"

Kerrick stepped toward the blowgun man before stumbling and falling. Two men seized Lacy and dragged her from the room.

She kicked and clawed and managed to pull a man to the ground before one of them started choking her. She struggled to get out of his grasp, but he squeezed harder before everything went black.

In the far reaches of her consciousness, Lacy heard water splashing. What was going on? Her last moment of awareness filled her mind. The man had placed his hands around her throat and choked her. He didn't want to choke her to death, just deprive her brain of oxygen long enough to make her lose consciousness. She'd heard about that practice before.

She opened her eyes and looked around the room. The two torches hanging in sconces cast eerie shadows onto the walls. The room was similar to the one she'd been in before, but now, of course, she was alone. Movement caught the corner of her eye. Maybe she wasn't alone.

"*Habla español?*" a voice floated across the room.

Lacy saw a tub in the middle of the room, and a middle-aged woman stepped forward to dump a bucket of water into it. The splashing water. *A bath. Why do they want me to bathe?* She shivered at the possibilities.

She figured if she told the woman she didn't speak Spanish, her old pal Freddy would have to come in and watch her bathe. "*Sí. Un poco.*" She did speak a little Spanish. More than a little, but now was not the time to test her limits.

Lacy didn't recognize every word the woman said next, but she knew the lady was telling her to take off her clothes and get in the tub. *I'm not getting naked in front of anyone.*

"*Necesitas al señor* Freddy?

Do I need Freddy? You've got to be kidding. "No."

Lacy removed her clothes and sat down in the tub of hot water. The woman poured water over her and began massaging her head as soap ran down her face. Lacy reached back and snatched the soap from the woman's hand. *I can bathe myself, thank you very much.*

While beginning to wash her own hair, Lacy struggled to remember her Spanish. She put together a few words, probably sounding more like a preschooler, but she made her point.

"Why am I bathing?"

Dread flooded her as she finally understood the woman's reply. The Spanish words "*la ceremonia*" and "*la elegida*" were clear to her. *The ceremony. The chosen one.*

The consummation ceremony. Oh, my God. I've got to get out of here. She started to get out of the tub. Lacy knew she could take care of this woman with one punch of her fist, but then what? She couldn't take down every warrior. If she was going to get out of this alive and help her friends escape, she needed to use her head.

What about Kerrick? They shot him, but she only remembered one dart hitting him. Just like José. *He's sleeping, Lacy. Don't go crazy.*

Lacy plopped back down into the water. She turned her head at the sound of the door opening. Another Coatepec woman walked in with a colorful dress. It was beautiful. Beautiful like a wedding dress. *Uh, not going to happen.*

Lacy's personal maid held it up for inspection. "*Para ud.*"

Of course, it's for me. I'm not a total idiot. How do you ask for a towel in Spanish? Come on Lacy.

"Uh…towel… por favor?"

The woman grabbed a towel from a table Lacy hadn't noticed. Maybe a little Spanglish worked after all, or maybe this woman knew English. Probably not. *Probably, the English word towel is close enough to the Spanish version.*

Lacy stood and wrapped the towel around her wet body. "*Otra?*" Lacy asked motioning to the towel.

The woman grabbed another towel and handed it to Lacy. She rubbed the towel vigorously over her head and looked around for her clothes. Gone. The other woman must have taken them. She eyed the colorful dress. *That will have to do.* She looked at the woman staring at her. *Do you have to stare? Can't you at least turn around? No?*

Lacy dropped the towel and pulled the dress over her head. The woman motioned to a chair and said a few words in Spanish. Lacy recognized *sit* and something about her hair. She sat down and the woman began working with Lacy's hair.

She tried to remember if anyone had ever brushed her hair. Maybe her mother, when she was a little girl, right? She closed her eyes and forced herself to review the current situation. She was going to have to figure out how to escape. Maybe, when they came to get her, she would make a run for it.

❦❦❦❦❦❦❦

Kerrick pulled himself to the wall of the empty room. What happened? Oh, yes. The dart. Where was everyone? He remembered Jon and José being taken out, and then they came back for Lacy. He tried to get to his feet, but he had no energy and collapsed. He had to find Lacy.

He crawled over to the jug of water. Whether or not the water was clean enough to drink crossed his mind, but he guzzled it anyway. He ate a tortilla and sat near the door, waiting for his opportunity. When someone opened the door, he was going through it.

What were they doing with Lacy? Was she scared to death? No, not Lacy. She was tough. If he knew her, she had mouthed off at them, maybe even decked a few of them.

He sat up straight as a thought entered his mind. *Consummation! What if the chief has already...No! Not yet. Freddy said the game came first. The sacrifice. Maybe, they took Jon and José to see the other team.*

An hour or more passed before Kerrick heard someone on the other side of the door. He crouched as close to the door as he could. He still felt a little off, but he prepared to attack.

The door scraped against the hard floor, and Coatepec warriors pushed Jon and José through the opening. The two men crashed into one another, falling to the floor. A woman entered and sat a flat piece of wood on the ground. A pot of refried beans and more tortillas sat on the word, still warm. She quietly exited the room, and the door slammed shut.

"Jon!" Kerrick cried out. "José! What's going on? They took Lacy."

"Are you okay?" Jon asked.

"I got one of the frog darts," Kerrick said. "I still feel a little out of it, but I'm okay. They took Lacy away right after making you leave."

"Patli said she was being prepared for the ceremony," José said.

"What does that mean?"

Jon sat down on the floor against the wall, grabbed a tortilla, and scooped up some beans from the pot. "We have no idea. You guys should eat."

Kerrick looked at the food and shook his head. "I don't feel like eating. Did you see the other team? I mean, the people we have to play against in the game?"

Jon turned and looked at José. "It's not going to be that way, Kerrick," he finally replied.

"What do you mean?"

"We are the team," Jon said. "Both of them."

Kerrick stared at Jon. What did he mean? Both of them?

"José and I have to play each other. The loser will be sacrificed."

"You're joking, right?"

"I wish. I don't think the rest will be released, however. Patli said everyone else will be set free in the jungle, but we know for a fact he plans to keep Lacy. I don't think any of us have a chance of getting out of here alive unless we escape. Only problem is, we can't escape without Lacy, and there's no telling where she's being held."

"This is crazy!" Kerrick shouted. He paced back and forth and continued ranting. "These people are insane. When is this contest? How much time do we have? I'm so messed up. I don't even know what day it is."

Jon looked at his watch. "Well, we've been here almost twenty-four hours. We know the contest is in two hours. They took us to the ballfield and showed us how to play."

"Jon, we can't play along with this insanity," Kerrick insisted.

"We're not planning on it," Jon assured him, "but we have to cooperate until we can figure out a way to escape. Patli told us the court would be lined with armed warriors. He said if we tried to escape or didn't play the game, you would be killed first, and then, José and I would go next." He looked down at the ground. "They'd keep Lacy because she's the chosen one."

"The chosen one?"

"Yes. He says her coming was prophesied. She's supposed to be the mother of the promised one."

"The mother?" Kerrick turned and faced the wall before looking back at Jon. "This guy is crazy! Who's the father? Never mind. Patli! Right? That little—"

"Kerrick!" Jon interrupted. "We're not going to let it get that far. Patli said we're to play the game this evening, and the sacrifice will happen in the morning."

Kerrick thought back to their visit to El Tajin. He remembered seeing the ballcourt and the sacrificial altar. He also remembered the guide telling them the sacrifice was done by beheading with a machete. He felt sick.

José joined them and dropped down beside Jon. He reached for a tortilla. "Kerrick, I think our best option is to go along with the game and figure out where they're keeping Lacy. I'm sure they'll bring us something else to eat after the game, and we can make a move at that point."

"I agree," Jon said. "Hopefully, they'll drop their guard a little. We'll have to overpower the warriors without being shot by those blowguns."

"Easier said than done," Kerrick replied, rubbing the sore spot on his neck.

An hour later, the door scraped open. Coatepec warriors filled the room. They moved behind Jon, José, and Kerrick and tied their hands. Kerrick knew José could take out several of them with his feet, but the Spaniard didn't seem to have immediate plans to do that.

They were led through the dark passageways of the inner parts of the ancient city. Now and then, Kerrick noticed carved structures that appeared to be a mix of stone, gold, and silver. He saw the sparkle of jewels for eyes or necklaces.

After a few minutes, he realized they were out of the cave and marching under the thick canopy of jungle growth. Somehow, this whole city was hidden away in the jungle, but how? Had Patli used something man-made to hide the place or had something natural covered it up? He saw stones piled along the sides of the road and around buildings.

Who were Patli and these crazy people? He knew the answer.

This group was a cult. They were worshipping this strange goddess and killing people without a second thought. Freddy was caught up in it, and now, they were all going to die.

Not if he could help it. He had to live. He had to save Lacy. They all had to get out of this mess.

The guards at the front stopped. Kerrick looked and saw the ballcourt ahead. It looked so much like El Tajin. The sides of the rectangular court were lined with stone terraced seating, and Kerrick saw the Coatepec people arriving for the show. In the center of the terrace to the right was a prominent seat, and Lacy and Freddy stood next to it. She wore a colorful, indigenous dress and had flowers in her hair.

One of the warriors grabbed Kerrick by the arm and pulled him to a pole at the end of the field. Someone cut the ropes around his wrist and retied his hands and feet around the pole. He realized he had no hope of escaping. Patli made sure he would have a front row seat to watch the game.

Chapter Thirty-six

The Game

Lacy gasped as she saw Kerrick thrown to the ground and tied around a pole. *What are they doing to him?* "You, let him go, you creep," Lacy said to Patli, who had taken a seat beside her.

Patli laughed and inspected Lacy from head to toe. She shook with rage. If she could get her hands on this man…As if reading her thoughts, Freddy grabbed her arm.

"Don't do anything stupid. It's all prophecy, Lacy. You didn't come here by mistake."

"You're delusional," Lacy said through gritted teeth. "Just like the rest of them. I'll kill you, too."

"Don't try it," Freddy said as he nodded toward armed warriors surrounding the court. "If you try to touch the chief, you're dead."

Lacy looked around and saw men with blowguns and spears at the ready. One guard was only five feet away with a spear pointed in her direction. *Surely José has a plan. They're not just going to go along with this craziness.*

Chief Patli stood and began some kind of incantation. Men in long, black robes lit fires at each corner of the field, and all of the people began to chant. This blood-thirsty game was not their first. Wearing colorful masks that looked like a bird's head, the men danced around the fire chanting something Lacy couldn't understand. She thought they must be the priests of this crazy cult. The chanting of the crowd grew louder and louder before Patli waved his hand, and the people became silent.

One of the priests climbed to the top of the hill behind the opposite side of the stadium. For the first time, Lacy noticed something large covered by a cloth. The priest grabbed the cloth and pulled it aside. She gasped when she saw a huge stone head with golden eyes. The dome of the carved head was also made of gold.

Chief Patli began a short speech that brought about cheers from the crowd. A man beside the chief turned toward Lacy and Freddy and translated it to Spanish. Lacy could understand some of it, but Freddy began to translate.

"May the gods be honored today with this act of obedience and sacrifice. I call to the gods of the earth, the wind, the fire, and the rain. I cry out to Coatilcue, the goddess of the mountain. You've blessed us by bringing the mother of the promised one. We sacrifice today in celebration of his consummation. Now, may the blood of the loser of this game bring us the favor of Coatilcue."

Patli turned to the field and shouted something in Nahuatl. He didn't bother to translate it into Spanish, but Lacy saw a ball thrown onto the field. It was smaller than a soccer ball. She watched as Jon kicked it to José who deflected it with his hip.

Lacy knew Jon was an excellent soccer player, and she'd heard him speak of José's skills on the field as well. She had no idea who would win this game and couldn't believe this whole scene was happening. To her surprise, Jon fell to the ground as José knocked the ball to a ring affixed to the side of the court. It was like a stone basketball hoop turned sideways. The ball hit the wall and bounced up into the crowd. The crowd cheered. *These people are crazy.*

One of the robed men threw the ball back onto the field. Lacy watched as Jon and José knocked the ball around several times. José fell to the ground as Jon kicked the ball, missing the goal by at least fifteen feet. Lacy was stunned. She'd seen her uncle kick a soccer ball at a soda can on the deck rail of the Pirate's Cove house. He knocked the can off in one try. Perfect aim. How had he missed this time?

A priest threw the ball back to the middle of the field, and once again, the two men began working the ball around the court. José kicked the ball, and it flew up into the stands again.

Lacy stood up and stared down at the field. *He meant to do that. He meant to miss. And so did Uncle Jon. They're both trying to lose.*

Fifteen more minutes of play passed, but Jon and José didn't improve. They were both terrible, and Lacy knew it was on purpose. She looked at the chief. He wasn't fooled.

Patli stood and shouted something to the men surrounding the field. One of the priests grabbed the ball and turned to face the chief.

Freddy stood beside her and translated as Patli shouted a warning. "You both must want to die."

He was right. Both men were trying to lose. Why? They were trying to lose so their friend could live. Tears filled her eyes. *Why are you trying to lose? We're going to escape. Do you not believe we'll get away?*

She focused on Freddy as he translated again. "We will change the rules. The one who wins will die as a sacrifice."

Freddy was stunned as well and sat down beside Lacy. "They're trying to lose aren't they," he said.

"It appears so," Lacy answered.

"I don't understand. Why does your uncle want to lose?"

Lacy turned and looked toward the field. Jon and José were talking in the middle of the field as the priest walked toward them with the ball. Lacy looked back at Freddy. "Because my uncle loves his friend."

"And José loves your uncle," Freddy said.

Tears flowed freely down Lacy's face again. "They're closer than brothers. Uncle Jon will gladly give his life for José."

Freddy sat down. He didn't understand what was happening.

"Freddy, you know we will not be set free, regardless of who wins or loses. Why are you going along with this craziness?"

"Chief Patli don't lie. You will stay, but the others will go."

The priest backed away from the two men and play resumed, but the game had changed. They were transformed by the new rules, and Lacy watched unbelievable moves. Just when José was about to score, Jon hurdled himself through the air and touched the ball with his fingertips, causing the ball to miss. After another ten minutes of play, Jon scored a point.

Jon and José appeared to be losing strength, but they refused to give up. Thirty more minutes flew by, and both men were covered with dirt and sweat. Jon's arm was bleeding, and blood ran down one side of José's face. Jon's wound on his head from earlier looked like it was bleeding again. Chief Patli stood and called for the four priests to move onto the field. *Is the game over? Did Jon win?*

The whole court seemed to be spinning as Lacy sat down and put her head in her hands. On the edge of her mind, she heard José shouting something, but nothing registered. She looked up to see a warrior unmoving on the ground, but several more restrained José. To her shock, one of the warriors stood beside Kerrick with his spear raised.

"No!" Lacy shouted. "What are you doing?"

José knelt on the ground, and everything became clear. José had begun to fight the warriors, and they threatened to kill Kerrick. Just like that. José could have taken out ten of those men, but he refused to endanger Kerrick.

Lacy froze as Jon turned to look at her. He said something, but she didn't understand. She cupped her ears and leaned toward the field.

"Tell Meg I love her," he shouted.

Several men grabbed his arms and tied him up. One of the Coatepec warriors grabbed her arm and led her away. She fought him and screamed every Spanish curse word she'd ever learned. The man grabbed her and threw her over his shoulder. Her foot was free, and she landed a few blows to his abdomen before another man grabbed her feet. The two carried her off.

Lacy looked back toward Patli and saw Freddy staring at the field. It was clear he had no idea about true sacrifice or real love.

❖❖❖❖❖❖❖

Coatepec men pushed Kerrick and José into their room and slammed the door behind them.

"What are we going to do?" Kerrick asked. "We can't let them kill Jon."

"We won't," José answered. "The problem is the blowguns, but we can surprise them before they have a chance to get us with the darts."

"What do you mean?"

"They will be coming to the room at some point tonight to bring us something to eat. You sit in plain view, but I'll sit here by the wall. In the past, only one person brought food in, but at least one other was outside in the hallway. I'll let the person come in with the food and take him out. If others come in, I'll deal with them, but I may need some help if one of them has a blowgun."

Kerrick tried to remember whether someone else was in the hall. Probably. Regardless, they wouldn't send anyone to the cell unarmed. He couldn't imagine how he would stop a man with a blowgun, but he would try.

"I'll do my best," he promised.

Kerrick thought back to being in the arena and watching them carry Lacy off. Where did they take her? He had no idea how to find her, but they couldn't wait around any longer. He'd go to every room in this place if he had to.

What about Jon? They must have him locked up somewhere. But why? They were supposed to kill him in the morning, but that wasn't going to happen. No way.

Kerrick thought back to José and Jon going onto Coral Cay to rescue Lacy. Jon didn't hesitate to risk his life. Kerrick would now do everything in his power to save Jon Davenport.

"How will we find Lacy and Jon?" Kerrick asked.

"I'm not sure, but we will," José assured him. "Hopefully, whoever brings us dinner will speak Spanish. We'll make him tell us."

Kerrick had no doubt José could make someone release information. José could be quite persuasive, and this wouldn't be the first time he had forced someone to reveal a secret. He had served in an elite Spanish military group and had ways of getting information

Kerrick sat down against the wall opposite the door. He didn't know what would happen. This may be his last night on earth, but he would die trying to save Lacy and Jon. If he had to, he'd give everything so they could live.

Chapter Thirty-seven

Serious Talk

Meg sat up in bed with a jerk. Her mind was fuzzy, but she knew something was wrong. Had she been dreaming? She checked the clock. Midnight. She'd been asleep for only a little over an hour. Had Carla cried out? Meg threw back the covers and peeked in on her little girl. Sound asleep.

She returned to her room and looked around. Her eyes landed on the empty side of the bed. She'd waited for Jon's phone call all day, but it never came. It wouldn't be the first time he got busy with something and failed to call. This time, however, Meg was unsettled. She'd chided herself all evening for being a worry wart, but Jon and the others should be back by now.

Don't worry, Meg. You know worrying doesn't help. Her pastor once said, "Don't worry about anything; pray about everything." He was right. Most of the things she'd worried about in the past never happened; however, this situation seemed different.

Her mind went back to the last phone call she received from her first husband before he was killed in Afghanistan. She remembered feeling a sense of foreboding then, too. A shiver ran down her spine, and fear began to grip her. *Don't worry about anything; pray about everything.*

Meg sat down on her bed. She bowed her head and poured her heart out to God. Tears rolled down her cheeks as she thanked God for His gifts. Jon was certainly a gift.

She entrusted her husband into His hands, the best place for him to be.

She believed in prayer. She'd found great comfort through the years when she talked to God about the things on her mind. Her silent phone was on her mind, and the potential of Jon being in danger tormented her. *He'll be okay. He always is. Come on, Meg. You're being dramatic. He's probably laying back in a hammock having the time of his life. He'll call tomorrow on his way home.*

Meg smiled to herself. *Home. I'm not even at home.* The thought crossed her mind that her home was with Jon. Location didn't matter. Jon and Carla were home. She just needed Jon to come back. She laid her head on the pillow and closed her eyes. If she hadn't heard from Jon or the others by tomorrow, she'd alert Alejandro.

@◆@◆@◆@◆

Jon sat on the floor of his room grateful the guard left an oil lamp burning. He stared at Meg's necklace he'd been carrying in his pocket the whole time. How had Patli's men missed it? They took everything else.

A small prism danced on the wall behind him as light reflected off the small diamond. Poor Meg. He loved her so much, and it broke his heart to think he may not see her again. She would be devastated. And Carla. Oh, Carla. She would grow up without a father. He brought the diamond solitaire to his lips. He would do everything in his power to get away. If he couldn't get away, he'd trust God to take care of his family.

He turned in time to see Freddy step into his room. Jon stuffed the necklace into his pocket. He looked at his watch and saw it was eleven fifty-three. How long had he gone without sleep?

Just before Freddy pulled the door closed, Jon saw at least two armed men in the hallway. Dealing with Freddy would be easy. Could he handle two men with spears or blow guns? What if there were more than two?

Jon noticed Freddy had food and water, which he sat on the floor. "I figured you'd want something to eat after the game. I'm sorry it took me so long."

"Thank you, Freddy." Jon looked the younger man in the eye. "You don't have to stay here and accept all this baloney about the Coatepec people. Patli will be caught, and you will be put to death with his cronies."

"Chief Patli is a good man, a holy man."

Jon looked down at the pot of refried beans and tortillas as his stomach growled. He rolled up a tortilla and scooped up some of the beans. As he chewed, he thought about how to approach this subject. Freddy was deceived, and Jon knew he needed to help him see it.

"Why did you come to Mexico, Freddy?"

Freddy didn't respond for several minutes before turning to Jon. "Looking for something, I guess. Like I had a hole in my life and couldn't fill it. I tried a lot of things. Drugs. Girls. Nothin' worked."

"I can relate," Jon agreed. "I tried a lot of things early in my life. Football was like a god to me. Girls were a close second." Jon chuckled, "Okay, so maybe sometimes girls were first."

"I heard about Los Unidos from friends in D.C.,"
Freddy continued. "I thought I'd find 'em, you know. Join
up and all."

"You realize the Cartel is about trafficking drugs and
sex? Murder?"

"I do now. I went to Mexico City and met a guy. He got
me connected. My first job was to take some girls to the border. At first, I thought it was no big deal until I saw these
girls. One of them was only nine years old. The rest were all
between ten and fifteen. They were like girls, man. I
mean…" He turned his head and stared toward the corner
of the room.

"The Cartel is evil. They destroy people so they can pad
their pockets with more money."

"I know," Freddy said. "At least I do now. I snuck away.
I couldn't go with them to the border. I thought they'd come
after me, so I went to Veracruz to hide out. I met a guy from
there, and I knew he'd help me."

"Did he?"

"Yeah. He got me to his uncle's house where I stayed
for a while. His uncle introduced me to someone else who
took me to Chief Patli."

"Why'd he take you to Patli?"

"I think he believed I could hide out here from the Cartel. He believed Patli and the Coatepec had been ripped off.
He made sense, Man. He told me how Coatlicue led his life."

"Coatlicue? The mountain goddess?"

"Yeah."

"Has she helped you?"

Freddy thought for a few minutes. "I suppose."

"How?"

"Well, she led me to Patli."

"Really? How many hikers do you suppose Patli has killed in the last year? Innocent hikers. Does that sound like a man worth following?"

Freddy didn't speak for a bit, so Jon continued to eat. He was famished. If he were going to try to escape, he'd need his energy.

"Why did you do it?" Freddy broke the silence.

"Do what?"

"The game. You tried to lose and then tried to win. If you'd have just played at first, you'd be the one being set free in the jungle tomorrow."

"For starters, I doubt Patli is setting anyone free in the jungle tomorrow. Regardless, I had no alternative."

"Man, I know José is your friend and all, but they're going to chop off your head in the morning. You know that, right?"

Jon leaned against the wall. He knew being killed was a possibility. "Freddy, it goes back to love."

"Love?"

"Yep. Love. A few years ago, I had a life-changing experience that showed me the purest form of love I'd ever seen. It happened when my first wife was sick. She was dying with cancer, though neither one of us believed she would die. For the first time in my life, I reached out to God for help."

"He didn't help you. She died, right?"

"She died, but He helped me a lot. He helped both of us. I started reading the Bible, and for the first time, I discovered what it means to love someone. That realization changed everything. I'd always been selfish and judgmental. I learned real love is selfless and giving. I was a taker, but I wanted to be a giver. I had a hole in my heart as big as Texas. My wife and I both made a decision to trust God and love like He wants us to love."

"You a preacher or somethin'?"

Jon laughed. "Nah, I'm just a guy whose life was changed. A lot of verses stick in my mind from those days. One of them says, 'There is no greater love than to lay down one's life for one's friends.' The interesting thing is the guy who said that knew he was about to die—not just for his close friends, but for every person who had ever been born and ever would be born."

"Now you gettin all religious on me."

"Nope, not religious. I think of it as a relationship. That guy who said those words wasn't just any man. He was called the Son of God. I believe that. I believe that more than I believe in a mountain range that sort of looks like a woman lying on her back."

"So, that's why you want to die?"

"I don't want to die. I have a wife and daughter I love so much. It breaks my heart I may never see them again in this life. But I also know if I die, they'll be okay. Because someone died for me many years before I was even born, the least I can do is to love the same way."

"And die for your friend."

"That's right. It's kind of tied to my purpose. I have a purpose for living, and I guess you could say I have one for dying."

Freddy stood. "This is too heavy, Man. I gotta go get somethin'. I couldn't carry it and the food at the same time."

He opened the door and left Jon alone in the flickering lamplight. Was he really going to die? If he had to, he would, but he would do everything in his power to return to Meg and Carla. He loved them so much. It broke his heart to think of her having to face the next years alone.

Emotions welled up inside, and he longed to talk to Meg, but he couldn't dwell on the fact he might never see her again. He had to figure out a way to get out of this place. He needed a plan.

The door opened, and Freddy stepped back into the room. He carried a carved mask. It looked more like a helmet. Jon examined it and saw it looked like a giant bird's head. He remembered seeing the priests wearing them before the game began. He noticed red splotches on the back of the mask. *Blood. Someone's worn that mask before.*

Freddy sat the mask on the ground and stared at Jon. He turned to leave.

"Freddy?"

The young man stopped and looked back at Jon.

"I may die in the morning, but if I die, I will know I have lived my life on purpose. I also don't believe that will be the end. You will still be alive searching for purpose. I hope you find it."

Freddy didn't say a word. He turned and walked out of the room.

Jon sat back on the ground. He needed a plan. Maybe he would die tomorrow, or maybe he would die tonight trying to escape. The odds of Patli letting José, Lacy, and Kerrick go free were nil. The problem was Lacy was being held in a different place than José and Kerrick, and Jon had no idea how to find any of them. If he somehow managed to get away from Freddy and whatever muscle awaited him in the hallway, how would he find the others before the whole place was alerted?

He bowed his head. Prayer had become an important part of his life over the last years. Although Jon didn't know what to do, he knew someone who did.

Chapter Thirty-eight

Hope

Lacy sat up on the little cot where she'd managed to doze. How long had she been asleep? *What time is it?* She looked at her wrist but remembered they'd taken her watch.

She jumped when she saw Freddy standing inside her room. She'd not heard him enter.

"You want to tell your uncle goodbye?"

"Where's he going?"

Freddy didn't reply. The silence pierced her heart. "No! You can't let them do this!"

He turned to walk out of the room, Lacy hot on his heels. When she stomped into the hallway, two men grabbed her arms. Their fierce grips made her hands grow numb. They dragged her down a corridor, taking several turns along the way. When they stopped at another closed door, two men stepped forward and removed the long wooden dead-bolt.

When Lacy stepped through the doorway, she saw Jon tied up in the corner of the room. "Jon! Are you okay?" Lacy hurried to her uncle and wrapped her arms around him. Tears spilled down her face."

"I'm fine," Jon said as she clung to him. He whispered, "Keep hugging me. I've got something to say, and I don't want them to hear."

Lacy squeezed him and began to sob.

"Lacy," Jon said into her ear. "I need you to listen. I'm going to try to get out of here, but I may not make it. You need to escape. Somehow. I don't know where José and Kerrick are, but find them if you can. If you can't, you have to figure out how to get out of here. If I don't make it, tell Meg…"

Jon's voice broke and Lacy knew he was about to cry. She'd never known her uncle to cry. Her vision clouded again with fresh tears.

"Tell Meg," he continued, "I love her, and tell Carla I love her. I'm sorry I got us into this mess. I love you, too, Lacy. I believe in you and believe you are going to make the right choices in life. Listen to Meg. She will always guide you well. She's the wisest person I know."

"Oh, Jon," Lacy murmured, "don't give up. I'm going to do everything I can to get you out."

"Lacy, listen to me. I want you to get away. Someone has to get away. Now, do as I've said."

Lacy felt strong hands clutch her and pull her away. "Jon! No. Uncle Jon." She sobbed as hopelessness filled her heart. He was going to die. "I love you, Uncle Jon, I love you."

The men dragged her from the room and carried her back to her cell. She collapsed on her cot and wept.

At least half an hour passed before she heard the door to her room, her cell, scraping open. She turned to see Freddy, again. She'd been so distraught, she hadn't prepared her attack, her escape.

"Lacy," he said quietly. "Come on."

She stepped from the room and was surprised no other guards were around. *I can take this little runt.* She thought back

to a self-defense class she'd taken during her first semester
of college. The instructor showed a video and taught them
some moves, but nothing that prepared her to attack
someone from behind. Freddy suddenly stopped, and Lacy
bumped into him.

"Listen," he whispered.

Why is he whispering? Weird.

"You gotta be quiet through this hallway up ahead.
You're being too loud."

"Too loud for what?" she whispered back. "Where are
we going?"

"To the others."

Lacy's heart and mind raced in different directions. *The
others? To Kerrick and José?* She couldn't believe it. She'd be
with Kerrick and José!

Were they all going to be killed together? Maybe they'd
know how to attack these creeps, but maybe she should try
to get away. Maybe not, if Freddy was taking her to Kerrick.
Why did he tell me to be quiet? Who is he hiding from?

They stopped at a wooden door, similar to the others,
similar deadbolt. Where were the guards? If this was the
place José and Kerrick were being held, then why wasn't the
door guarded? Maybe, they trusted the door was secure.

Freddy removed the wood, swung the door open, and
stepped inside. Lacy heard commotion inside with grunts
and pleas. She stepped into the room and saw José holding
Freddy, his hand over the skinny kid's mouth.

"Kerrick!" Lacy hurried over and wrapped her arms
around him.

"Lacy? How did you get here?"

Lacy noticed Freddy was no longer struggling in José's grip. "Freddy brought me. I'm not sure why. There are no other guards around."

"What's going on, Freddy?" José asked. "Can we talk?"

Freddy nodded his head before José removed his hand. Lacy knew he could yell for help, and their one good chance for escape would be gone.

"I'm going to show you how to get away," Freddy said in between gasps for air. "We need to hurry. Patli said you'll die after Jon."

"We can't leave Jon," José said.

"Don't worry about Jon. I'll take care of him. Follow me, but be quiet."

Can we trust him?

Lacy took Kerrick's hand and followed Freddy out of the room. They crept through several passageways before coming to a tunnel.

"This tunnel will wind around for a ways beneath the city, but then you'll start climbing. It empties out at a trail not far from the rim of the volcano. Follow it almost to the top and take the trail to the left. Careful, though. People will be able to see you from the city at one point on the trail."

"And Jon?" Kerrick asked. "What about Jon?"

Freddy looked at the ground for a long minute. "I said I'd take care of Jon. He'll have to come out a different way. Hurry before you're caught."

"Tell Jon we'll wait at the top for him," José said. "And Freddy, thank you."

Freddy didn't reply. Lacy hugged him and watched him walk away. She turned to see José motioning her to follow him through the tunnel.

Nearly an hour passed, and she checked her wrist for the hundredth time. She didn't have a watch. "What time is it?"

"Almost six thirty," José answered, "which means the sun's up."

The group came out of the tunnel and walked across a narrow ledge overlooking the city. Rays from the morning sun filtered through the growth overhead. Freddy wasn't kidding about being exposed to people in Coatepec. She realized if anyone happened to be walking through the city, they could look up and see them trying to escape.

Safely off the ledge, Lacy stopped and leaned on her knees. She took several deep breaths and asked José if they could stop for just a second. They walked several feet to a place where they were hidden by vegetation where Lacy sat down on a large rock.

"Shouldn't Jon be free by now?" Lacy asked. "It seems to me if Jon escaped, someone in the city would know it, and the place would be going crazy. I don't notice anyone moving down there."

Although they were high above the ancient city, they could still see the roads and structures. She peered around the edge of the growth to the main road of the city. She could see the ballcourt and was stunned to see people sitting at one end of the terraced area, not far from where she sat during the game the previous day. *What were they watching*?

She realized the people had gathered to watch the sacrifice, but she couldn't see the altar. Drums began to beat in the still morning. Lacy cocked her head and squinted through the morning light. Why were the drums beating? Would they stop when they discovered the man they were going to kill had escaped?

Lacy moved back to a spot that offered a better view. She felt the blood drain from her face when she spotted guards escorting a man wearing a giant bird-like mask. The clothes and the look of the prisoner were all too familiar, and she knew at once Freddy had not planned on setting Jon free.

"Jon!" Lacy shouted and turned toward the ledge that would take her back to the city. It took them nearly an hour to climb out, but she had to save her uncle.

Kerrick grabbed her. "Lacy! You can't go back down there."

"I've got to. We can't just let them kill him. I know that's him."

"Stay here!" José ordered. He didn't wait for a reply but sprinted toward the ledge they'd just crossed.

The drums got louder. Lacy could no longer see Jon, but she saw people rising to their feet. She jerked away from Kerrick and raced toward the ledge.

Just as she was about to reenter the tunnel, the drums stopped, and the small crowd cheered. Lacy stumbled and fell forward, scraping her hands and banging her head on a rock. Her face was wet with a mixture of tears and blood when Kerrick dropped to his knees and pulled her against him.

"Let me go. I've got to get to Jon."

Kerrick's grip tightened. "We can't save him, Lacy. I'm…" His body jerked with a sob. "We're too late."

Despite his hold on her, Lacy's body went limp, and she collapsed onto the ground. This couldn't be happening. Jon was the finest man she'd ever known. And what about Meg? She would be devastated. The crowd began to chant, and Lacy felt her whole world spinning out of control.

After several long minutes, Kerrick took Lacy's hands and pulled her to her feet. "We need to get back across the ledge while no one is looking."

She looked at Kerrick and remembered Jon's final words to her. *You need to escape. Somehow. And tell Meg and Carla I love them.* They were both right, of course, but she had no desire to leave, no desire to get away. No desire at all.

Lacy turned to look back in the direction of the altar. Kerrick tried to keep her from looking, but he wasn't fast enough. She gasped and started to crumple again, but Kerrick's strong arm tightened around her.

She didn't want to think about what she'd just seen. The Coatepec warriors had thrown a headless body onto the funeral pyre. They were about to burn Jon's body. She felt sick. This couldn't be happening.

José raced out of the tunnel. "We have to go. Men are coming up the tunnel."

Kerrick pulled Lacy to her feet, and they bolted for the trail that would lead them to safety.

Chapter Thirty-nine

Casa de las Montañas

Meg's cell phone rang as she pulled the tiny, pink shirt over Carla's head. She looked at the caller I.D. and pressed the speaker button to answer. "Hey Ann. How long you been up?"

"I've been awake a while. The morning is beautiful. The butler served me coffee on the patio, and I read a while. I could get used to all this pampering," Ann said with a laugh. "You ready for breakfast?"

"Yeah. I was just finishing up with Carla. You better enjoy your quiet mornings while you still can, though you'll have to serve yourself coffee when you get back home."

"True," Ann agreed, "at least true on the enjoying the quiet while I can. My time is coming. But José serves me coffee, so I'll be spoiled even at home." Ann paused and looked at the floor. "I'm guessing you still haven't heard from Jon?"

"No, and I'm getting concerned. I don't want to be like the worry wart wife, but we should have heard from them by now. I can't fight this feeling something's not right."

"So, you think something's wrong? Oh, no. I knew I shouldn't have agreed to José going off."

"It's okay, Ann. Everything's probably fine. Don't start worrying on me."

"Didn't you just say you were worried?"

"I said I was concerned. That's different than worrying."

"Sounds like the same thing to me."

"Well, it's not. They're okay, so don't start panicking. I'll just ask Alejandro about it. I'm sure they're fine. We'll be down for breakfast in a few minutes."

Meg disconnected the call and ran her hand through her hair. She shouldn't have told Ann that she was concerned. Her best friend was beautiful and brilliant. She had many fine qualities, but she had a tendency to worry about everything.

She sat Carla down on the floor and paced across the room. She twisted the front of her tee-shirt in her hands and stopped in front of the full-length mirror near the bathroom door. She had dark circles under her eyes and looked a little pale. If she slept during the night, it wasn't much. She spent most of the night praying for Jon and the others. She knew worrying never solved anything, but it was hard not to be concerned.

Meg knelt in front of Carla and took hold of her little hands. "Do you want to pray for Daddy with me?"

Carla babbled something that Meg took for a "yes," so she bowed her head and once again asked God to give her husband strength. When she finished, she picked up her little girl and headed for the dining room.

"You look like something the cat dragged up," Ann said as Meg strapped Carla into the highchair.

"Should I take that as a compliment?" Meg asked and blew a strand of hair out of her face.

"Let's just say I think your *concern*," she gave the last word air quotes, "kept you up all night."

"Ann, you've been my best friend for a long time. You know I don't always have everything together, and I can worry just as much as the next person."

"I knew I should be worried."

"Listen, Ann. We don't need to go getting emotional and start making up horrible things we don't know are true. I'm sure there's a good explanation. I'll ask how to get in touch with Alejandro, and he'll give us some great insight."

A woman dressed in a white uniform came in through the kitchen carrying coffee cups. "*Buenos dias, señoras.*"

"Good morning, Maria," Ann replied.

Meg thought for a moment before attempting to ask her question in Spanish. "Maria, is it possible to speak with Señor Alejandro?"

When Maria replied, Meg didn't understand everything, but she understood enough to know Maria would check and let them know. Maria returned with a breakfast of eggs, refried beans, and plantains and handed Meg a piece of paper with a phone number written on it.

"Señor Alejandro no…no available," Maria said in broken English. "Phone *número de celular*, uh, cell phone." She smiled as if proud of her English.

"Thank you, Maria," Meg said. "I'll call him."

"Uh, *llámalo después de las diez y media*, uh…ten thirty, more ten thirty."

"After ten thirty?" Meg asked. "Did you say I should call him after ten thirty?"

"*Si*…yes. You welcome."

Meg smiled. "Thank you, Maria."

Ann leaned toward Meg. "So, what do we do?"

"We wait until after ten thirty and call this phone number."

"And in the meantime?"

Meg picked up her coffee cup and took a sip of the hot drink. "In the meantime, we don't worry."

The morning crawled by like a slug on a frozen pond. Meg thought ten thirty would never arrive, but the alarm on her phone chirped at ten thirty to let her know it was time to call Alejandro. Unfortunately, he didn't answer. Meg left a message asking him to call her as soon as he could.

Something wasn't right. She knew it, felt it. She pulled out her phone and dialed Jon's number again. Nothing—like the last twenty times she'd called him. At ten forty-five, she called Alejandro again and left another message as she stared out at the lawn from the back patio.

"Still nothing?" Ann asked as Meg continued staring at the yard. "Meg?"

Meg didn't say anything but shook her head slowly.

"Meg," Ann said, placing her hand on her friend's shoulder. "Are you okay?"

Meg turned to face her friend. "Uh, yes. I'm okay. And yes, I mean no. Still no answer."

"This isn't right, Meg. You know it's not. We've got to do something."

"Okay, listen, Ann. For starters," Carla started bawling as she toppled onto her hands and knees.

Meg ran over and picked up her little girl. "Oh, Sweetie. I'm sorry. Mommy wasn't paying attention."

I cannot let myself come apart. Come on, Meg. Get it together. Your little girl and your best friend need you. We've got to do something to keep us from dwelling on the negative possibilities.

Kneeling beside Meg, Ann asked, "Is she okay?"

"Yeah. She's fine. A little skinned knee, but it's certainly not the first time."

"And it won't be the last."

Meg smiled. "You want to go back to the market for a while? I'm sure Alejandro will call back shortly, but in the meantime, there was a dress I wanted to get for Carla."

"Another one?"

"I can't resist. Besides, I'll have better cell signal in town."

Nearly an hour later, while weaving through the narrow aisles of the downtown market, Meg heard her phone ring. "Hello?"

"Mrs. Davenport? My name is Sophia Ortega. I am Mr. Morales' assistant. Mr. Morales asked me to call and tell you he is in a meeting, but he will call you at three o'clock. Will that be okay?"

Meg looked at her watch. *Almost two o'clock. Only an hour longer.* "Yes. Thank you, Ms. Ortega."

"Ms. Ortega?" Ann asked as Meg disconnected the call.

Meg looked at her friend who held the stroller containing a very sleepy Carla. "Yes. Alejandro's assistant. Let's get back to the villa so Carla can take a nap. Alejandro will call at three o'clock."

At exactly three o'clock, Meg's phone rang. "Hello?" Meg put the phone on speaker so Ann could hear.

"Mrs. Davenport. This is Alejandro. I'm very sorry I've been unavailable today. I had to fly to Mexico City this morning to meet with the president. Is everything okay?"

"I'm sorry to bother you, Alejandro. Everything is probably fine. It's just that…well, I haven't heard from Jon in a few days. More like four. I'm starting to get a little…" Meg looked up at Ann. "A little concerned."

"Oh, Mrs. Davenport. I'm sorry. You should have interrupted me this morning. Didn't they go off to Catemaco?"

"Yes. They went across the lake and spent the night at The Reserve. The last time I talked to him was when they were near Santa Marta."

"The village or on top of the mountain?" Alejandro asked.

"The village. Cell service was bad, but he called from above the village. He told me they were going to spend the night in the village and maybe hike up Santa Marta or go toward The Goddess."

"If they hike The Goddess, it's more than a day's hike from Santa Marta. It's true cell service is very bad in that area, but I'll have some men fly around to see if they can find them. They may be able to land near Santa Marta and look for them in the village. We'll find them, Mrs. Davenport."

"Thank you, Alejandro. It's probably nothing. I'm just starting to get a little worried." Meg's eyes rose to meet Ann's. Her face was ashen as she bit her bottom lip.

"What are we going to do?" Ann asked as Meg laid her phone on the table.

Meg took Ann's hands and stared into her eyes. "We're going to wait here for a phone call and trust they are okay.

Ann, you've got to tell yourself that José is fine. Don't create a crisis until there is one."

"You're right, Meg. I just can't help but think of all the things that could've happened."

"I know, but don't think that way," Meg insisted. "Remember there might be one hundred reasons why they haven't called yet, and only one of them is a crisis. I've always held onto two words when I'm afraid: trust and believe."

Ann's hand rested on Meg's shoulder. "You're so strong, Meg. I need to be more like you."

Meg turned her head and caught her reflection in a mirror. The image she saw didn't look strong. She looked scared to death.

Ann stayed with Meg all night, and neither one slept much. Meg constantly checked her phone to make sure she hadn't missed a call or a text. She knew that sometimes text messages went through when phone calls didn't. Maybe Jon couldn't call but would text. So far, nothing.

They heard a knock, and Meg hurried to open the door. A woman dressed in white rolled a cart into the room with coffee, fruit, and sweet bread. Meg figured Alejandro must have had breakfast sent up to her room.

"*Muchas gracias*," Meg said.

Eating was the last thing on Meg's mind, but coffee might help. As she lifted the cup to her lips, her phone split the silence just as Carla called from her room.

"Hello," Meg said with a tremble in her voice. She debated for a split second whether or not to put her phone on speaker but knew Ann needed to hear everything. She touched the speaker icon.

"Mrs. Davenport? This is Alejandro Morales."

"Alejandro. Have you found them?"

"My pilot just called and said they've spotted some hikers in the jungle heading toward Santa Marta."

"Oh, thank God. Are they okay?"

"He told me a man was carrying a woman with blond hair. It's possible she's injured. My men are searching for a place to land and said they'd get back with me as soon as possible. I'll call you back as soon as I know more, but I'm about to board a plane. I will have access to a phone for most of my flight."

"Should we go to Catemaco?" Meg asked.

"No. I'll have them flown back to the villa. I'm leaving Mexico City, now. I'll be at the villa in a little while."

As Meg hung up, tears flowed down her cheeks. Carla began to cry out from the adjoining room.

"So, Lacy's hurt?" Ann asked.

"Sounds like it."

"Didn't he say a man was carrying a woman? Why didn't he say three men, and one of them was carrying a woman?"

"I'm sure that's what he meant," Meg said as she rose to get her little girl.

Chapter Forty

Despair

Meg heard a helicopter landing outside and rushed to the window of her room. She saw Alejandro scrambling from the helicopter toward the villa. Ann moved toward the bedroom door as Meg grabbed Carla and followed her.

"Have you heard anything?" Meg asked, winded from their sprint downstairs.

"They should be here shortly," Alejandro said. "I just spoke with the pilot a little while ago. He landed and some other men were going after them."

"Are they all there?" Ann asked. "I mean, you said the pilot saw a man carrying a woman. He didn't say anything about three men and a woman."

Alejandro opened his mouth to answer and paused. "I didn't ask if they were all there, but I assume so. I told the pilot to get them here as quickly as possible and to stand by in case…" he looked at Meg. "What is your niece's name? It appears she has an injury."

"Lacy. Her name is Lacy."

"Yes. Lacy. I told the pilot to stand by in case we need to take her to the hospital."

Alejandro's helicopter lifted into the air and flew north. Meg figured it left to make room for the other helicopter. She returned to the dining room table as an attendant served more coffee and pastries. Meg had no appetite.

She flashed back to when an army officer and chaplain came to her door years ago to tell her Steve had been killed in combat. Her first husband was adventurous and daring just like Jon. She knew dread and fear would swallow her if she gave into them. She had no reason to think something like that happened to Jon.

She had to control her emotions. She wouldn't be a babbling, emotional mess when Jon returned. She had blown this whole thing out of proportion. Lacy was injured, and they took longer to get back. That's all.

Meg had never known Lacy to be so accident prone, but this injury was Lacy's third one in the last three months. Of course, Miguel was responsible for the first two, so maybe Lacy shouldn't be blamed.

Nearly thirty minutes later, Meg jumped to her feet when she heard another helicopter overhead. She raced to the door and looked out to the landing pad. Ann came to stand beside her, Carla on her hip.

As soon as the helicopter was on the ground, the side door opened and Kerrick jumped to the ground. He turned around to take Lacy in his arms, but she slid from the helicopter to land on one foot. Kerrick slipped his arm around her waist to help her limp toward the house.

José came out next and ambled toward the house. *Where's Jon?* Meg looked for him to jump down next, but one of the soldiers closed the door.

Her heart sank.

The wind from the helicopter's rotors whipped around Lacy's head as she tried to put weight on her sprained ankle. After discovering Coatepec men were coming after them, they ran for at least two miles before she tripped and fell. José hid them in the brush just as the men charged by. It turned out Lacy's sprained ankle may have saved their lives.

Trying to take a step on her injured leg, she groaned in pain until she noticed Meg. She locked eyes with her aunt standing on the patio of the villa. Meg stood frozen, studying them. Expectant. Confused. Suspicious.

How could Lacy tell her aunt Jon was gone, that she was a widow for the second time? Tears made it impossible for Lacy to focus.

She felt Kerrick's strong arm come around her as José stepped to her other side. They were there for her. She glanced at them both, their expressions unfaltering, stable.

Not so with Meg. Looking back toward the house, Lacy saw the stricken look on her aunt's face. She knew.

One of Alejandro's attendants from the kitchen stepped up beside Ann and took Carla into her arms. Ann hurried across the yard into José's embrace as Lacy hobbled toward Meg. She had to tell her what had happened, but how?

Before Lacy got to the patio, Meg took two steps backward and lowered herself onto a wicker loveseat. Lacy's face twisted and another sob escaped her lips as she stepped onto the patio. "Aunt…Aunt Meg." Sitting down beside Meg, Lacy wrapped her arms around her aunt and wept. She could hear faint, whimpering sounds coming from the woman she loved more than anyone else in the world.

"He's not…" Meg stopped as she shook with a sob. "He's not…coming back?"

"Mama?" Carla said as Meg began to cry.

@♦@♦@♦@♦

Lacy looked toward the steps leading up to Meg's room. Meg had been closed up in there for over an hour. Although Alejandro's cook prepared a huge meal, none of them ate much, and Meg excused herself early.

Poor little Carla. She was so confused. Lacy knew there was no way her cousin understood what was going on, but the little girl knew her mother was upset. When Ann laid her down for a nap, Carla eventually cried herself to sleep. Lacy had cried so much that she thought she had no tears left.

Earlier, they each gave their versions of the story to Alejandro and a couple of military officers who flew in from Veracruz. Even before all of the details of the last few days came out, one of the officers was on his phone relaying orders to someone. Lacy picked up a few of the Spanish words and understood he was readying soldiers to go find Coatepec.

When José told how Jon died and how they saw his body burning, Meg lost it. Lacy had never seen her aunt lose control, and she couldn't bear watching her in such pain. She held Meg in her arms, and they both fell apart. They all fell apart.

As José, Kerrick, and Lacy described Coatepec to Alejandro, Alejandro found it hard to believe that no one had discovered the city before. One of the officers pointed out the city may have been hidden until the earthquake a few years earlier, or maybe until after tremors later caused rock-slides in the area.

"What do we do now?" Ann asked, bringing Lacy out of her thoughts.

Alejandro placed his coffee cup down on the table and cleared his throat. "Our men are moving toward Coatepec now. The jungle was too dense to land helicopters, but they should be in the area shortly. They'll arrest the whole bunch. How many people did you say were there?"

"Probably fifty or sixty," Lacy said. "Maybe more. We didn't see everyone."

"Are you sure about the golden statues and jewels? And the lake of gold?" Alejandro asked.

"We didn't see everything," José reminded him, "but we saw a number of treasures that has to be worth millions. I hope you warned your officers of the find. That much gold can make a man do crazy things."

"Evidently," Alejandro replied. "This Patli character certainly went crazy."

Ann readjusted herself in the chair and turned back toward Alejandro. "I meant what do we do? As in us. Should we return to the United States? I know Meg is hoping your men will find Jon's body, but it sounds like there is no body." She stopped and took a deep breath. "No body to find."

"If you don't mind staying for another day or so, it will help us with our investigation. If you want to leave, we understand."

"I'm sure Meg will want to plan a memorial service for Jon," Ann said while trying to stifle a sob. "And we've got to get hold of his family. I don't even know how to do that."

"I have called President Johnson," Alejandro told them. "He was heartbroken and demanded we find these people. I assured him we would."

"We'll talk with Meg," José said. "She'll want to stay here as long as you need her. I'm confident she will want to help with the investigation as much as possible."

The next couple of days crawled by as more information poured into the villa, which had become a command center. When the soldiers arrived in the ancient city, they discovered it mostly deserted. A couple of men were shot while trying to escape with a golden statue of a bird, but no other people were found.

Meg decided to have two services for Jon. One would be held in Georgia and open to the public. President Johnson planned to attend, and he told her a number of dignitaries would be present. Jon had touched a lot of people through his life, so they expected a crowd at their former church in Canton.

Lacy dreaded attending the first service, but the second would be more difficult. The second service was to be held at Pirate's Cove on Great Exuma in the Bahamas. Jon and Meg loved their home; they were married there. The soldiers returned a box of ashes to Meg that everyone knew was probably more than just Jon's. She told Lacy she wanted to take the ashes to Conception Island and sprinkle them in the cave.

Tears spilled out of Lacy's eyes when Meg mentioned the cave, causing them both to have yet another good cry. The cave was the place where Meg and Jon sought refuge from a hurricane, where they hid from their kidnappers before they were married, and where they went every year for their anniversary. The cave was where Carla was conceived. Christopher Columbus had named the island hundreds of years earlier, but Jon and Meg's love for each other had given the island's name a new meaning.

At dinner, Meg announced to the group they should leave the following morning and return to Atlanta. Lacy thought she'd never be glad to return to Georgia, but she was ready to leave Mexico. She hoped never to return. This place would always carry too many sad memories.

Lying in bed that night, she found it difficult to sleep. She sat up, turned on the bedside lamp, and reached for her phone. She was fortunate to have it back. The soldiers found a bag with her phone and a few other items, but her camera was gone.

She scrolled through the phone and stopped on a picture of her and Jon. Lacy smiled at the memory of Jon telling her he loved her and believed she was going to be a wonderful, godly woman. She had laughed out loud, and now, she wondered if she was laughing at the word *wonderful* or *godly*. Neither was true. He had kissed her on the top of the head, and they'd turned for Meg to take their picture.

Her vision blurred with tears, and once again she began to sob.

Lacy had no idea how long she had been crying when she realized Kerrick was sitting on the bed beside her. "I look," she sniffed and reached for a tissue. "I look terrible." She smiled up at her wonderful man.

"You look great to me," he said and leaned in for a gentle kiss. "I heard you crying from my room next door."

"I was that loud?"

"Maybe I was just paying attention."

"To answer your question, no. I'm not okay. I don't know if I ever will be."

Kerrick wrapped his arms around her and held her. He looked at her, and she stared into those blue eyes she loved so much.

She felt loved. Cherished.

"I love you, Lacy Henderson. I hurt when you hurt, and I know you're hurting."

Another tear slipped from her eye. He reached up and brushed it away. She needed a tissue as she felt her nose running. This was about to get ugly.

"I'm sorry, Kerrick. I don't want to be such a baby, not to mention a bother."

Handing her a tissue, Kerrick brushed her cheek with his knuckles. "You're not a baby or a bother. We're going to get through this together. That's exactly what Jon would want. We're going to help Meg and Carla get through it, too. We're family, Lacy."

Lacy stared up at Kerrick. *We're family?* She leaned her head against his chest and reveled in his warmth. His love. Her idea of family for the past few years hadn't been good, but if being family included Meg, Carla, and Kerrick, count her in.

Lacy wished she could enjoy Kerrick's warmth all night, but she knew neither of them had much sleep for the past few nights. "You know, Meg would have a stroke if she knew you were in my bed."

"I'm not in your bed. I'm on it. I have a feeling Meg would want you to be comforted, and that's what I'm doing."

"You really are comforting me, Kerrick. Thank you. I could enjoy it all night long." She looked into his eyes again and felt pulled deep into his soul. "I want to enjoy it all night long, which is a problem."

Kerrick kissed her. "You're right." He pulled her to him again, held her for a moment, and slipped off the bed. "I just wanted to make sure you're okay."

Lacy held his hand, not wanting to let go of it. "You know, Kerrick, if it hadn't been for Jon, I wouldn't know you. I can't imagine not knowing you."

"I will always be grateful Jon picked me to work on his boat this summer," Kerrick said as he walked slowly toward the door. He paused and stared at her silently. His silence communicated volumes. Her heart was broken but full.

I love you, Kerrick Daniels.

Chapter Forty-one

The Silver Necklace

Settling into her seat in the first-class cabin, Meg reached over to make sure Carla's travel seat was buckled. She looked across the aisle where Lacy and Kerrick sat staring into each other's eyes. *Oh, boy. How can I make sure they save themselves for marriage without Jon helping me?* She wiped away another tear. Going home without Jon wasn't right.

She noticed Kerrick wiping Lacy's face. This ordeal wasn't easy on any of them. Poor Carla kept asking for Dada. She was so confused. The flight from Veracruz to Houston was only two hours, and then they'd head to Atlanta. They should be at her mother's house by dinner tonight, and the drama would start all over again. How would she be able to face the next few days?

The loud noise of the engine diminished. Meg had flown enough to know that was not a good sign. They hadn't even backed away from the terminal. Could it be engine trouble? They may not make it to Georgia by dinner after all.

A flight attendant stepped from behind the wall by the door and walked toward Meg. "Mrs. Davenport. Would you come with me, please?"

"What's wrong?" Meg looked toward Lacy and saw her niece unbuckling her seat belt.

"Hopefully nothing is wrong. The captain called and said we were asked to delay takeoff. Someone has a message for you."

Meg had never known a flight to be delayed for someone to deliver a message. Then again, she and her family were guests of the president of Mexico.

She turned around to Ann. "Will you watch Carla for a moment? I have to get off the plane. I'll be right back."

Meg followed the attendant to the door, Lacy and Kerrick close behind her. The stairs had been rolled back into place, and as her feet touched the tarmac, she noticed Alejandro standing at the door leading back inside the terminal.

Halfway to the terminal, she turned around and saw José coming down the steps, followed by Ann and Carla. A door on the side of the plane was open, and a baggage handler pulled her luggage out of the plane. *What is going on?* She looked back toward Alejandro and noticed his face was as white as a sheet—like he had seen a ghost.

"Alejandro? What's wrong?"

"Nothing is wrong, Mrs. Davenport. I have something I need to talk with you about."

Lacy stood next to Meg and reached down to hold her aunt's hand. "I don't understand."

A man opened the door and motioned to Alejandro to come inside.

"The plane needs to take off, so we have to go inside," Alejandro said. "We have a room down the hallway where we can talk. Follow me."

The whole group followed Alejandro back inside the terminal. He said he had something to talk about. Meg felt perplexed. What else is there to talk about? Maybe they'd found Patli. Finding the chief would be great, but it wouldn't bring

Jon back. She saw Morales stop at a door halfway down the hallway. He held it open for everyone to step inside a small, comfortable room.

"Sit down, Mrs. Davenport. Everyone sit down."

@◆@◆@◆@◆

Meg sat down and Lacy sat beside her. Lacy slipped her hand into Meg's and squeezed to give her aunt reassurance. Meg's hand was shaking. Her whole body was shaking. Lacy looked up at the Mexican official. "What's going on, Mr. Morales?"

Alejandro pulled a chair up and faced the small group. "I received a phone call from a clinic in Tatahuicapan last night. Actually, my phone call was from the president, but someone contacted his office from this clinic."

"Tatahuicapan?" Meg asked.

"It's a small village southeast of Catemaco, not far from the Gulf. Someone arrived at the clinic last night with a badly injured man. They are transporting him to the hospital in Coatzacoalcos, a large port city."

Lacy felt like her heart was about to beat out of her chest. She looked at Meg who appeared to be in shock. Poor Meg. Lacy knew what she was thinking: Jon. It couldn't be Jon. They'd seen his body burning. Maybe the injured man was Patli.

Tears streamed down Meg's face. "Is it Jon?"

"We don't know, Mrs. Davenport. As I said, he's badly injured. He's not conscious, and his face, well…his head is…well, injured. We think he is American, but he has no papers to identify him."

Lacy tried to figure out what Morales was saying to them. Someone had been beaten to a pulp and left him for dead, so badly he was unrecognizable?

"Some young men found him at the river a little north of the village. It appears he had been in the river but managed to get to the riverbank. It also seems he had been lying on the riverbank for a while."

"How do you know he'd been there a while?" Kerrick asked.

"For one thing, his clothes were dry. His body is also covered with sores from bites of some kind."

Lacy jerked as if she'd been slapped. The man had been so out of it he wasn't even aware that insects or small animals had been eating on him?

Alejandro continued. "He was barely alive when they brought him to the clinic. I learned of all this last night, but you must understand. Finding injured and murdered people is…I mean, we have crime in Mexico as you do in the…"

"You must think this is Jon, or you wouldn't have taken us from the plane," José interrupted.

"Late last night, the father of these boys returned to the village. This father is an honest man. A Godfearing man. It seems when the boys found this body, they also found something with him. The boys kept it, but the father insisted it be returned to the man. I received word of this discovery early this morning, and one of my men was in Coatzacoalcos planning to return to Veracruz this morning. I asked him to bring it along."

Alejandro reached into his pocket and pulled out a silver necklace holding a single diamond solitaire. Meg gasped.

Holding the necklace out to Meg, Morales said, "I believe this is yours."

Lacy stared at the single diamond dangling from the end of a silver chain. Meg's cherished necklace.

"We don't know if this man is Jon," Alejandro continued, "or if he is someone who took the necklace from Jon. I'm sure we can find out later today, DNA and such, but I thought you may want to fly to Coatzacoalcos. I have a plane waiting."

Nearly an hour-and-a-half later, Alejandro led them toward the front door of the Coatzacoalcos hospital where they were greeted by a man in a white lab coat. He explained the condition of the man, and Lacy realized he was preparing them for what they were about to see. This injured man's face had been badly beaten, and his whole head was swollen. The doctor thought he had been physically brutalized, but he had also hit his head on rocks in the fast-moving river.

The doctor talked with Alejandro as they guided Meg, Lacy, and Kerrick to an area Lacy figured was like the Intensive Care Unit. Ann and José wanted to come, but it was best that Carla stay in the waiting area on the first floor. Lacy felt a shiver. The place reminded her of her episode in Veracruz only two weeks earlier.

They stopped in front of a door, and Alejandro eyed Lacy. He motioned with his hand for her and Kerrick to stay outside. *Not a chance.* He led Meg into a small, dark room, and Lacy and Kerrick followed.

Over Meg's shoulder, Lacy could see the swollen body of a man in the bed, tubes coming out of his body. Lacy couldn't make out his features. She needed to get a closer look.

Meg took two more steps toward the bed and choked out a sob. She fell to her knees. "Jon!"

❦✦❦✦❦✦❦✦

Meg felt weak but somehow managed to stay on her knees. She needed to get up to check on Jon, but she couldn't move. This moment wasn't real. It couldn't be, but the man lying in the bed was Jon. She didn't need to see the scar under his chin, the mole on his right side, or the tiny birthmark on his lower back. She knew her husband, and he was alive!

"Meg?" Lacy squatted beside her aunt and wrapped her arms around her. "Are you okay? It is Jon, isn't it?"

Meg heard the hesitation in Lacy's voice, but she had no doubt. "Look under his right arm on his side, high up near his armpit. You'll find a small mole."

Kerrick hurried around the bed and did as she said. "There's a mole all right. It is Jon. He just looks so…bad."

Lacy put her arms around Meg and helped her stand. Alejandro pulled a chair up for her.

"He's alive, Aunt Meg," Lacy cried. "I can't believe it. We saw what they did to his body, but…"

"Mrs. Davenport," Alejandro said. "If this is your husband, we have some decisions to make. The doctor will need to talk to you. I'm confident he will suggest you have him transferred to another hospital."

Meg didn't want to put him in a hospital in Mexico, but she didn't think she'd have a choice. She had known people with head injuries. If his brain was swelling, they'd have to act fast. She took Jon's hand in hers. She bowed her head. "Thank you, God; oh, thank you."

A doctor stepped into the room to talk about Jon's condition. He had numerous contusions on his face and a severe concussion. The doctor believed his brain was swelling and recommended they transfer him to Centro Médico ABC in Mexico City. Alejandro assured her they could have medical transport ready in thirty minutes, or less. They would fly Jon to the airport in a helicopter and take him by plane to Mexico City. Meg and the rest of the group would fly in a separate private plane to the capital city.

"As soon as we get him to Centro Médico, I'm sure the doctors will need to do a procedure to relieve pressure on his brain," the doctor told Meg. "Will you sign this paperwork giving them permission to do it, Mrs. Davenport?"

Meg felt overwhelmed. A few hours earlier, she had been discussing funeral plans, and now, she was signing consent forms to do a procedure to save his life. *Is this real?*

Twenty minutes later, emergency personnel rushed Jon to the helipad. Lacy relieved Ann from baby duty. While Lacy took care of Carla, Ann stood by her friend.

"It's a miracle, Meg," Ann said. "We have witnessed a bona fide miracle. Now, we just need to get him healthy enough to travel back to the States."

"Oh, I wish we were at a hospital in Atlanta," Meg said. "Maybe Piedmont or Emory."

"I heard someone say Centro Médico is one of the best hospitals in the world. He'll be fine."

José stepped up beside them and placed his arm around Ann's shoulders. "I want to know what happened. We saw what they did to him. I would have sworn they killed him."

Meg smiled up at him through her tears. "Evidently, it wasn't him."

Chapter Forty-two

Living on Purpose

Lacy and Kerrick walked into the hospital room and saw Meg spooning soup into Jon's mouth. Lacy's sprained ankle had almost healed. Jon, however, still looked bad, but five days of medicine, medical procedures, and rest had done wonders. Everyone was dying to know what happened in Coatepec, but the doctors kept him in an induced coma to help his brain heal. They'd begun to wake him last night, and Meg got to talk to him for the first time in the wee hours of the morning.

When Jon saw Lacy, he smiled until his eyes closed in pain.

"Don't smile, Jon," Meg ordered, though she couldn't contain her own smile. "We're not supposed to upset you."

"Not upset," Jon said with labored speech. "Happy. Thought I would never see any of you again."

Lacy couldn't contain her smile or her tears. "You told me to stay alive, and I did. We did. But we saw them…," Lacy's body heaved with emotions, and she reached for a tissue. "We didn't actually see them, uh, kill you, but the crowd cheered when it happened. We saw them burn your body, Jon. It was your clothes. I knew it was you."

Jon lay still, and a tear rolled down the side of his face. "Wasn't me." He closed his eyes again and didn't move for several minutes.

"Maybe we should come back later, Uncle Jon," Lacy said.

"That's probably a good idea," Meg agreed.

Jon's hand reached out and took hold of Lacy's arm. "Was so afraid for you, but knew you were strong." He opened his wet eyes and stared into her face. More tears covered his cheeks.

"That's enough," Meg insisted. "Lacy, you guys need to go so Jon can rest. He can tell us the whole story later."

"We'll see you tomorrow, Uncle Jon. President Diaz is treating us like royalty, so don't worry."

A slight grin lit Jon's face, and he waved to them. Lacy and Kerrick left the room and headed toward the elevators. Alejandro arranged for them to have a private tour of Chapultepec Castle, and a car awaited them at the front entrance of the hospital. Lacy was eager to know the whole story of Jon's miraculous escape, but it would have to wait another day.

When Meg returned to the home President Diaz provided for them in Mexico City, she gathered everyone to explain what the doctors told her. Jon was making great progress, but she requested no one come to the hospital the following day so he could have a complete day of rest.

Finally, a full seven days after he entered the hospital, nurses moved Jon into a private room. One of the president's staff offered to keep Carla that evening so everyone could visit Jon together. Jon had requested they all come so he could tell his story to all of them at one time.

Lacy pushed open the door to Jon's room and saw Meg had already arranged the room with enough chairs for everyone. "You sure look like a new man, Uncle Jon."

"Thanks, Lacy. I feel like a new man."

"He's not one hundred percent, so we don't need to stay too long," Meg insisted.

"I'm fine," Jon said. "I graduated from the bed pan to the toilet this morning with a little help from my bride, who has now declared she's my head nurse." He looked up at Meg and winked. "My new nurse sure is prettier than all of the rest combined."

Meg grinned and leaned over his bed for a quick peck.

"I'm hoping tomorrow we can get really adventurous and try a shower," Jon added.

"I don't think you need to rush the shower," Meg said.

Jon grinned. "Just like that, she turns into Attila the Hun."

Lacy moved her chair closer to the bed, and José stood and stepped closer as well. This whole experience seemed unreal, impossible. It was like Jon had risen from the grave. Lacy stared at her uncle. He looked better, but he had a long way to go.

Lacy, avoiding the IV needle, took hold of Jon's hand. "Uncle Jon, we've got to know how you got away. We saw them leading you to the altar, and then we saw them throw your body on the pyre. They burned your body."

"Here's what I know for sure," Jon began. "I talked to Freddy for a while, and then he retrieved this large bird mask I was supposed to wear. It looked like a wooden helmet with a beak and feathers."

"We saw some like that before the game," Lacy said. "The priests, or whatever those guys were, had them on, and we saw you wearing it as you walked toward the altar."

"Correct," Jon said. "Well, correct except for the part about me wearing it. After Freddy left my cell that night, he returned later with clothes. I'm not sure where they came from, but he told me to put them on and leave mine behind. Then, he said he would show me how to get away."

"I knew Freddy had something to do with your release," Lacy said.

"We went deeper into the mountain where he explained how I could find the steps that would lead me out of Coatepec. It sounded like the steps we'd used that first day. Freddy told me he had to get back, and I should climb the steps to get out of the volcano."

"You mean the steps that led down to the lake of gold?" Kerrick asked.

"Yes. I didn't know where Freddy was going, so as he was walking away, I asked him. He said he was going to fulfill his purpose."

"What did he mean?" Lacy asked.

"We had talked earlier about living on purpose. I thought he was referring to becoming a Coatepec, but I think something different now."

"It was Freddy who wore the mask," José said as a matter of fact.

"I'm sure of it," Jon said. "I think he went back to my cell, put on my clothes, and hid his true identity with the mask. He…" Jon faltered. "He died instead of me."

Lacy's breath caught as she imagined Freddy laying his head down on the altar, knowing he was about to be killed. How would they tell his poor mother? "Why would he do it?"

"He asked me a lot of questions about why José and I were both trying to lose knowing the loser would be killed." Jon looked at José and choked up a bit. "I think I'm getting soft in my old age."

José reached over and placed his hand on Jon's shoulder. Lacy saw that José's eyes were wet, too.

"I told him that verse that says no greater love is expressed than when a man lays down his life for his friends." Jon looked at Lacy. "I have hope, real hope, because someone did that for me many years ago. He did it for all of us."

Lacy stared at the floor. She knew exactly what and more importantly who he was talking about.

"If someone died for me, how could I not die for someone I love?"

José squeezed Jon's shoulder, and Meg reached out to take his hand.

"I encouraged Freddy to leave Coatepec and discover his purpose. I told him God made us all for a purpose, and we couldn't find fulfillment until we discovered it."

"So, Freddy went back to your cell, put on your clothes and the mask, and waited to be taken to the altar to die in your place?" José said.

Jon's face pinched with emotions as he whispered, "That's what I think."

"But why did Freddy have to die?" Lacy asked. "He could have just helped you escape. No one would have known it was him."

"Maybe they would have known," Jon said, "or maybe he knew guards would be looking in on me throughout the night. By putting on the mask and sitting in the room, Freddy bought me time to get away."

The room was silent for several minutes before Lacy finally spoke. "Did you find the stairs?"

Meg grabbed a tissue and wiped Jon's eyes. He took the tissue and blew his nose before grimacing in pain.

"I found them," he said. "The only problem was three men came down the steps as I approached them. Let's just say I had a lot more to fight for than they did. I killed two of them when I managed to get one of their spears. The last one hit me in the head with a club and about knocked me out. Fortunately, I got back to my feet and thrust the spear in him as well. He got away, but he was in bad shape. I was too. He probably didn't get far."

"Climbing the stairs must have been horrible," Kerrick said.

"I heard more voices, so I went down the golden stairs to the lake. When I heard the men coming, I swam out as far away from the steps as possible. The water was warm, like a bath. I felt current and realized it's not just a lake but a river. I saw more men coming down the stairs and decided to literally go with the flow."

"Unbelievable," Lacy whispered.

"I don't remember a lot of what happened after that. Everything was pitch black. At one point, I went underwater and thought I'd drown. I had the sweetest peace. I also re-member hitting my head on rocks. More than once. The last thing I remember is lying on some sand and having a head-ache the size of Texas." He looked over at Meg. "I knew I was going to die, so I wanted you to be my last thought. I still had your necklace. I pulled it out."

A nurse walked into the crowd and said something in Spanish so quickly Lacy couldn't understand her.

"She says we're causing the patient too much stress and need to leave," José translated.

Jon cleared his throat. "Tell her thank you, but we'll be fine. You guys can leave in a minute."

José talked to the nurse, and she left shaking her head. Lacy stepped to the bed and took Jon's hand in hers. "I think your purpose is not fulfilled yet, so we got you back."

"Sounds like it to me," José agreed.

"For one thing, we've still got to find that sunken treas-ure ship near Eleuthera," Kerrick said with a wink.

"True," Lacy added. "We found the old gun. What's it called?"

"Arquebus," Jon said with a weary smile.

"Yeah. The arquebus. We know there's treasure there, Uncle Jon. We can't just give up on that search."

"Maybe." Jon looked around the room and squeezed Meg's hand. "If Carla and Judy were in here, I'd say I have all the treasure I need right here in this room."

Meg leaned over and kissed him again while everyone stood silently. Lacy wiped her eyes.

The quiet was broken by Ann blowing her nose into a tissue. "Sorry."

Everyone laughed.

"You guys are the greatest," Jon said. "If you're up for it, maybe we can go back to Eleuthera."

"Whoa, whoa, whoa," Meg said, all kidding aside. "Let's get you well and back home. We can think about treasure hunting later. Way later."

"Speaking of home," Ann said. "We heard from Diego. Pirate's Cove didn't suffer too badly from the storm. He said the roofs were damaged on both houses, and the yard's a mess, but all-in-all, the place did all right."

"Miami is shut down for a while," Meg added. "The University is trying to get classes up and running online by next week." Meg looked down at Jon and stroked his cheek. "We're going to get you home and make you lie around for at least a month or two without any more excitement."

Jon pulled Meg's arm, and she fell on top of him. He kissed her. "I love you Mrs. Davenport," he said when they came up for air. "I'll rest for a while, but we've got a few more adventures in us. Why don't you take this group back to the house and go to bed? You need a good night's sleep. In the meantime, I'm going to lie here and think about all the ways I can love you for the next one hundred years."

Lacy watched them kiss one more time. *There is no greater love.* She looked at Kerrick to discover he was looking down at her. Would he love her like Jon loved Meg? He smiled and grasped her hand. She looked into those deep, blue eyes that offered promise, hope, love. She had many adventures left, too, and she hoped they all included Kerrick.

A Word from the Author

Thank you for reading my book, *No Greater Love*. I hope you enjoyed reading it as much as I enjoyed writing it. Most of the places I wrote about are real places I've visited in doing research for Books 5 & 6 of the series. Although lost cities may still exist in Mexico, Coatepec exists only in my imagination.

If you enjoyed the book, will you please take a moment to leave a review on Amazon? If you have missed reading any of the previous books of the series, you'll find descriptions on the following pages. You can pick them up from Amazon or your favorite retailer.

I created a prequel to the whole series entitled "A Girl Can Always Hope," and I offer it to my readers as a gift. If you would like a free pdf copy of a story about Jon and Meg as teenagers, visit my website and click on the "free gift" tab (judahknight.com).

If you would like to contact me for any reason, I'd love to hear from you. You can reach me through my publisher (greentreepublishers.com) or through the contact page on my website (judahknight.com). I look forward to hearing from you soon.

Thanks again for taking the time to read *No Greater Love*. I'll see you in the next adventure.

Judah Knight

The Davenport Series

Book 1: *The Long Way Home*

He had a boat. She needed a ride. A simple lift turned into the adventure of a lifetime. Jon Davenport and Meg Freeman had a chance encounter in Nassau that would change their lives and destinies.

Book 2: *Hope for Tomorrow*
Our tomorrows can be different than our yesterdays!

Jon Davenport invited Meg Freeman, along with her friend Ann, to join him in searching for sunken treasure in the Bahamas. Though Meg thought that she was simply searching for gold, the treasure she found was far more valuable.

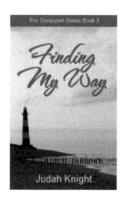

Book 3: *Finding My Way*
Bitterness. Betrayal. Brokenness. Can the search for ancient gold help her find lasting treasure?

Meet Jon and Meg's niece, Lacy Henderson, as she joins the adventure in the Bahamas, along with summer intern, Kerrick Daniels.

Book 4: *Ready to Love Again*

She had given up on love until…
Lacy Henderson went to the Bahamas
to help her aunt and uncle in a boys'
program, but she seems to be the one
who had the most challenging and
thrilling summer of all.

Book 5: *Love Waits*

The Dream of a Lifetime…or a nightmare in disguise?

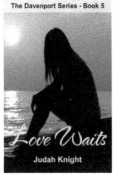

Though the summer is completed,
Lacy's and Kerrick's relationship is far
from over. The two join with Jon and
Meg Davenport on a search for lost
treasure that takes them from the Bahamas to Mexico. Lacy learns that love
hurts, but also, love waits.

Prequel: A Girl Can Always Hope

In *The Long Way Home*, we learn that the
two main characters knew one another
as teenagers, and Margaret Robertson
(Meg Freeman in *The Long Way
Home*) had a crush on her brother's best
friend, Jon Davenport. This book is
available as a gift on the author's website: judahknight.com.

CPSIA information can be obtained
at www.ICGtesting.com
Printed in the USA
LVHW010249090621
689713LV00028B/1854